I0723397

THE LONG-FORGOTTEN WINTER KING

ANNETTE MARIE

BOOKS IN THE GUILD CODEX

UNVEILED

The One and Only Crystal Druid
The Long-Forgotten Winter King
The Twice-Scorned Lady of Shadow

SPELLBOUND

Three Mages and a Margarita
Dark Arts and a Daiquiri
Two Witches and a Whiskey
Demon Magic and a Martini
The Alchemist and an Amaretto
Druid Vices and a Vodka
Lost Talismans and a Tequila
Damned Souls and a Sangria

DEMONIZED

Taming Demons for Beginners
Slaying Monsters for the Feeble
Hunting Fiends for the Ill-Equipped
Delivering Evil for Experts

WARPED
with Rob Jacobsen

Warping Minds & Other Misdemeanors
Hellbound Guilds & Other Misdirections
Rogue Ghosts & Other Miscreants

STEEL & STONE UNIVERSE

Steel & Stone Series
Chase the Dark
Bind the Soul
Yield the Night
Reap the Shadows
Unleash the Storm
Steel & Stone

Spell Weaver Trilogy
The Night Realm
The Shadow Weave
The Blood Curse

OTHER WORKS

Red Winter Trilogy
Red Winter
Dark Tempest
Immortal Fire

THE GUILD CODEX

CLASSES OF MAGIC

Spiritalis

Psychica

Arcana

Demonica

Elementaria

MYTHIC

A person with magical ability

MPD / MAGIPOL

The organization that regulates mythics and their activities

ROGUE

A mythic living in violation of MPD laws

THE LONG-FORGOTTEN
WINTER KING

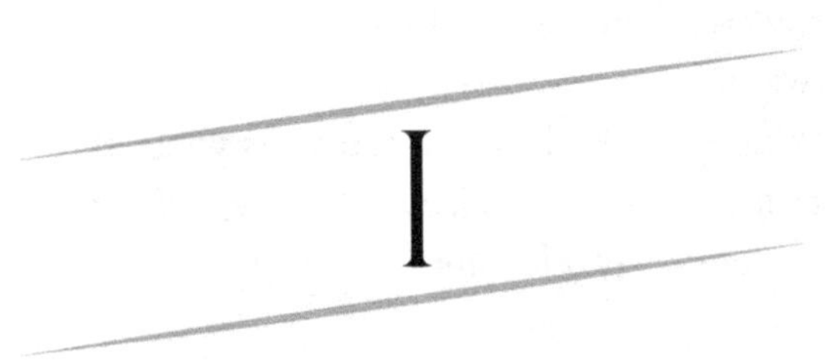

DRUID.

The rough voice slithered into my head, and my feet stopped moving. I gazed down at the dirt between my hiking boots, then slowly looked up to find a sunlit path bordered by towering trees.

Confusion bubbled in the pit of my stomach.

The unfamiliar voice pushed into my mind a second time. *You are a druid, yes?*

My stare rose. Perched on a branch twenty feet above the trail, a large black raven tilted its head side to side in question.

"I'm not a druid." As I spoke, disorienting memories clawed through my detached daze, challenging my flat statement.

I would treat with you, druid, the raven said.

"I'm not a druid."

Not a druid? The bird ruffled its feathers. *You insult me.*

"I—"

I sense your power.

"I'm not—"

The raven let out a furious caw that shattered the quiet with unnatural volume, and the ear-splitting sound obliterated my numb detachment. My senses snapped back, my awareness sharpening and adrenaline dumping into my veins.

I retreated a step, my left arm jostling in its sling, and took in the towering spruce and fir trees bordering the dirt trail. Where was I?

Clacking its beak, the raven spread its wings threateningly. *I came to treat, and you insult me. A disrespectful druid does not deserve the courtesy of a bargain.*

"Wait—"

I will take my boon instead.

It leaped off the branch, and my right hand shot into the pocket of my jeans for the handle of my switchblade. But my pocket was empty.

The bird flew at me, and as it came, its body changed—swelling to four times its original size as a second pair of enormous black wings split from the first. Two more heads sprouted from its massive shoulders.

I leaped sideways and landed in an awkward roll. Pain flared through my cracked collarbone. As the raven's huge, curved talons tore through the earth where I'd been standing, my back slammed into a tree, my limbs positioned wrong to leap up.

The bird pivoted to face me, its four gargantuan wings stretched out, caging me against the tree. Its three avian heads with red crests lowered menacingly, beaks open and forked tongues darting out.

Delicious druid, three voices croaked in my head.

It reared back to strike—and coldness rushed over me.

In a flash of white feathers, an albino hawk plummeted out of the sky, talons extended. He crashed full tilt into the raven's broad back, and thick shards of ice burst from beneath his feet. The raven screamed in either fury or agony as the ice rushed over its entire body, encasing everything except its four broad wings. Its hoarse cry cut off, leaving my ears ringing.

Pale azure light rippled over the hawk's feathers. The temperature plunged. Frost bloomed across every surface, the air sparkled with tiny ice crystals, and the raven's icy prison creaked and groaned.

Then it exploded.

I recoiled as ice peppered me—ice and frozen black feathers. The frosted shards tumbled to the ground, and with them, pieces of the raven. Its body had shattered along with the ice.

The white hawk fluttered to the path, landing at my feet, and fixed a steady, blue-eyed stare on mine.

Saber.

Ríkr's low, clear voice was so familiar, yet now that I'd heard it with my ears instead of only inside my head, it sounded like a stranger's.

You have … returned, he added, a slight hesitation on the last word.

I knew why he'd faltered over his word choice. He wasn't referring to my physical whereabouts; he was talking about my mental state. I'd "returned" to normal.

This wasn't the first time I'd dissociated and lost track of the world around me, but I didn't usually end up in the middle of a forest with no clear recollection of how I'd gotten there. Pushing forward onto my knees, I glanced around for a landmark.

We must speak, dove, Ríkr said after a moment. *It cannot wait any longer.*

"Speak?" I repeated roughly, my attention swinging back to him. "We aren't going to *speak.* I never want to hear your lying voice again."

As you've told me several times, but I disregarded those commands, as I will for every foolish order you may deign to throw at me.

Rage ignited in my chest, and a familiar grind of impending violence scraped across my ribs. "You've been deceiving me for *seven years,* and now you're calling me *foolish?*" I shoved to my feet, my teeth bared at the fae. "You arrogant, lying son of a—"

There are no bitches in my lineage, he interrupted. *But I will admit my unfortunate predilection for both arrogance and deception.*

I sucked in air through my nose. Straightening my sling, I strode away from him, hoping it was the opposite direction to wherever I'd been heading before returning to my senses. I had no idea where I was.

Straining my mind, I sorted through vague memories from the past day or two—feeding the rescue's animals, eating dinner with Dominique and Greta, and meandering around the pastures. It was like watching old video footage through a dirty window with no sound. I recognized the places and activities, but I felt no connection to the memories.

The last clear memory I had was of the orchard covered in ice. I vividly remembered the cold against my skin, the sharp sting of Lallakai's claws at my throat, and Ríkr's voice in my ears as he'd warned her to keep her hands off his druid.

His druid.

Meaning me.

Saber.

Footfalls padded after me in a four-legged rhythm, and I glanced angrily over my shoulder to find a white-furred, blue-eyed coyote. At the sight of his canine form, a fresh wave of disbelieving horror crashed over me, just like in the orchard when I'd realized the depth of his deceptions.

Saber, he repeated firmly, projecting his telepathic voice into my mind. *We need to speak, if for no other reason than more fae will seek you out, and we must—*

"*We* aren't doing anything. Leave me alone, Ríkr."

I will not. The coyote trotted up to my side, one azure eye canted up toward me. *I will not casually abandon my role as your guardian now, just as I have not these past four days.*

I missed a step. "*Four* days?"

He was silent for a moment. *Too much accosted you in too short a time. Your mind retreated.*

My chest expanded with a deep breath, and I blew the air out slowly. I didn't normally dissociate for that long, and fear for my mental state unfurled in my gut—but I quashed the feeling. In a matter of days, my entire life had been uprooted, my home and freedom had been threatened, and my past had become my present. I'd regained my repressed memories all at once, reliving the worst betrayal of my life as though it'd happened that very day instead of ten years ago. Shortly afterward, I'd battled the heart-stealing Dullahan for my life.

The final straw had come two days later: the revelation that Ríkr, the only being I'd trusted without question, had been lying to me since the day we met. I didn't remember much beyond that, so I must've dissociated afterward.

"I won't forgive you," I barked at my familiar.

I deceived you, he replied, *but I also protected you—for seven years. Is that worth nothing?*

I shook my head. "I don't want to hear more of your lies."

He darted in front of me, forcing me to a halt on the path. *Whether you want to hear what I must say is irrelevant. The raven fae is a harbinger of what will come, dove. You cannot hide from this.*

"Hide from what?"

Yourself. His ears swiveled toward the surrounding forest. *You cannot hide from the power within you that is calling my kin from miles yonder.*

"What power?"

Your druidic energy.

"I'm not a druid." I stepped around him to continue down the path. I still didn't know where I was. Dappled sunlight warmed the top of my head, and I guessed it was mid-afternoon. Depending on when I'd begun this trek, I could be anywhere.

The soft thump of paws followed me. *You are a druid, dove. I found you seven years ago by following the call of your power.*

"I'm a witch," I said flatly. "I've been a witch my whole life. My parents were witches. They would've known if I was a druid."

I have no explanation for what your parents taught you, but to my senses, your true nature is utterly unmistakable.

"Then your senses are wrong. I'm a witch. A weak, incompetent witch who can barely perform a balancing ritual."

Of course you struggle with the banal rituals of witches. Druids neither need nor use them. A pause. *And you were weak due to my interference.*

"What the hell does that mean?"

You had no power because I was consuming it.

I stopped dead on the trail. "You were *what?*"

Consuming your druidic energy, as my kind does. The white coyote padded up beside me, and his clear, vibrant blue eyes met mine. *By sunrise following our first meeting, I had devoured all your power but the faintest spark. Every day hence, I drained it as swiftly as it welled within you.*

My heart thudded in my throat, choking me. "You … were stealing … my power?" My good hand curled into a tight fist. "You *fucking leech.*"

He'd been feeding off me like a goddamn vampire? If he was right that I was a druid, that explained why I hadn't suspected I was anything more than a witch. He'd been draining me of power since we met, and before that, I'd spent three years in prison with my magic suppressed like all the other convicts. And before that …

Before that, I'd always worn the river-stone pendant my parents had given me, which had hidden my spiritual energy from fae.

You do not recall, do you?

My focus snapped back to Ríkr. "Recall what?"

The wish you shared with me the day we met. You said you wished nothing more than to be a normal person and live a normal life.

A flicker of memory danced through my mind: sitting on a fallen log, looking out at the mountains bathed in the first sunset I'd seen in three years. I'd been thinking about the impossible task of assimilating into a coven of witches who all knew I was a murderer.

I *had* told Ríkr I wished to live a normal life, but I'd been referring to being a convict, not a druid.

The breeze ruffled his white fur. *You told me your desire, and I granted it. I rendered you as human as possible, so never would you possess enough power to interfere in your pursuit of a "normal" life.*

Shock and fury battled inside me. "And you did that purely out of the goodness of your fae heart, did you?"

Oh, it was highly beneficial to me, he replied without the slightest hint of contrition. *We both benefited, dove. I gave you the simple life you desired, free of the dangers that come with your power, and devoted myself to protecting you since I was depriving you of the means to protect yourself.*

I forced my feet back into motion, leaving him to follow. His explanation was very …Ríkr. He hadn't apologized because he felt no guilt. The benefits to us both, as he measured them, far outweighed the harm he'd done to me.

His telepathic voice brushed my mind, quiet and determined. *Though I did not share the nature of our bargain with you, I have held to it all these years. I protected the life you were building.*

I couldn't respond. It was too much to process when I'd barely begun to grasp the magnitude of his actions, of how he'd shaped my life over the past seven years—and what my life would have looked like if he hadn't.

"What changed?" I asked abruptly. "Why did that raven fae attack me?"

He trotted up beside me again, his furred tail held low and still like a wolf's. *I haven't consumed your spiritual energy since Lallakai's assault. Your power builds, and it calls my kin to you.*

"You stole my power for seven years. Why stop now?"

His ears flicked with surprise. *Consuming your power was only a boon to you when you believed yourself a witch. To continue now would benefit me alone.*

"So you want my permission?"

Permission?

"To consume my power."

I am not seeking your permission. You need to establish your territory and arm yourself with offensive magic to—

"No." My limbs tingled with low-level adrenaline. "I don't want a territory or fae drooling over me like I'm a dinner buffet. I don't want to be a druid."

But you are, and you cannot unknow that.

"You know what it took for me to build this life—appeasing the coven, making it through college, getting a job, fitting in at the clinic. I finally have a life I enjoy and a home where I want to be. I won't lose that. A *druid* can't live with humans or volunteer at a rescue or fly under the radar. I don't want any part of that life."

But you do want power. You always have.

I slashed a glare at him. "Do you still want my druid energy?"

I do not want to deprive you of your only defense against my kin.

"*You* would be my defense. That's what you've been doing all along, isn't it?"

Does this query mean you wish us to remain companions?

I hesitated. Was that what I wanted? To put myself back in his power, knowingly and willingly? To put my entire life in the hands of a fae I'd known for seven years—but barely knew at all?

Halting on the path, I pressed my lips together. "How can I ever trust you? How do I know you aren't hiding more secrets from me?"

I am most assuredly hiding more secrets. He gazed up at me, his canine face revealing nothing. *I have centuries of secrets to keep and no intention of revealing them all to anyone, especially a human.*

My eyes widened. *Centuries* of secrets? How old was he?

Not even to my favorite fierce and bloodthirsty druid, he added regretfully.

I stood for a moment longer, then continued forward. As the trail curved, I spotted a tangle of fallen trees I recognized as part of Lodge Trail in Minnekhada Regional Park, not far from the rescue. Reassured, I picked up my pace; the trailhead was only a few hundred meters away.

"Who are you, really?" I asked the coyote, who was easily keeping pace with my long strides.

Would you like the condensed version, he asked with a cant of his head, *or the painfully detailed one?*

"The whole thing."

I warn you, the tale is dry, sordid, and paints a poor image of my long-ago grandeur.

I snorted. "Have you always been such a pompous ass?"

For time immemorial, dove. You are not the first to describe me so.

"I probably won't be the last either."

I hope not.

My calves burned with exertion as I strode into a small gravel parking lot. A familiar quad waited for me, and when I dug into my pocket, I found the keys.

"I need to think about all this," I told him, stopping beside the quad. "If you still want to be my familiar, then consider this your trial period. Prove to me why I should trust you—and if you lie to me again, we're done forever."

He flicked his ears thoughtfully. *Two caveats. First, I reserve my right to privacy. I will be forthcoming only with knowledge and intentions directly relevant to you and your future.*

I considered that, then nodded. "Fine."

Second, this will not be a "trial period" for my role as your familiar. That designation has expired. His blue eyes sharpened. *It shall be a trial for your role as my consort.*

His words took a moment to sink in. "*My* role?" I repeated incredulously. "As *your* consort?"

I offer now to take you as my druid consort, he declared formally. *And before you attempt to pummel the life from me, I would add it is not a relationship of undue intimacy. It is a commitment of mutual protection and empowerment.*

"Empowerment?"

A blue shimmer rippled over him, and he shrank into the form of an albino hawk.

So, dove, dedicate this time to your assessment of me and what I offer. His white wings spread, and he launched off the ground. *I will await your answer with eager patience.*

I squinted up at him as he spiraled into the sky, the sun burning my eyes and my head reeling.

2

THE DRIVE HOME WAS SHORT. Consumed with thoughts of Ríkr and his offer, I barely noticed the familiar farmland zooming past until I reached a large sign that read, "Hearts & Hooves Animal Rescue." I'd come so close to losing this place forever. Losing my home. Losing everything I cared about.

Being a druid might cost me all of it.

Passing through the open gate to the farmstead, I turned the quad toward the house—and my heart lurched at the sight of two vehicles parked beside Dominique and Greta's old Ranger. One was an unfamiliar silver jeep and the other was my white and teal truck. I'd abandoned it at my coven leader's house a week ago.

As I pulled the quad into the yard, the jeep's passenger door opened and a large, leather-clad man climbed out. Pierce had a bristling beard, beefy tattooed arms, weathered skin, and a criminal record like me. He was also a nature-loving witch and the closest thing I had to a friend in our coven.

I parked the quad and swung off it as Pierce strode over.

Wariness rolled through me, and I kept my expression cold. "What are you doing here?"

A slight movement: his serpentine familiar, Gleer, poked its head out from beneath the collar of his leather coat. The snake flicked its tongue.

Pierce tossed me a key—the spare key to my truck that I kept hidden in the wheel well. "Returning your truck. I called first but you didn't answer." He squinted at my sling. "What happened to your arm?"

"Riding accident."

"And what happened to Laney?"

"No idea."

His eyes narrowed even more beneath his thick eyebrows. "We got the news yesterday. About how her body was found up at the crossroads, mauled by fae." He waited a moment. "You're not going to tell me anything, are you?"

"You didn't tell me the coven planned to ambush me and put me on trial."

"I didn't know," he said gruffly. "They knew I'd warn you."

Watching his eyes, I absorbed his statement, then relaxed. Letting go of my cold wariness, I tucked my key in my pocket and said softly, "Thanks."

His beard twitched as he smiled, and he scooped me into a brief hug. "Glad you're okay, girl. I was worried about you."

"I was worried about me too."

He rested a hand on my good shoulder. "I'm afraid I didn't just come to return your truck. I have news as well, and it isn't good. The coven is disbanding. With Arla and Laney dead, the others decided the coven wouldn't be the same and that it's time to move on."

They were disbanding? I shouldn't have been surprised, but with everything else going on, I hadn't given the coven's future a second thought. I was more concerned about my present.

"All right," I said.

"That means," he added, giving my shoulder a gentle squeeze, "the MPD will have to relocate you."

All my muscles locked down.

"Someone else could've taken over your rehabilitation after Arla's death, seeing as you only have two years left, but with the coven disbanding …" He trailed off, frowning unhappily. "I'm sorry, Saber."

Why hadn't I realized my rehabilitation was in danger? My parole required a specially licensed guild—or in my case, a coven—and a trained rehabilitation supervisor, both of which the MPD selected for me. There were no other guilds near Coquitlam, let alone ones licensed for convict rehabilitation. Once the MPD assigned me to a new guild and supervisor, I'd have to move away from the rescue.

As my breathing sped toward hyperventilation, another memory pushed through the chaos in my head—an older man in a suit, an MPD badge resting against his chest and a sheet of crisp white paper in his hand. His voice echoed in my mind, ordering me to present myself at the Vancouver precinct for questioning within seventy-two hours.

Seventy-two hours. Three days.

Ríkr had told me *four* days had passed.

I'd missed my deadline—and that meant I was officially a rogue in violation of MPD law.

A faint tremor ran through my limbs, and I longed for the comforting feel of my switchblade in my hand. Its absence only deepened the feeling that everything was spinning out of my control. The list of catastrophes in my life now included losing my sense of identity, my guild, my home, *and* my freedom.

"I …" Swallowing, I pulled myself together. "I just realized I'm late for something. I need to go."

Concern pinching his brow, Pierce stepped back. His familiar peeked at me over his shoulder, flicking its tongue again.

"Saber …" He gave me a strange look. "Can I ask … are you really a witch?"

For a second time, my limbs seized.

"Gleer swears you were a witch last time he saw you," he added, watching my expression. "But now he says you're radiating energy just like a—"

"No," I cut in flatly. "Gleer is mistaken."

Pierce's concern deepened. Witches had an extremely limited ability to detect other mythics of the Spiritalis class; Pierce had to rely on his familiar's assessment of me, and he had no reason to doubt Gleer.

"Please don't, Pierce," I said quietly, almost pleading.

He sighed. "All right. Take care of yourself, girl. And let me know if you need anything."

I nodded. He climbed into the jeep's passenger seat, and as the vehicle reversed, I glimpsed the driver, a stocky man cut from the same biker mold as Pierce. The jeep roared down the drive toward the main road, and I stood unmoving until the sound had faded away entirely.

The farm was quiet, the warm summer air tranquil. My gaze roved across the weathered farmhouse to the outbuildings, garden, and orchard. Our resident escape-artist chicken bobbed across the far side of the yard, and the high whinny of a horse drifted from the turnouts on the stable's far side.

The days I'd lost in my detached haze hung over me, confusing and unreal. Had it really been four days since a shadowy eagle had perched on the roof, or a magnificent blue-roan stallion had roamed the pasture, or shaggy wolves had prowled among the trees? Had it really been four days since a dark-haired, green-eyed druid had haunted my home?

It felt like minutes. It felt like years. It felt like I'd dreamed it all and they'd never existed.

I strode toward the stable. Through the back door, up the stairs. Into my small apartment above the tack room.

A folded blanket and spare pillow were stacked neatly on the end of the sofa, and I halted, staring at them. Trying to remember. But no matter how much I strained, I couldn't remember when in the past four days he'd left.

Shaking myself, I swept into motion again. Stripping off my clothes. Showering. Drying my long dark hair, attempting to brush it into a ponytail one-handed, then giving up and leaving it loose. Dressing again in my nicest pair of jeans and a black tank top, the ugly white sling strapped to my chest. My wallet and keys went into my pocket, then I picked up my phone from my nightstand.

When I woke the screen, it revealed the last thing I'd had open: a message conversation with "CD." The most recent text was from six days ago, the night we'd faced the Dullahan. Zak had stayed at the rescue for at least two more days after that—until Ríkr had revealed I was a druid and I'd gone off the rails. After that, I didn't know.

But he was gone now, and that was all that mattered, wasn't it?

I tapped the menu. My finger hovered over the "Delete" button, then I hissed angrily and swiped the messaging app away. I stuffed my phone into my other pocket, then grabbed the folded piece of paper off the table, added it to my pocket, and marched out of the apartment.

When I strode into the yard, a white hawk was perched on a fence post, watching me.

I faced the fae. "If I were your consort, you would protect me, correct?"

Without question. He ruffled his feathers. *Though with some limitations.*

"Will you protect me from the MPD?"

He went very still. *The MPD?*

I was the prime suspect in my coven leader's death, but Zak's pet agent, Kit Morris, had promised to prove my innocence by the time my seventy-two-hour grace period was over. I'd missed the summons deadline, but I could still present myself at the precinct and hope Agent Morris had followed through on his promise.

"I don't know what will happen, but I'm not ready to go full rogue." I gestured at the farm. "If there's a chance I can stay here, I need to try to do it Morris's way."

You will risk everything on the word of an agent?

"No, I'm risking everything on you."

His eyes gleamed. *In that case, dove, it would be my pleasure to guarantee your safe return from this MPD venture.*

WHY DID I FEEL like I was about to walk to my own execution?

I stared at the MPD logo stamped on the glass doors in front of me. Behind me was a small, enclosed lot that could only be accessed through a parking garage entrance off the street.

Though the precinct was in the heart of downtown Vancouver, there was little chance a human would stumble on this building.

My breath rushed through my nose, and I fought to slow it.

I hadn't been inside this precinct in ten years. The day after I'd murdered my aunt, a pair of MPD agents had shown up at the Vancouver police department where I was being held, transferred me out, and brought me here. I could feel the cold handcuffs digging into my wrists. I could hear the oppressive silence in the car as they drove. I could see their emotionless faces as they pulled me out of the vehicle.

Ríkr's small claws pricked me. He was perched on my shoulder in the form of a white ferret, and his whiskers tickled my cheek as he leaned forward.

Say the word, and I will unleash a wintry nightmare upon the weak fools inside. He bobbed his small head. *An unrestrained slaughter would be refreshing.*

A faint shiver ran through me. Ríkr had been making grandiose, violence-loving remarks since the day I met him, but they were far less amusing now that I suspected he could enact them.

"How powerful are you, actually?" I muttered.

How does one quantify power?

"Can you get me out of there if it goes bad?"

It would depend. He paused as though assessing his odds. *Though my magic is highly effective against humans, I might struggle to overcome an entire MPD force.*

"You *might*," I repeated dryly.

Fear not. If you need me to extract you from their foul clutches, I will hold nothing back.

Rolling my eyes, I opened the door and entered a rectangular lobby. Two rows of back-to-back chairs ran down the center of the long space, half a dozen occupied by waiting mythics, and to my right, visitors stood in a short line in front of a service counter.

Pulling my summons paperwork from my pocket, I got in line. My nerves tightened like coiled springs, adrenaline buzzing through my veins. Every muscle in my body was primed for fight or flight, and I battled the rapid-fire thoughts building up in my head.

Would they arrest me? Would they lock me in a cell? Would they send me back to the correctional center? Would they convict me of murder and execute me? The longer I stood there, politely waiting for strangers to condemn my life again, the more I felt like a terrified teenager.

The person in front of me moved away. Suddenly I was facing the service counter, a thirty-something man with blond hair and a goatee sitting behind it.

My feet wouldn't move.

"Next," the man said, waving at me to approach.

Panic flooded me, and I felt like I was outside my body, looking down at myself standing three feet from the counter with my pallid face blank and empty—then Ríkr bit my earlobe, his tiny teeth like needles, and the pain snapped me back into myself.

I stepped forward and set my paper on the counter. The man unfolded it and peered at the summons. I waited for him to realize I was a day late, but he merely turned to his computer screen. He typed on the keyboard, clicked the mouse, then picked up the phone beside him and hit a button.

"A summons is here," he said without preamble. "Saber Orien. Yeah. Okay." He hung up the phone. "Take a seat. Someone will come get you."

I backed away from the desk, then walked woodenly to the nearest seat and dropped onto it. My breath huffed out, and I reached up to touch my ear, almost dislodging Ríkr from my shoulder. A smear of blood stained my fingertips, but I didn't complain that he'd made me bleed.

"Mom," a high-pitched voice said in that loud "whisper" tone children used. "Mom, look! That lady has a rat!"

"What? Where?" a woman yelped. "Oh. That's a ferret, sweetie."

A rat? Ríkr muttered in an insulted tone.

I glanced at him out of the corner of my eye. *Are you visible right now?*

Yes. The MPD should know you are not facing their mercy alone.

A quiet flare of affection warmed the painful mistrust that had tainted our relationship. Like most fae, Ríkr preferred to remain undetectable to human senses. Usually, I was the only one who could see him—and other witches and druids, if they were paying attention.

The mother and daughter duo sat at the end of the row, farthest from the entrance, the little girl bouncing impatiently in her seat. Scattered around the lobby were a dozen other civilians, most of them in business-casual dress, as though they'd stopped by after work.

At least I didn't have to worry about my job. Before my four-day bout of non-responsiveness, I'd arranged to take two weeks of paid vacation time, using my broken collarbone as an excuse for the lack of notice. I doubted anyone at the clinic was happy to be suddenly shorthanded, but I wasn't absent without leave.

"Mrs. Colbert?"

At the front desk agent's call, the woman with the little girl got up, holding her daughter's hand. She started across the lobby toward the service counter.

BAM!

A metal door at the back of the lobby crashed into the wall. A tall man with a messy beard and stained overalls flew through the threshold, charging straight for the mother and daughter.

"Out of my way!" he roared, swinging his thick arm.

His limb slammed into the mother, throwing her off her feet. The little girl's high-pitched scream rang out as the woman hit the tile floor, and the man ran past without a backward glance, heavy shoes pounding. He sprinted toward the lobby doors.

My good hand closed over the back of the empty seat beside me. As the man raced past, I whipped the metal chair into his path.

It crashed into his shins, and he fell with a pained shout. Clutching his knee with one hand, he started to shove himself up—then flattened again as I dropped the back of the chair on his head. I planted my hiking boot on the other side of the metal and leaned my weight down onto it, Ríkr hanging from my shoulder.

The man's arms spasmed as he awkwardly grabbed at the chair flattening his skull into the floor. "Stop! *Stop!*"

The same door banged open a second time, and a woman rushed through, wearing a leather jacket with her ash-brown hair pulled back from her face in a long ponytail. Two men with MPD badges trotted after her.

"You got him!" she exclaimed, hastening toward me. "The bastard gave me the slip—"

Two steps away, she came up short, her eyes widening as she gawked at my face. "Mairead?"

I went rigid. In that moment of stillness where we stared at each other, I felt something else—a shift in the sour, lifeless energy of the concrete-entombed earth around us. An intangible swirl of vibrancy and life emanated from the woman, softening the air with power, confidence, tranquility, and command.

I'd only felt that kind of power from one other person.

"Druid?" I whispered, the word slipping out.

She blinked—then the two agents caught up to her. One of them glanced at my foot on the chair with arched eyebrows. Recovering my composure, I used the toe of my shoe to flip the chair back up onto its feet. The two agents pounced on the man, one pinning him while the other cuffed him.

"Come on," one of the agents told the woman as he and his partner hauled the escapee to his feet. "Let's get him booked."

"Right. Thanks for nabbing the runaway," she added, tossing the words over her shoulder as she walked off.

I didn't move, staring after the woman as she and the two agents retreated to the door they'd come through, their prisoner spitting curses. She'd called me Mairead—my mother's name. That woman had known my mother.

That *druid* had known my mother.

My head spun, thoughts reeling. My parents had raised me as a witch, and now that I knew the truth, questions ripped at me. Had they known I was a druid? Why had they hidden it? Why had they lied? Who were they? Who was I?

They couldn't answer my questions—but that druid had looked at me and seen my mother.

I launched forward, speeding toward the door where the woman had vanished, barely managing not to run.

Ríkr's small paws gripped my shoulder. *As supportive as I am of all forms of insurrection, this isn't an ideal time to ignore instructions.*

I pulled the door open—and found myself staring into a pair of bright blue eyes. The man on the other side of the threshold looked me over from head to toe, then flashed a grin I had no idea how to interpret.

"Heya, Saber," Agent Kit Morris said lightly. "You're late."

3

I FOLLOWED AGENT MORRIS down a utilitarian hallway lined with doors. Other agents bustled along in the opposite direction, but I didn't see the druid or the runaway brute.

"There was a woman," I said tersely. "Tall, brown hair. She chased a man into the lobby and two agents helped her arrest him."

"Okay?" he drawled in bemusement as he led me to a pair of elevators.

"Do you know who she is?"

He prodded the call button. "Is she an agent?"

"I don't think so. She's a druid."

His eyebrows shot up. "And did her tag look like he walked out of an episode of *Deadliest Catch*?"

I frowned. "I don't know what you mean, but he was wearing grimy overalls."

"Then my best guess is Josephine Pisk. She's a bounty hunter. She uncovered a gang of mythics involved in an illegal fishing scheme up in the Lighthouse Park area, and she's been dropping off sea-salty rogues all week." He cocked his head. "Why do you ask?"

Remembering I was speaking to an MPD agent I didn't trust, I cooled my expression and said nothing. His eyebrows crept higher as the elevator door chimed and slid open.

We exited the elevator on the second floor, and with each step, I expected Morris to shove me into a cold, concrete interrogation room like the one I'd been locked in ten years ago. Instead, he led me to a door with a red first-aid symbol on it, rapped on the wood, then swung it open without waiting.

The cramped space inside held three medical bays, their partitioning curtains open. The hospital-style beds faced a long counter loaded with medical supplies, where a gangly man with long red hair tied back in a ponytail sat in front of a computer.

At the opening of the door, he looked up with a questioning expression.

"Hey Scooter," Morris said amicably.

"What is it this time, Kit?" the man asked, crossing his arms. "Burns or bullet holes? Wait, let me guess. You got your ass thrown around by another demon."

"You say that like it's a regular thing, but don't worry, my favorite demon is on holiday."

Scooter's attention shifted to me, taking in my sling. "Are you the patient, then? What's broken?"

Morris waited, and when I didn't speak, he said, "Collarbone."

How did he know that?

"It's cracked, not broken," I muttered stiffly. "And it's fine. I don't need—"

"—use of both arms?" Morris interrupted. "Sure, right. Can you fix her up, Scooter?"

The man had already pushed out of his chair. He opened a cabinet. "Lie down on a bed. Doesn't matter which one."

I wasn't keen on accepting "free" healing services from the MPD, but the risk of owing Morris was worth two functioning arms. Walking to the nearest bed, I gingerly lay down on my back. Ríkr hopped onto the partition curtain, the fabric swinging, and climbed up it until he was perched on the rod suspended from the ceiling. Morris squinted up at the small fae.

Selecting a long roll of what looked like either stiff paper or thin cardboard from the cabinet, Scooter strode over to the bed. He set the roll beside me, then unclipped my sling, pulled it away, and straightened my arm at my side.

He gently prodded my clavicle. "Normally, I'd take an x-ray to confirm it doesn't need to be set, but I'm assuming that's been done?"

"Yes."

"Then I'll get straight to repairing it."

He unrolled the paper, revealing a complex series of circles marked with unfamiliar symbols. An Arcana spell. Witches and druids weren't the only humans with magic in the world. There were mages, sorcerers, alchemists, psychics, and more, including healers like Scooter.

He slid the prepared spell under my shoulder so the center was lined up with my collarbone, then chanted in a low voice. I held perfectly still, unable to feel anything magical, but I wasn't gifted in Arcana magic.

After a few minutes, he stepped back. "That needs to charge for half an hour. Don't move. I'll be back shortly." As he headed for the door, he called to Morris, "Make sure she stays put!"

"You got it, doc."

The door clacked shut. Sitting on the neighboring bed, Morris smiled in a friendly way I didn't trust.

"Why am I here?" I demanded.

"You mean, why haven't I tossed you in a holding cell?" His smile took on an edge. "It's not like I put my neck on the line only for you to blow off your summons deadline."

I stared back at him stonily.

He sighed. "I get that you don't like agents. You have lots of reasons to hate the whole system, but I'm trying to help you."

"Are you?"

"The Judiciary Council is made up of a bunch of dried-out carcasses with Grinch-sized hearts and zero empathy, but I still can't believe they convicted you. You didn't deserve a twelve-year sentence, and you sure as shit don't deserve another one."

"I killed my aunt."

"Your guardian was the criminal, not you. I read the report."

My jaw tightened. If he'd read it, then he'd seen the results of the medical examination I'd been subjected to—the bruises, burns, and broken bones from the last beating Ruth had given me, and the evidence showing years of similar abuse.

"If you know that," I said icily, not wanting to discuss my past with him or anyone else, "then you know why I was convicted."

"Killing her was self-defense. They should've sent you to therapy, not prison."

"I went back," I snapped. "That's why they convicted me. I'd already escaped, but I went all the way back to that house, and I walked over to where she was sitting in the living room, and I stabbed her in the throat. Then I stabbed her over and over and over as she died, because I *wanted her dead so badly it was killing me.*"

He met my glare with sympathy instead of revulsion. "That's still self-defense in my books."

I looked away. "How do you know Zak?"

"I tried to arrest him."

His cheerful tone made me blink. Against my wishes, my head swung back to him.

"What happened?" I asked warily.

"Got my ass handed to me." He grinned. "But it turned out we had similar goals. One thing led to another, and the next thing he knew, I'd convinced him to team up to save a kid's life."

Such altruism, Ríkr remarked from his perch near the ceiling. *In their alliance, who do you think exploits whom?*

I wanted to say Zak was the one using Morris, but I wasn't sure. There was something strangely disarming about Morris's warm blue eyes—and something dangerously cunning hiding behind his smile.

"And after that, you decided to become Zak's loyal lackey inside the MPD?" I asked with a hint of a sneer.

"I think of myself as more of a Nick Fury than a Count Rugen." He gave me a considering look. "Do you think Zak should be arrested and executed?"

"No, because I want to kill him myself."

"Does he know you want to kill him?"

"Yes. And he knows he fucking deserves it."

His eyebrows arched. "Brave man."

"What?" I snapped.

"Nothing."

Silence stretched between us—or rather, I was silent. Morris, gazing aimlessly around the room, was humming the jingle from a cereal commercial I'd heard on the radio.

The door opened, and Scooter returned with a bottle of dark powder. I spent the next hour lying uncomfortably still while Scooter adjusted the spell, then tugged my tank top partway down and drew on my chest, on and around my clavicle, with a wet marker of some kind. He sprinkled several powders in various spots on me and the spell sticking out from under me, then performed another long chant. Dull pain throbbed through the bone.

While he worked, my thoughts returned to the mysterious druid. Josephine Pisk. I had a name, but not much more. I chafed at the slow healing process, though I knew that, healing or no healing, Morris wouldn't let me search the precinct for her. At least, not without an explanation—and I wasn't telling him shit.

"All right," Scooter announced. He tugged the spell out from under my shoulder. "You're done. Take it easy for the next few days, and the bone will be good as new."

I sat up, my muscles stiff, and prodded my clavicle. Though tender, it no longer hurt to move my arm. Scooter handed me a damp towel, and I wiped away the lines and runes he'd drawn on my skin. As I finished, Ríkr scuttled down the curtain and jumped onto my shoulder.

Morris, who'd passed the time tapping on his phone, pushed to his feet. "Let's get going then, shall we, Saber?"

I stood, not particularly excited to proceed to the interrogation phase of my visit. On the plus side, I felt steadier now that both my arms were working.

"Thanks, Scooter," Morris called with a wave, simultaneously nudging me toward the door. "See you later."

"Sooner probably than later, knowing you," Scooter retorted.

I stepped out into the hallway, and Morris joined me, closing the door.

"Now," he said, his humor replaced with grimness. "It's time for the hard part."

I met his gaze with defiance, and Ríkr's small claws gripped my shoulder in readiness. If Morris planned to take me to a holding cell, I'd only have a few minutes to decide my plan of action.

Morris led me back to the elevator. I expected him to select a basement level—where the holding cells were located—but he surprised me again by choosing ground level.

On the main floor, I cautiously followed him to the far corner of the building. Halting in front of the last door, his broad shoulders blocking my view of the plaque just beneath the small frosted window, he tapped lightly.

"Come in," a woman barked.

He swung the door open and stepped aside so I could go ahead of him.

A simple rectangular desk took up most of the large office, and filing cabinets filled the space behind it. Framed certificates decorated the walls. Seated behind the desk was a woman in her forties with short, wavy blond hair and elegant, mature beauty sharpened by an aura of stern authority. Her blue eyes, a shade lighter than Morris's, raked over me.

My hackles rose, and I bristled with instant challenge, the shards of my past grating in my lungs.

The door clacked shut, and Morris stepped up beside me.

"Afternoon, Cap," he said, casual despite the woman's harshly assessing stare. "This is Saber Orien. The one I was telling you about—the druid."

I jolted. I was registered in the MPD's system as a witch. How did he know I was a druid?

He waved a hand up and down me like I was a mannequin dressed in an unusual outfit. "See what I mean?"

The woman gave me another once-over, then leaned back in her chair. "Perhaps."

I crossed my arms. "What the hell is this, Morris?"

A corner of his mouth twitched. "Saber, this is Captain Blythe. She's the big boss of the precinct."

"I know." My cold stare held the captain's. "I remember her standing in front of the Judiciary Council during my hearing and recommending a minimum three years of prison time before I could be offered rehabilitation."

The woman's expression didn't change. "Why are you registered as a witch, Miss Orien?"

"Ask my parents. They registered me."

Silence settled over the room like a cold miasma.

Morris cleared his throat. "We can't place Saber with just any rehab supervisor, and we can't throw her back in prison. If we try, that fuzzy ferret on her shoulder will obliterate us and half the precinct."

An accurate prediction, Ríkr crooned silkily, though no one but me could hear him.

"She has two years of rehab left," Morris continued, sliding his hands into his jeans pockets. "If we don't handle this right, she'll slip straight into the criminal underground. The last thing we need is another rogue druid on the loose."

As if Morris wasn't partly responsible for their existing druid problem.

"We need a *perfect* placement for her. And," he concluded, rocking back on his heels, "I see only one option."

The captain's stare bored into his for a long, tense moment, then she said flatly, "Make the arrangements, Agent Morris."

"Yes, ma'am." He nodded toward the door. "Let's go, Saber."

I didn't move, all my instincts warning me of a trap. "What arrangements?"

"I'll fill you in later."

"Fill me in now," I snapped.

The captain turned to her computer monitor. "Out, Agent Morris, and take Miss Orien with you."

Morris stepped toward the door, waving me to follow in a "stop being difficult" way.

I still didn't move. "What about the murder charges?"

"We aren't charging you," he replied with a note of exasperation. "We can't prove you're innocent, but we can't prove you're guilty either. Arla Collins, Laney Collins, and Jason Brine are all dead, and unless Jason reappears as a lethal secret-agent amnesiac at war with the agency that—"

"Morris," the captain growled warningly.

"Long story short, there's no evidence. We can't link you or anyone else to the murders." He shrugged. "So we aren't placing charges. You're in the clear. Why are you still asking questions about this?"

I caught my lower lip in my teeth, unease tinging my wary relief. Jason had gotten himself killed when he'd called the

Dullahan through the crossroads, and I'd killed Laney to stop her from giving Zak's name to the lethal fae. But I had no idea who had given Arla's name to the Dullahan.

Without another word, I pivoted on my heel and strode to the door.

"Miss Orien."

I stopped with my fingers on the door handle but didn't turn to face the captain.

"I recommended three years of prison time," she said matter-of-factly, "because if you'd gone immediately into rehabilitation, you'd have either run away or killed someone else, and in both cases, you'd have had no chance at a future."

I curled my lip. "You say that like you know a single fucking thing about me."

Shoving the door open, I walked out.

Morris caught up to me in the hallway. As he fell into step beside me, I slashed an angry glare across him. "What arrangements are you making?"

"We can't just let you wander around without supervision for the next two years, so I'm arranging a new guild for you."

My gut tightened with nerves. "What's the guild?"

"I'll let you know once it's confirmed." He eyed me sideways as we entered the lobby. "If I can make it happen, this will work for everyone, including you. I'm on your side, Saber."

Lips pressed thin, I pushed through the doors. He followed me outside, and I turned to face him. Did he know what it was like to be helpless in the power of someone who could control—and destroy—your life? Did he know what it was like to have everything you valued held over your head?

My fingers closed around the front of his t-shirt, and I yanked his face down to my level.

"The MPD," I hissed, "has never been on my side, and neither are you."

Shoving him away, I pivoted on my heel and strode into the parking lot, Ríkr riding on my shoulder.

"Have a little faith, Saber," he called after me, sounding unfazed. "And don't leave town, okay?"

I didn't bother to reply.

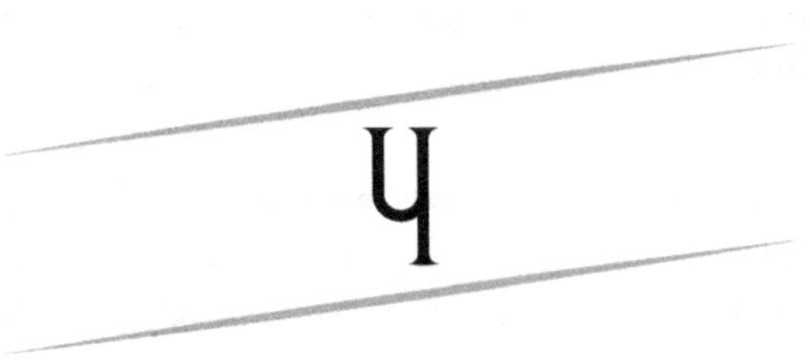

MY TRUCK RUMBLED DOWN Marine Drive in West Vancouver. I could've taken the highway and arrived at my destination a few minutes faster, but I'd chosen the scenic route. The water of the Burrard Inlet sparkled in the early evening sun on my left, and the city was a thin strip of land far across the waves.

So, Ríkr drawled from his spot on the passenger seat, lounging in cat form, *we have set upon a new quest.*

"If that's what you want to call it," I muttered.

Seeking the mysterious druid who called you by your mother's name, with naught but a general location in which to look? How else would you describe this mission?

"Are you complaining?"

Not at all. Onward to adventure, dearest dove.

As I guided the truck along the bends of Marine Drive, my thoughts skittered back to Morris and the new guild he was arranging for me. Should I have told him how important it was that I live at the rescue? How crucial it was to my sanity? Should I have explained how a new guild full of judgmental strangers was more than I could handle right now?

I shook my head. What was the point? Whatever Morris claimed, my comfort was his last priority. I was a druid—one of the most powerful and unpredictable types of mythics. The MPD would place me in a guild where they could monitor and control me. They didn't want another rogue druid, like Morris had said.

Later, I'd think about how he—and now all of the MPD—had found out I was a druid, who must have told him, and how I could add "selling me out" to that person's towering list of betrayals.

But right now, my priority was finding Josephine Pisk.

Turning off Marine Drive, I directed the truck onto a narrow road that resembled a back lane more than a city street. It wound past properties hidden by dense greenery before the private land gave way to mature coniferous trees that towered a hundred feet tall. I'd entered Lighthouse Park, where Morris had said Josephine was working on a bounty-hunting case.

The road ended in a gravel lot half filled with vehicles. I parked my truck beside a minivan, shut off the engine, and let out a deep breath. Then I reached down to the floor in front of the passenger seat and lifted a small, plain paper bag. I withdrew a slim black box, pried it open, and upended it over my palm.

A switchblade landed in my waiting hand.

My fingers curled around the cool, olive-green handle. I rubbed my thumb across the switch, then pressed it. A double-edged black blade snapped out, sharp and beautiful in its simple symmetry.

Its weight in my hand eased the pressure compressing my lungs, and I took a deep breath—a deeper breath than I'd taken since losing my knife almost a week ago.

It wasn't normal. It wasn't healthy. But I needed it anyway.

A fine new weapon. Ríkr arched his feline back in a stretch. *But perhaps insufficient for a druid. We must promptly increase your armaments.*

I didn't reply. If I agreed to become his consort, one of my requirements for our new bond would be that he consume all my power again. I had no intention of embracing the druid lifestyle.

Impatient with my minute examination of my new blade, Ríkr hopped off the seat. His form blurred through the truck door, and before he landed on the ground outside, he'd transformed into a crow. The white bird soared up into the trees.

I pushed the switchblade box back into its bag and tucked both in the glove compartment. Switchblades were a prohibited weapon—though you could buy them if you knew where to shop—and I didn't want to leave evidence lying in plain sight.

Flinging open the truck door, I climbed out. As my feet met the gravel, another notch of tension released from my spine. Old nature was the most magnificent landscape for a witch—or a druid—to walk. The sleepy but powerful life force of this ancient forest emanated from the land like a warm embrace, tinged with the fiercer power of the ocean currents that surrounded it. I stood beside the truck, letting it soak into me, then shut the vehicle's door.

Ríkr, can you sense the druid? I asked, heading toward the trailhead.

Not currently, he reported from a lofty perch in a cedar. *I shall search farther afield.*

He flew toward the tops of the towering trees, and I strode down the path, my hands tucked in my pockets and my fingers loosely curled around my switchblade. My muscles relaxed, but even the forest's soothing influence couldn't calm my mind.

Since Ríkr's revelation that I was a druid, I'd lost four days in a shocked haze. Now that I was back to myself, the pressing need for answers burned inside me like an ever-present flame, feeding off my confusion and doubt. My parents had raised me as a witch, but they'd given me the river-stone pendant to hide me from fae. Why would a witch child need such a powerful artifact? They must have known I was a druid.

So why had they lied?

I needed the truth, but my parents were dead, my aunt was dead, and I didn't know any other relatives or family friends.

But Josephine had known my mother. And Josephine was a druid.

The possible implications of that connection made my gut twist, and anxiety drove me into a faster pace. I had to find her. She might be the only person alive who could provide the answers I needed.

At the end of the trail, I found myself standing on a slab of thick rock that jutted into the ocean waters. The Howe Sound stretched as far as I could see, distant islands on the horizon. The salty breeze washed across my face, cool and tangy with a sour undertone of wet things and rot. The energies here were different, the immense and immutable power of the ocean blending with the ancient steadfastness of the forest.

I exhaled slowly. Racing around the park would be a waste of effort. I should calm down and wait for Ríkr to find Josephine. He could search far more efficiently than I could.

A few more deep breaths settled me, and as I watched the waves splash against the rocks, a soft tune came to my lips.

"*Twas Friday morn when we set sail, and we were not far from the land,*" I sang, picking up a pebble. "*When the captain, he spied a lovely mermaid*"—I pitched it toward the water—"*with a comb and a glass in her hand.*"

The pebble landed with a splash, and still singing, I headed north along the shore, not caring where I ended up.

"*And up spoke the mate of our gallant ship, and a well-spoken man was he.*" I climbed along the rocks at the water's edge. "*I have me a wife in Salem by the sea, and tonight she a widow will be.*"

Trailing off, I halted and squinted across the inlet. Fifteen meters out, beside a small rocky outcrop, a dark spot I'd assumed was seaweed floated on the waves. Shading my eyes with one hand, I peered toward it, wondering why it had caught my attention.

Not seaweed, I realized, but fishing nets. Discarded nets and rope, tangled together with aquatic debris to form a small, floating island of trash—and within it, something was moving. A large, dark flipper lifted out of the water, then splashed back down.

My breath hitched. Amidst the garbage was the hump of a sea turtle's shell. Was it caught in the netting? I looked around sharply, but the only boats in the area were distant specks.

Ríkr? I called with my mind. *Ríkr, come here!*

He didn't reply. Was he too far to hear me?

The turtle splashed helplessly. In a mess of netting like that, the more it struggled, the more entangled it would become. It would end up trapped beneath the surface and drown, or it'd slowly starve to death.

This wasn't natural selection. This was humanity destroying everything it touched.

I took my phone and keys out of my pockets, set them on a rock, then stripped down to my black sports bra and boy-short-style underwear. The cool ocean breeze chilled my skin as I faced the water, fingers gripping my new switchblade.

"*Three times around went our gallant ship,*" I sang under my breath. "*And she sank to the bottom of the sea.*"

Then I climbed down into the ocean waves.

I gasped as cold water engulfed me, gooseflesh erupting over my skin. It might be summer, but this far north, the Pacific Ocean was never warm. My bare feet touched slimy rocks, the waves sloshing against my chest, and I launched forward into a strong breaststroke.

Passing the rocky outcrop, I circled the garbage float. Rotting seaweed trailed off a massive clump of twisted blue fishing net, with bright orange lines knotted around it. White plastic bags, snagged on the net, rippled in the current like flags of surrender.

The turtle was on the west side, farthest from the shore. As I drew closer, I realized the distance and water had warped my perception of the turtle's size. It was a full-grown leatherback—and it was massive. Its ridged shell was almost as long as I was tall. Several loops of orange fishing line were wrapped around its left flipper.

The turtle stuck its head out of the water, one dark eye watching me as it blew out a breath and sucked in another one.

"Oh," I breathed. "You're beautiful, darling. You're going to be okay. I'm here to help."

Treading water, I reached for it. It ducked under the surface to get away from me, and the floating mess dipped as the sea turtle's weight—easily over a thousand pounds—dragged it down.

I dove with it and pressed my palm to its back, letting it feel my calm desire to help. Its beating flippers stilled, then it rose back toward the surface, lifting me with it. We broke the surface together, and I blinked salt water from my eyes.

"You'll be okay," I crooned, running my hand over its back, a white scar disfiguring its ridged shell—an old wound from a collision with a boat.

Humming softly to calm it, I slid my knife under the water-swollen rope cinched around its massive flipper and started sawing. The plastic bags, which resembled jellyfish—the leatherbacks' primary prey—had probably attracted the turtle to the garbage pile. But that was just one of the many ways this beautiful, ancient species had become critically endangered, with ninety-five percent of its population wiped out.

Legs kicking to steady myself in the rising and falling waves, I cut through a second loop. The turtle's flippers surged with growing urgency, and I hung on as I slid my blade under the last loop. With a sharp jerk, I cut the line, and the turtle dove in a rush, so huge and heavy that its momentum sucked me below the surface.

I kicked my feet—and realized I'd been wrong. The turtle hadn't pulled me under.

Something else had a hold of my ankle and was dragging me downward.

Pain erupted in my inner ears as I plunged into the depths too quickly. I swallowed to pop my ears, then kicked against the vise squeezing my ankle. It didn't loosen, and something grabbed my other foot.

I squinted into the murky water—and found someone staring back at me.

The large, glassy, dark blue eyes were set in a humanish face with pale, almost translucent skin and bold markings on the cheeks and temples. A tangle of long hair, braided with seashells, floated off its head. Its human torso, naked and sexless, morphed seamlessly into a smooth, dolphin-like tail with bold black and white stripes down the sides.

The merfae floated in front of me, and a second one held my ankles, its limbs slightly more delicate—a female?

Let me go! I threw the thought at the two fae.

Their dark eyes stared at me.

Release me! I shouted at them as my lungs burned. I hadn't gotten a proper breath before going under.

No reaction.

I blew out a slow stream of bubbles to quell my desperate need to breathe. As my lungs emptied, I bent at the waist and slashed my knife across the merfae's webbed fingers. Blood stained the water as she jerked her hand back.

With a sweep of his tail, the male merfae darted behind me, looped his slimy arm around my neck, and dragged me backward and down. The surface above me sparkled through the gloom.

I jabbed my knife over my shoulder and into his face.

He shoved away from me, and with the sudden release of pressure on my throat, the little air in my lungs rushed out in a stream of bubbles—and I compulsively inhaled. Water hit the back of my throat and my laryngeal muscles seized, closing my airways.

The urge to cough, gasp, and breathe obliterated my brain, and panic hit me like a breaking ocean wave. I kicked frantically toward the surface.

The two merfae gripped both my legs. Agony burned through my lungs and throat as they dragged me down. They were going to drown me and devour me. My vision narrowed to a pinprick, my entire body screaming for oxygen.

Amber light burst across my eyes.

Bubbles swirled as I revolved in the water, completely disoriented. My thoughts were fuzzy, my consciousness fading. Vaguely, I wondered which way was up.

Another flare of yellowish light. Water rushed around me. A hand squeezed my arm—someone pulling me through the current.

My head broke the surface. Cold air hit my skin. The waves pushed my body to and fro, my limbs limp and unresponsive.

My back met a hard surface. No more waves. I was dragged out of the water.

"Breathe!"

A hand hit me hard in the back, jolting my entire torso. My throat unlocked and I gasped in air—then doubled over, coughing violently. Dizziness rolled through me, my throat burning. As my diaphragm spasmed, my stomach jumped. I gulped it down before I vomited.

As the coughing fit subsided, I became aware of the arms around my middle that were keeping me from tumbling off the small rocky outcrop. I squinched my burning eyes halfway open. My legs were sprawled out in front of me on the slimy rock, my feet in the water. Another pair of legs, clad in soaked jeans, were braced on either side of me—masculine legs.

I was sitting between someone's knees, the other person's wet chest pressing into my back with each panting breath. But I didn't need to turn around to discover my rescuer's identity. I could sense his presence in the air—a subtle, electric sense of calmness and command.

I knew *exactly* who'd pulled me from the water.

5

MY FINGERS CURLED TIGHTLY around the cold, solid weight of my switchblade.

"What," I began slowly, the word rasping out of me as though dragged from my lungs, "are … you … doing … here?"

Maybe he felt my body coiling with tension, or maybe he knew my standard reaction to a threat, but his hand closed around my wrist, immobilizing my weapon.

"I know you can't resist knifing me anytime I save your life," he said, "but those merfae will drown us both if we end up back in the water."

The husky rumble of his voice plunged through my body and shivered in my bones. Days that felt like years. Years that felt like minutes. I didn't know anymore how long it'd been since I'd heard his voice. I didn't know why the sound reverberated through me like this—and the feeling made my fingers spasm around my knife with the urge to silence him. To silence his power over me.

My only comfort was being unable to see his face.

"Why the fuck are you here, Zak?" I growled, my throat burning with each hoarse word.

"Why were you swimming in merfae waters?"

"None of your goddamn business." My limbs were trembling, either from rage or nearly drowning. "You don't seem to grasp that the only circumstance in which I want to see your face is to identify your mangled corpse in a morgue."

"According to Kit, you want to kill me yourself."

My upper lip curled. So he and his pet agent *were* talking to each other about me. Morris must've tipped Zak off about my possible whereabouts after I'd left the precinct.

They both needed a knife in the gut for thinking they could mess with my life.

With that thought, I tried to twist my wrist free, but Zak tightened his grip—and his other arm constricted as well, pulling me harder against him. His chest was hot, his skin slick with water. He wasn't wearing a shirt—and I was nearly naked.

I glanced at the shore, fifteen meters away. It wasn't far—but far enough for aquatic fae to drown me.

"Can't you deal with the merfae?" I demanded.

"You've never met a merfae before, have you?" Zak replied with a low snort. "They hate humans. Including druids. They won't even acknowledge me."

So, what then? We were stuck out here until the merfae gave up and went home? As if they'd leave when there was not one but *two* tasty druids stranded on this stupid rock.

Zak's hand pressed into my bare stomach as though I might leap recklessly into the water if he didn't stop me. "Why are you out here?"

"I fancied a nice Northern Pacific swim."

"Funny."

"Why are *you* here?"

"You haven't guessed?"

I exhaled—then twisted violently, my wrist tearing free from Zak's grip. We grappled, slipping on the rock, then he went rigid as I touched my razor-edged blade to his throat.

We were pressed together, legs tangled, me half on top of him. His vibrant green stare pierced me as deeply as his voice had, his dripping black hair plastered to his forehead and his jaw darkened by stubble from a missed shave.

My gut tightened uncomfortably at the sight of his face, conflicting emotions battering me, but I shoved it all aside and brought my fury to the surface.

"Is this a game to you?" I snarled. "Am *I* a game? Show up for no fucking reason, taunt me, torment me? See how long it takes me to snap?"

"That's not why I'm here."

I leaned down, getting more in his face. "Then *why?*"

"Get the knife off my throat first."

"Answer first so I can decide how much I want to watch you bleed out all over this rock."

He tilted his head up, exposing more of his throat. "Go ahead, then."

I stiffened, caught off guard. He gazed at me, unflinching, his expression cool, almost disinterested. His arms were slack at his sides. He wasn't even trying to defend himself.

"If you want to kill me so badly, do it," he said. "Slit my throat."

A quiver ran through my hand, my knuckles white around the handle. I should. Just cut his throat, shove his bleeding body into the water, and swim for shore while his death throes distracted the merfae.

"Kill me."

"Don't act like a guilt-ridden martyr," I spat. "I'm not buying it."

"I'm not acting like anything." His hand rose, and he curled his fingers over mine so we were both holding the switchblade. "I know you won't do it."

"Don't underestimate me."

"You killed someone to save my life, Saber. You don't want to kill me."

I stared down at him. His water-speckled skin stretched taut over hard muscles, his curved biceps flexing. The flat planes of thick pectorals met the smooth ridges of his abs. Every line of his body spoke of strength and power.

This deeply masculine adult man overlapped in my mind with the slimmer, softer teen boy I'd first met, and the longer I looked at him—at them—the more I felt myself unraveling. The past and the present were colliding in front of my eyes. Two unreconcilable beings, the boy he'd been haunting the man he'd become, both looking at me with the same green eyes.

They were both hurting me. The past and present, gouging out my heart.

"I want to."

The words were a hoarse whisper. My hand shook in his hold. He wasn't stopping me from pushing the knife into his throat. The only thing stopping me was myself.

"I want to kill you."

This time, I gasped the words. My whole body was trembling. On this stupid rock in the ocean, trapped and surrounded by fae who wanted to drown us, I told myself to just do it. Just kill him. Just end it forever. End this tearing, shattering pain I felt.

"Why can't I?"

I hadn't meant to speak those words. Hadn't meant for them to scrape from my abused throat. Hadn't meant for him to hear them.

His enigmatic eyes watched me, unreadable and unfathomable.

White wings beating, a hawk swooped down out of the sky. Ríkr circled over our heads in a tight arc.

What is this? he asked sharply. *Why are you at sea?*

"Where have you been?" I barked, withdrawing my knife from Zak's throat.

Fetching the druid, as you requested. The other druid, he added.

Startled, I looked toward the shore. Standing on the rocks beside my pile of clothes with her arms folded was Josephine. Even at that distance, I could see that her eyebrows were arched.

Can you do something about the merfae? I asked Ríkr silently.

I'm afraid I cannot, dove.

My frustration reignited. *Why not?*

I dislike getting wet. He swooped another circle. *Also, I am not well suited for aquatic combat.*

Suppressing an aggravated snarl, I looked back at Josephine.

"Need help?" she called from the shore.

I hesitated, then shouted back, "There are merfae."

Her short laugh echoed across the water. "My familiar will distract them, so go ahead and swim back."

Her familiar? I couldn't see or sense another fae. Come to think of it, I couldn't detect Lallakai's presence either. Was she not nearby protecting her druid?

I glanced at Zak. Since the alternative was staying on this rock with him, I swallowed against the painful burn in my throat and plunged into the salt water. The cold shocked my system all over again.

No merfae appeared as I swam for shore, but the short distance exhausted the last of my strength, and I was breathing hard as I pulled myself up onto the rocks. Water sluiced off me as I stumbled to my feet. Josephine caught my arm, steadying me. The druid was in her late-thirties with a warm, golden-ochre complexion, expressive full lips, and bold eyes that, with a mere glance, evaluated me on every level—and revealed nothing of her assessment.

"Looks like you were having fun out there," she remarked.

Drawing on long years of practice, I dredged up my "nice Saber" smile in response.

With a splash, Zak climbed onto the rocks a few yards away. He straightened to his full height and fixed a green-eyed stare on Josephine.

"Tempest Druid," he rumbled.

"Crystal Druid," she replied frostily.

I glanced between them. "You two have met?"

"No," they replied in unison—and with equal hostility.

What's their problem? I silently wondered.

Ríkr landed on a boulder beside me. *Druids are territorial, dove. They rarely rejoice in encountering another of their kith.*

Josephine raised her eyebrows slightly—and a sudden gale tore across the shore. From the shimmering wind, a figure materialized. The tall, slender fae wore gray and silver robes that trailed thin black ties, the silk ribbons snapping in the gusts. Long, pale lilac hair swept around him, his androgynously beautiful face dominated by large, pupilless opal eyes.

Threads of glowing silver magic spiraled around his delicate fingers as he raised them toward Zak.

Zak gave the fae a dismissive glance. Despite being shirtless, shoeless, unarmed, and as far as I could tell, completely alone, he seemed unconcerned for his safety. As he turned toward the Tempest Druid, I glimpsed the tattoos on his left forearm. Each of the five dark circles contained a colorful magic rune.

"Are you sure you and your wind master want to pick a fight with me, Tempest Druid?" he asked coolly.

"Why are you back?" she demanded. "You abandoned your territory."

"I took a vacation." He smiled without humor, showing his teeth. "And this isn't your territory either."

"Can we call it neutral ground, then?" I asked with a hopeful smile. Zak glanced at me, then did a double take when he saw my pleasant expression. "I'd like to speak with you, Josephine. If possible?"

The Tempest Druid frowned in answer. Still smiling, I tilted my head toward Zak—and out of her line of sight.

"Fuck off," I mouthed silently.

His eyebrows shot up. A faint smirk crossed his lips, and without comment, he picked up his shoes and shirt, discarded on the rocks where he must have pulled them off before jumping in the water to save me from the merfae. I belatedly noticed that his stab wounds from a week ago, courtesy of my knife, were completely gone. He must've found a healer in the past few days.

Which of us was more twisted—me for stabbing him only to save his life shortly afterward, or him for saving my life after I'd stabbed him?

Belongings in hand, he walked into the trees. I watched him go with narrowed eyes.

"Hm," Josephine mused, also observing Zak's silent retreat. "He's not what I expected."

Saying nothing, I turned to grab my clothes—and found myself facing her familiar. Or was he her consort? His fathomless opal eyes flicked across my face, then a salty breeze rushed off the water, and with it, the wind fae disappeared into shimmers of air.

Perched on his rock, Ríkr ruffled his feathers in irritation.

I yanked my clothes over my wet skin, then hastily turned back to Josephine. "I'm sorry for bothering you. I just wanted to ask you … about my mother."

"Mairead," she said. "You look just like her—except taller. Much taller." She pursed her lips. "I heard that Mairead passed away."

"Yes, eighteen years ago."

"I'm sorry for your loss." She offered her hand. "Should we introduce ourselves? I'm Josephine Pisk, the Tempest Druid, but my friends call me Jo."

I shook her hand. "Saber Orien. Should I … call you Jo, then?"

"If you want." She smiled. "I considered Mairead a friend, and I think she felt the same way. Who knew she had a daughter! What—yes, I'm asking her. Don't distract me."

I blinked in confusion.

"Sorry. Niavv likes to natter in my head while I'm having conversations with people."

I peered around the rocky shoreline, but I couldn't see the wind fae, not even when I focused my vision on the misty fae demesne.

"He's adept at concealment," she added, watching me with amusement. "He wants to know your druid name. He's convinced he knows all the druids in the area, and he's frustrated that he doesn't recognize you."

"I don't have a druid name."

Her full lips quirked down. "Are you a practicing druid?"

I hesitated, unsure how much I wanted to reveal. "No."

"Oh. That's a shame. I really admired the Meadowlark Druid, and I bet you'd be just as talented."

My gut dropped, and I felt like I was underwater again, my lungs empty and my mind spinning from lack of oxygen. "The Meadowlark Druid?"

"She was something else," Josephine mused, gazing out at the water. She hadn't noticed my reaction. "The way she sang … unbelievable. I've never heard anything like it before or since. Fae would stop whatever they were doing to listen. Mairead was truly gifted."

Her voice sounded very far away, her words sliding through my ears, scarcely heard.

As soon as Ríkr had revealed I was a druid, I'd wondered. Either my parents hadn't been my parents at all, or one of them had been a druid too. And when Josephine, a druid, had called me by my mother's name, I'd suspected I knew which parent.

Now I had confirmation—and it rocked the very foundation of my world. Every memory of my mother shifted, cast into a different light. I remembered her gentle smile, her blue-gray eyes just like mine. I remembered her voice and the way it flowed through every molecule of my body when she'd sing.

The Meadowlark Druid. My mother had been a druid.

My hands shook and I curled them into fists. "How did you know her?"

Only after I'd spoken did I realize I was interrupting Josephine. She glanced at me, concern pinching her eyes. She opened her mouth, then reconsidered whatever she'd been about to say.

"We met … the year before she died, I guess it would've been." She clasped her hands together. "I'd just started bounty hunting, and I was tracking a black witch who'd been killing fae on Vancouver Island before fleeing inland. He was heading for Kamloops, but I lost him in the Coquihalla Pass."

She smiled ruefully. "I was bumbling around, drawing all sorts of fae attention, and Mairead showed up to find out what young, idiotic druid was kicking up such a fuss."

It was so easy to imagine: my mom would've crossed her arms, one hip cocked, and arched her right eyebrow in that lofty, knowing look that always meant someone—usually me or my dad—was about to get in trouble for doing something foolish.

"When I explained what I was up to," Josephine continued, "she offered to help. The rest of the story is pretty mundane. It took us a week to catch the guy, and I learned a ton from her while we worked together."

The ache inside me deepened. It seemed territorial druid instincts didn't preclude any possible friendship between druids. Josephine's hostile reaction to Zak probably had as much to do with his dangerous reputation as his druid status.

I brought up another false smile, thankful I had so much practice hiding my real face. "Did my mother ever mention me or her family?"

"She didn't, but that's no surprise. Druids are often very private—or secretive, depending on how you look at it." She shrugged. "I'm not fussy about secrecy, myself. It's hard to be a bounty hunter and not earn a reputation."

Zak, too, had kept his druid identity a secret. I remembered from his bounty listing that his rogue alias and his druid name had only recently been connected as the same person.

"Mairead didn't tell me where she lived," Josephine added, "though I assume her territory was somewhere nearby. Again, typical for many druids."

I nodded as though I were familiar with the ways of druids. Keeping my pleasant mask in place was a struggle as the pillars of my existence quaked and crumbled.

"This might be an odd question," I began haltingly, "but do you know why a druid might raise their child as a witch?"

"Some druids will register as witches with the MPD to protect their identities. Fae predation is our biggest killer, but there are territory disputes with other druids, conflicts with other mythics, abduction, enslavement—yes, Niavv, I was about to tell her that many druid lines live in complete secrecy. Only the fae in and around their territories know who and what they are."

Understanding trickled through me. My mother must've raised me as a witch to protect us. Children didn't understand secrecy, so it was safer to wait until I was older to tell me the truth about what I was.

Except she'd died before she could.

My parents hadn't made any arrangements for me in case of their deaths, or none that the MPD had discovered. Aunt Ruth had been my only living relative—and not even a blood relative. She'd been married to my father's older brother for three short years before he died, and she hadn't kept in contact with her in-laws. The first time I met her was the day she picked me up from MPD foster care.

Pulling myself from dark thoughts of the past, I offered Josephine my hand. "Thanks for answering my questions. I appreciate your time."

"Sure thing." She shook my hand, but her expression was oddly critical. "Feel free to tell me to butt out, but your aura is a mess."

"My aura?" I repeated blankly.

"It's your choice if you want to practice druidry or not, but you should at least utilize basic aura reflection. Who did you appren—no way, Niavv," she said abruptly, interrupting herself.

"No way what?" I asked.

She grimaced in embarrassment. "He asked if you've had any training at all. Rude, I know."

My false smile stretched my lips. "I guess I'm just rusty since I don't practice."

She frowned slightly, then cleared her expression. "Fair enough. Just be careful in less urban places like this—and watch out for the Crystal Druid. Again, none of my business, but he's Trouble with a capital T."

"Why didn't you try to capture him?" I asked curiously. "Since you're a bounty hunter?"

She snorted. "Because I don't want to die today. I'm good, but I'm not *that* good—which means he could rip you apart."

I held my smile with effort. Little did she know he already had.

6

STANDING AT THE EDGE of the water, I watched the amber sunset dim, the sky darkening to shades of purple and indigo. Every breath scraped my raw throat and the broken shards inside me cut at my lungs.

I sank my hands into my damp hair. My fingers curled, nails dragging over my scalp. Tilting my head back, I drew in the deepest breath I could, and with it I gathered all my uncertainty, my fear, my grief, my hurt, my loneliness. I filled my lungs with everything I felt until my chest was about to burst.

Then I unleashed it all in a scream.

The sound split the quiet evening air and tore through my throat. I embraced the pain as I let loose the storm inside me in the only way I could. I screamed until I ran out of air, then I sagged forward, still clutching my head as though I could hold myself together.

My anguished cry echoed across the water, softly fading, and part of me wished I could fade away too.

I'd wanted answers about my parents, and now I had one—but knowing my mother had been a druid was worse than knowing nothing. My parents, my childhood, my past. Nothing was what I'd believed. I didn't know who I was, who I should've been, or what the hell I was supposed to do.

Everything was spinning inside me like a maelstrom. The boy who'd betrayed me, back again. Memories I'd lost, returned. My magic, a ticking timebomb threatening to explode the life I'd built. The threat of losing my place at the rescue, of the MPD and the new guild Morris was arranging for me. Zak. Ríkr. My mother. Lies and betrayals and secrets.

A tremor ran through me. I couldn't handle all this right now. I had to go home before I lost it.

I hiked swiftly along the shore in the fading light, and by the time I reached the path, a white coyote had joined me. He hadn't been far. Ríkr might struggle to understand my human emotions, but he'd always had good instincts for when I needed space.

The parking lot had emptied while I'd loitered on the shore, and there were only two vehicles left: my old truck and a newer black pickup. I angled toward my truck with long, desperate strides, but as I reached the driver's door, a prickle ran along my spine.

A faint but familiar sensation of otherworldly power teased my senses.

Coming to an abrupt halt, I looked again at the black truck twenty feet away—and saw what I'd missed the first time.

A dark figure leaned against the door, dressed in black clothes, arms folded.

No. I'd waited this long so he'd be gone. So I wouldn't have to face him again while I was so unbalanced—but here he was anyway. Waiting for me. Forcing his presence on me. Making me relive the past. Making me hate him and hate myself and hate everything just like I had ten years ago.

"Why are you still here?" I asked hoarsely.

He pushed off the truck, watching me. Seeing me fragile. Seeing me weak. Seeing me on the verge of breaking.

"*Why are you here?*" The furious question burst out of me. "You're right, okay? I can't kill you. You deserve it. You fucking deserve it, you coldhearted bastard, *but I can't do it.*"

My tormented shout filled the parking lot, absorbed by the quiet forest. The boy who'd broken me was standing right there, *right there*, and even though everything inside me wanted to hurt him, to destroy him, I couldn't.

"I admitted it!" I flung my hand out. "You win! You fucking *win!* So leave me alone! Just go and never come back and leave me in peace."

My vision blurred. Tears had filled my eyes but I blinked them away. I wouldn't cry in front of him. Never.

"You can't live in peace."

His rumbling voice was closer than I'd expected, and I roughly swiped my hand over my eyes to clear my vision. He'd moved toward me and stood ten feet away.

"Druids don't get to live in peace. No matter where you go, fae will find you."

A sob tried to push out of my throat and I choked it back. "Go *away!* Just go—*go go* GO!"

The last word was a hysterical shriek. I was losing it. I was falling apart, and I couldn't let him see. I whirled blindly toward the truck. I hadn't locked it. The door yanked open under my hand, and I scrambled into the driver's seat. My fumbling fingers found the keys in my pocket and I shoved them into the ignition.

I couldn't see through the tears blurring my vision. My chest heaved with the sobs I was fighting. I turned the key anyway.

The engine stuttered, coughed, and died.

I twisted the key again.

Another stuttering cough. The engine didn't turn over.

"No," I gasped, wrenching on the key. "No, no, no!"

Why? Why now? I needed to get away, to move, to flee, to go home—home, I needed home, I needed it now, my safe place—but the truck wouldn't start and I was trapped—

Pain registered on my senses. I was hitting the steering wheel. Pounding it as hard as I could, tears streaming down my face. I was screaming wordlessly as I slammed my fists down over and over, and everything hurt so much that I didn't even feel the impact.

Hands closed around my wrists, stopping me.

I wrenched one arm free and drove my fist into Zak's stomach as hard as I'd been hitting the steering wheel. He took the blow with a muffled grunt, then grabbed my wrist again and heaved me out of the truck.

I fell into him, and for a second, the barest second, I sagged against his warm, solid chest.

Then I shoved off him with a shrieked curse. *"Leave me alone!"*

He pulled me into him and wrapped both arms around my upper torso, pinning me to his chest, my hands trapped between our bodies.

"*No!*" I was screaming, struggling, crying. I couldn't stop. I wanted to stop. He could see, hear, feel every heaving sob, and I couldn't bear it. I was breaking. I was imploding.

"Let me go!" I kicked his shin. Stamped his foot. Headbutted his shoulder. He didn't let go. "Let me go, you bastard!"

His arms tightened instead.

I let out a wordless shriek. "I hate you! *I hate you, Zak!*"

"I know," he whispered, so quiet I almost didn't hear it.

"Then let me go!"

"No."

My rage burst apart and exhausted despair swept in. I crumpled. He took my weight, holding me tightly. I silently shook, waiting for numbness, the wonderful, glorious numbness that would deaden the pain and emotions.

But all I felt was exhaustion so deep that drowning would've been a welcome escape.

Zak uncurled one arm from around me and reached into the truck. A metallic jingle as he pulled my keys from the ignition. A creak and a thump as he shut the door. A dull clunk as he locked it.

His arm guided me into motion. I dragged my feet, too tired to fight him anymore.

The black truck's door opened. Hands gently pushed me into a seat. I sagged into the leather, staring at nothing. The door closed.

Movement at my feet. A white cat stood on the floor mat between my boots, gazing up at me with pale blue eyes. Ríkr rose on his hind legs, front paws braced on my knees, and studied me again, uncertain. Then he hopped up onto my lap and carefully lay down, a warm weight across my thighs, facing the driver's side door as it opened.

Zak climbed into the seat. His door thumped shut. The truck's engine rolled over smoothly.

Neither the fae nor the druid said a word as we drove away from the park.

I WAS MOVING, but not from the vibrations of the truck rushing along the highway. It was the slow sway of a human gait, and strong arms held me against a warm chest, my head resting on a solid shoulder.

My eyelids fluttered, but I didn't open them. I wanted the dark unawareness of sleep. I didn't care that I had no idea where I was or where Zak was taking me.

His stride shortened, then he leaned forward, lowering me. My back met the firm give of a mattress, and as my head settled on a pillow, the familiar scent of my laundry detergent and shampoo filled my nose.

He'd taken me home. The thought fluttered sluggishly through my weary mind. Sleep was closing in on me again.

Now that she is returned to her abode, you must leave.

Ríkr's telepathic voice was distant; he wasn't directing his words at my mind.

"I'm not going anywhere," Zak rumbled, his quiet voice much closer. A blanket slid over me, and he tucked it under my chin. "I only left in the first place because you insisted she needed space."

She still does. Your return caused this. Whatever transgression you inflicted on her in the past, you left wounds too great for her to bear.

"What about you?" Zak whispered harshly. "You knew she had no idea she was a druid, but you hid the truth and sucked her power dry for *years*."

That is between us. The mattress vibrated as a slight weight moved across it—the press of Ríkr's feline paws. He stopped near my pillow, and when he spoke again, his voice had deepened with an echo of ancient power. *Heed me now, Crystal Druid. If you cause her distress again as you did this night, I will kill you on her behalf.*

Zak made a rough sound in his throat. "You're just like the rest of your kind, Ríkr. You don't get it."

Get what, pray tell? he hissed.

"Killing the people who hurt you doesn't fix anything." A rustle of movement, then near-silent steps receded toward the door. "Not for humans, at least."

The door closed with a soft click.

Ríkr let out a low, feline growl, and the mattress bounced slightly as he lay near my pillow. He grumbled a bit more before falling silent.

My eyes cracked open, dry and stinging, then slid closed again. Zak's words replayed in my mind, over and over, sinking deeper and deeper until the truth had entombed itself into my scarred heart.

Killing our tormenters wouldn't heal our wounds.

But that wasn't why I couldn't kill Zak.

7

I WOKE WITH MY LIMBS ACHING, my head throbbing painfully, and my skin stinging with scrapes. My throat was excruciatingly raw, my eyes felt swollen, and my nose was stuffed. I was dirty and grimy with dried ocean water.

Gingerly, I sat up. I was alone in my bedroom. Dragging myself out of bed, I grabbed an armload of clean clothes from my closet and crept to my bedroom door. Cracking it open, I found the main room empty. No Ríkr, and no sign that Zak had slept on the sofa.

I wasted no time getting into the shower. The water was hot and soothing, and as I soaked, my mind locked on the most important, most disturbing thing I'd learned yesterday: my mother's true identity as the Meadowlark Druid. I had the first answer I'd needed—which of my parents had been a druid—but I needed more. Much more.

I lathered shampoo into my hair. I still had to deal with Ríkr's offer to take me as his consort, but I wasn't deciding anything until I heard his whole story. And that could wait a little longer. If I wanted answers about my mother, I needed to get them before Morris finished arranging my future for me. Once I was placed in a specially selected, MPD-approved guild, my freedom would be restricted—assuming they allowed me any freedom at all.

After rinsing off, I got out of the shower and wrapped myself in a towel. Watching my reflection as I blow-dried my hair, I noted my red-rimmed eyes and hollow cheeks, my skin paler than usual.

Dressed in a tank top, a snug zip-up sweater, and jeans, I unearthed the pants I'd slept in and rescued my phone and switchblade. Stuffing them in my jeans pockets, I traipsed down the stairs and locked the door behind me.

Gravel crunched under my hiking boots as I strode into the yard. It was still dark, the sky tinged deep blue with the coming dawn. Shadows draped the farm, obscuring the large black pickup with dark-tinted windows parked a car length away from Dominique's old Ranger. My lips thinned.

A hungry horse neighed hopefully from its stall turnout, and I turned away from the black vehicle to head for the stable. No personal crisis could take precedence over the animals' care. As I headed to the feed room, my thoughts cycled through what I knew and what I needed to know.

An hour later, the sun was just breaching the mountainous horizon in the east, the animals were fed, and I was striding toward that black truck.

Movement in the back caught my attention. Four gleaming, blood-red eyes appeared—Zak's two vargs, sitting in the box like obedient dogs. Ignoring them, I cupped my hands against the tinted glass of the passenger window and peered inside, just able to make out a dark shape on the seat. I tapped on the glass. The dark shape moved, then the locks popped.

I opened the door.

Zak lay across the reclined seat. He'd changed into a fresh t-shirt and dark jeans, and his tousled hair was clean, his jaw smooth from a recent shave; he must have borrowed my bathroom last night.

He squinted blearily at me, then at the pink sunrise. "What time is it?"

His tone was one of extreme displeasure.

"Morris does favors for you, right?" I asked without preamble or warmth.

He rubbed a hand over his eyes. "What?"

"I want the MPD report on my parents' deaths."

Dragging his hand down his face, he exhaled roughly. "Next time you want a favor at the crack of dawn, at least bring me a coffee or something."

"Pain and adrenaline work better than caffeine," I informed him with sugary venom. "Would you like some of those?"

He fumbled for the lever on the side of his seat, and the back returned to its upright position. "I'll pass on the early morning knife play."

"Call Morris."

Letting his head fall back against the headrest, he gazed at me tiredly. "What do I get out of this?"

"I won't stab you today."

"Generous, but you'll have to do better than that."

Reaching out, I pressed my fingertips lightly to his cheek, looking deep into his eyes.

"Zak." His name was a soft, almost gentle murmur on my lips. "You could grovel at my feet for the rest of your pathetic life and still never make up for what you did to me. You owe me every beat of your black, soulless heart, and even that won't pay your debt." I bared my teeth in a vicious grin. "So shut the fuck up and call Morris."

His eyelids dipped over his vibrant green irises. He touched the back of my hand, then slid his fingers over my sleeve to my elbow.

"You don't own me," he said just as quietly, his voice lined with steel. "And I'm not here to grovel for forgiveness. If you want to talk about debts, then first we're going to talk about what happened ten years ago."

My lips curled with loathing. "I don't want your selfish excuses."

"I don't want excuses either. I want the truth."

A shiver rippled through me. The truth. The truth of what had happened—of his betrayal and how much of it he'd planned in advance. Of how Ruth had become aware that I would try to poison her and that the poison was fake. Of why Zak had come to meet me only to throw my treasured, broken riverstone pendent in the mud at my feet.

Out of everything weighing on me, drowning me, tearing me up inside, I couldn't face that in any way.

Zak's fingers tightened around my elbow. He could feel me shaking. My whole body was quaking at the very thought of that *truth*.

Sucking in air, I pulled my arm away from his hand. "Please ... help me with this."

The words were quiet, reluctant, and tinged with a hint of desperation. I hated that he was making me beg. I hated that I had no better options.

He watched me for a long moment, then pulled his phone from his pocket. I leaned down to watch the screen as he opened a list of contacts. There were no names, only numbers.

He selected one and started a new text conversation. "Your parents' names?"

"Killian and Mairead Orien," I whispered.

He typed out a swift message, hit send, and slumped back in his seat. "He probably isn't up yet." He scowled at the sunrise. "Most people aren't."

"You're cranky in the morning." I swallowed, then swallowed again before I could force the next words out. "Thank you."

He said nothing, eyes closing wearily. It occurred to me that he'd gotten a lot less sleep than I had.

"Why are you even here?" I asked, attempting a neutral tone.

"At the moment, I'm trying to sleep."

"In your truck," I observed. "*Is* this your truck?"

"It is now."

"It's stolen?"

"No idea."

"How do you not know?"

"I didn't steal it, but it might've been stolen at some point."

I scrunched my face. "You didn't answer my question. Why are you here?"

His eyes slid open again. Green irises moved across mine. "Why do you think?"

"I'm not your responsibility." I lost my neutral tone, anger hardening my words. "And I don't want to be. I just want to move on with my life."

He turned in his seat to face me, elbows braced on his knees. "How are you going to do that without learning to control your power? Did you arrange for training with the Tempest Druid?"

My mouth twisted before I could stop it. I hadn't even considered asking her to train me.

My reaction didn't surprise him. "Who will teach you, then?" he asked. "Ríkr? He's only good for leeching off you."

That was exactly what I wanted Ríkr to do. "If you think *you're* going to teach me, then you're out of your mind."

"If you think you can just carry on like nothing has changed, you're out of *your* mind."

"I don't want your help."

"You just asked for my help."

"To find out about my mom!" I yelled, my temper breaking free. "I don't want to learn how to be a druid! I don't want to be a druid at all!"

"You can't change what you are."

"Ríkr can!"

The words had flown out of my mouth before I could stop them. Zak's eyes widened—then fury hardened his features. He shoved out of the truck, towering over me.

"You mean he can suck your power dry so no fae can sense you're a druid?" Zak snarled. "Is that what you're saying?"

I held my ground, glowering up at him, his face inches away. "He did it for seven years and it worked just fine. If he—"

"You're a druid, Saber!" He seized my upper arms as though he wanted to shake sense into me. "You can't—"

The buzz of his phone vibrating interrupted him. He glared at me, then let out a harsh breath. Releasing my arms, he pulled his phone from his pocket and tapped in a rapid passcode to unlock it. I crowded beside him to see the screen.

Zak's message read:

```
Send me everything you can find on Killian
Orien and Mairead Orien ASAP
```

Beneath it, Morris had replied:

```
Cyber-stalking your new girlfriend isn't
cool, man. Especially her dead parents.
```

I scowled at the reply, but before I could get properly angry that Morris hadn't sent anything useful, the phone vibrated again with a new message.

```
I attached Killian's and Mairead's profiles
and the report on their deaths. I don't see
anything else on them, but I'll do a deeper
dive tonight after my shift. I have bad guys
to arrest first.
```

Three attachments had come through with his message. I was reaching over to tap the first one when a third text popped up.

```
Don't get me into any more trouble, okay?
```

"What trouble is he talking about?" I asked.

"Do you want to see the files or not?"

I snatched his phone out of his hand and selected the first attachment. He leaned over my shoulder to read, and I considered elbowing him in the gut … but it was his phone I was hoarding.

The attachment opened to reveal a standard profile document. My father's photo filled the top corner, and my heart contracted. He looked exactly as I remembered—light chocolate-brown hair, a thick reddish beard that accentuated his cheekbones, and walnut eyes. His bland expression was the only thing I didn't recognize. In my memories, he was always teasing and joking.

His mythic class identified him as a witch, and according to his records, he'd been a member of a guild I'd never heard of. A small notation identified it as a sleeper guild—a guild for mythics who didn't practice magic.

I devoured every tidbit of mundane information on his profile, then opened my mother's. When the document appeared, Zak drew in a sharp breath of surprise. I knew why. Mairead's photo could've been me, but instead of a severe line of bangs cutting across her face, her thick black hair was swept back, revealing the graceful arch of her eyebrows above her soft blue-gray eyes.

My eyes had never looked that soft.

As I'd suspected, she was also listed as a witch, and she'd been a member of the same guild as my father.

"She was your druid parent?" Zak asked.

"Yes. The Meadowlark Druid." My gaze darted to him. "Have you heard of her?"

He shook his head.

I studied her photo again, then pulled out my phone and typed in the last address listed under her residences. An apartment complex in Chilliwack, a town over a hundred kilometers east of Vancouver, popped up. I couldn't remember any details about where my childhood home had been located, but I knew we'd never lived in a town, and we'd definitely never lived in an apartment. Josephine had been doubly right about druid secrecy.

Pocketing my phone, I flipped back to Morris's message and tapped the third attachment—the investigation. A document loaded, filling the screen with small text. I skimmed through the initial information describing the date, location, persons involved, and purpose of the investigation.

My finger slid across the screen as I scrolled down. A cluster of photos appeared, and I had a second to register the rocky ground in the first one before the phone vanished from my hand.

Zak stepped back, holding his phone. "I'll read the rest for you."

"What?" I snapped. "Give me that."

"Those are crime scene photos. You don't need to see them."

"I can handle gore just fine."

"I know," he snapped back. "But your memories of your parents are precious. Don't taint them with images of their deaths."

My anger faltered, and his voice, a decade old but crystal clear, whispered in my memory, telling my fifteen-year-old self that he couldn't remember his parents.

I bit my inner cheek. All my memories of my parents were happy ones. Did I want to see their broken, devoured, decomposing corpses? Did I want those images to come to my mind when I thought of them?

I puffed out a breath. "Give me your keys."

He blinked. "Huh?"

"You read, I'll drive."

His confusion deepened. "Drive where?"

I arched my eyebrows and pointed at his phone. "Where else? To the place where they died."

I DRUMMED MY FINGERS on the steering wheel, impatiently watching the entrance of the gas station. We were ten minutes out of Coquitlam, and I wasn't pleased to be stopped. I wanted to keep moving.

In a flash of white fur, Ríkr hopped onto the center console in the form of a ferret. *Allow me to confirm my understanding, dove. We are journeying to the site of your parents' demise, yes?*

"Yes."

Where they perished nearly two decades ago.

"Yes."

And in that place, you hope to discover … what?

"I don't know." My tapping on the steering wheel increased in tempo. "But this is all I have."

He sat on his haunches, his whiskers twitching in thought. *I still do not understand. What do you wish to accomplish?*

"I don't want to accomplish anything in particular. It's …" I scrubbed my hand over my face, then flattened my bangs back down. "The last time I saw my parents, they dropped me off at a family friend's place so they could volunteer with a search and rescue for a lost hiker. I never saw them again. I never got to see my home again. With no warning, my entire childhood was just … gone. And now, knowing that my mother was a druid, it feels like the childhood I remember was just a dream.

I want answers about her and her secrets, but I also want to reconnect with her … with my past … in some way."

And this is all you have, he murmured, repeating my words.

The gas station door opened and Zak walked out, two disposable coffee cups balanced in one hand and a small paper bag in the other. He opened the truck door and climbed in, putting the two steaming drinks into the cupholders. After closing his door, he settled back, buckled up—and only then did he offer me the keys.

Irritated, I snatched them from his hand.

As he adjusted his seatbelt, Zak glanced at Ríkr on the center console, the dislike between druid and fae buzzing through the cab. Refocusing my eyes, I checked the rearview mirror; the two vargs were in the box, sitting just behind the window as they surveyed the small parking lot. I still hadn't seen any sign of Lallakai, and if Zak wasn't going to bring her up, neither would I.

I reversed out of the parking spot as he opened his paper bag and withdrew a fat muffin. He passed it over. I took it without comment and bit into the fluffy top. Blueberry. Not bad.

"It's an hour and a half to Chilliwack," I said, swallowing my mouthful. "How much farther to the place where their bodies were found?"

He pulled out a second muffin and peeled the wrapper off the bottom. "I'll load the GPS coordinates in a minute. You said that Chilliwack address was fake?"

"It's a real place, but we never lived there. I assume we lived in the area, though." Flicking on the turn signal, I took the entrance ramp for the highway and floored the accelerator. "Seeing Chilliwack might jog my memory."

"Maybe," he muttered before stuffing half the muffin into his mouth at once. With his other hand, he got out his phone and opened a GPS app.

Ríkr darted out a tiny paw and stole a blueberry from my half-eaten muffin. *I have not ventured from our territory since meeting you. It is an odd thing.*

"Have you been out this way before?" I asked curiously.

Some time ago, yes. He canted his ferret head, whiskers perked. *Humans were far fewer, and I do not recall these corridors of concrete.* He tilted his head the other way. *I remember trains. Foul, noisy machines. I detest them.*

Zak shot the fae a look of mild incredulity. "Trains, but no roads?"

"So, what," I muttered, "the late 1800s? You haven't left the Coquitlam area in over a century?"

I have not traveled in this direction, he clarified. *I did wander some before meeting you. To the north. I enjoy cool climates.*

No surprise there.

Finishing his muffin, Zak applied both hands to his phone. "It looks like … just over two hours from here until we run out of road. We'll have to hike to the actual spot."

I nodded. "What's our route?"

"From Chilliwack, we continue east on Highway 1 until Hope, then it's north into … Fraser Canyon."

At his hesitation, I flicked a quick glance at him. "What?"

His finger swiped across the screen. "This is …"

"*What?*"

"Fraser Canyon. Your parents died in Hell's Gate."

"Hell's Gate?" I repeated in confusion. "Isn't that some sort of tourist trap?"

"Not *that* Hell's Gate."

Are you certain that is our destination? Ríkr asked sharply.

"These coordinates are dead center," Zak replied.

Ríkr shook his small head. *Then we must abort this endeavor.*

"What are you talking about?" I demanded.

"Have you never heard of the most notoriously deadly region in the lower BC mainland?" Zak asked dryly. "That's the mythic Hell's Gate."

A swoop of cold chilled my limbs.

It is a wild place, Ríkr explained. *And rich with natural power. My kin have held dominion over those mountains for millennia, and rule there still. We cannot venture into those lands, dove. It would mean certain death.*

"I wouldn't say *certain* death," Zak mused. "It's safe enough to pass through, but the mythics dumb enough to wander around in Hell's Gate tend to disappear."

My hands tightened on the wheel. "If it's so dangerous, why would my parents go there?"

"I don't know, but since they died there, it was almost certainly a fae attack."

And it would be cruel irony for their daughter to perish in the same place and manner, Ríkr said, hopping onto the dashboard to see me properly. *Even with the most compelling and inescapable of reasons, I would urge you to turn back.*

Turn back now? When I'd only just set out? Giving up felt like forsaking my childhood—and losing any chance of finding answers about my mother. "Are you that worried we'll die?"

My concern is for you, dove. I am very difficult to kill. You are not.

Zak ran his finger across his phone, studying our planned route. "If you're craving a near-death experience, I can think of a dozen better options that are much closer."

I gritted my teeth. "I'm not turning back. You said it's safe to pass through, right? As long as we're quick about it, we'll be fine. I'm not planning to stop for a picnic lunch."

Haste is no guarantee of safety, Ríkr insisted. *This venture is an unnecessary and unacceptable risk.*

I pressed my lips together, trying to logically weigh it out in my mind—but logic wasn't working. "I need to do this, Ríkr. I know it doesn't make sense to you, but I need to."

He let out a tiny ferret sigh. *Then we must move swiftly.*

"We will," I promised. "In and out."

Zak leaned back in his seat. "This'll be interesting."

Most, Ríkr grumbled.

8

I'D ALWAYS CONSIDERED the mountains north of the rescue to be wild, but Fraser Canyon was wild in a completely different way.

The highway clung to the side of the canyon, weaving along the mountainside and cutting through tunnels. Untamed forest blanketed the slopes and trees clung to rocky cliff faces. The deeper into the canyon we drove, the steeper and rockier the mountains became. Every few minutes, a break in the trees would reveal brown water far below, swirling downstream in the opposite direction.

The Fraser River was the longest river in the province. It flowed out of the Canadian Rockies and into the Fraser Canyon, then bent west into the lowlands. It widened and slowed, passing Coquitlam, where I lived, and continued all the way to Vancouver, where it emptied into the Georgia Strait. Its erosive power had shaped this landscape for hundreds of kilometers.

"How much longer?" I asked, gripping the wheel tightly.

Zak checked his phone. "Forty minutes."

Crouched on the console between us, Ríkr watched the canyon walls flashing past with twitching whiskers. A jittery feeling climbed up my spine.

"Why do I feel like ants are crawling under my skin?" I muttered.

"The energies here are intense." Zak flipped back to the report on my parents' deaths. "I understand why fae like it."

"Fae might like it, but I don't think I do."

"Yeah," he agreed absently, scrutinizing the report. He'd already read it and provided me with a summary, but he kept skimming through it as though searching for something that wasn't there. "You get used to energy like this, but I prefer a more peaceful atmosphere."

I snorted. "*You*, the universally feared dark druid, like peace?"

"Says the homicidal, knife-fetishizing ex-witch who cuddles animals for a living."

"I don't *cuddle* animals. I rescue and rehabilitate them."

"And that doesn't involve petting them and singing to them?"

"I can sing to you, if you want—while I carve out your heart."

He smirked. "Knife fetish."

"Masochist," I shot back.

"No more than you are."

My eyes narrowed, and I refocused on the road. Intensely green forest pushed up against the pavement on the left, and on the right, glimpses of the valley's far side peeked through the trees. Other than the road and a long line of train tracks, there were no signs of human habitation.

"What are you looking for in that report?" I asked after a minute.

"I'm not sure. It just doesn't make sense. If the Meadowlark Druid's territory was in the vicinity of the Fraser Canyon, she *must* have known how dangerous it is. So why casually walk into the fae gauntlet of Hell's Gate?"

Is that not precisely what you two are doing? Rîkr complained.

"It's one thing to visit briefly. It's another to spend hours or days wandering around, searching for a hiker."

"It wasn't the first time my parents helped with a rescue operation," I said. "My mom must've thought it'd be safe—or safe enough."

He scrolled through the document. "Was her consort really powerful?"

"Her … consort"—I hesitated over the word, having always thought of her fae companion as a familiar—"was a water nymph."

Zak frowned. "Good at spells and enchantment, but they don't have aggressive temperaments, in my experience. I wouldn't count on one for protection."

Thinking back on the beautiful, blue-skinned fae who'd lived in the creek near our house, I couldn't disagree. She'd always been very gentle with me, and she and my mother had loved to sing together. They hadn't been battle-hardened warriors prepared to take on the dangers of Hell's Gate.

And the same went for me.

I bit my inner cheek, wondering if I was making a big mistake as I steered along the curving highway. The truck sped onto a bridge. Over a hundred feet below, the wide, sediment-laden river flowed through the gorge it had created. The bridge met the far side of the canyon and cut into the forest. Trees closed in on both sides.

A strange, uncomfortable pressure expanded inside me. My gaze darted across the view through the windshield. Wooden power poles had appeared, electrical lines slung between them.

A dirt track, almost a road, flashed past on the right. My foot lifted off the gas pedal.

On the left, a dirt parking lot with a small outhouse appeared. The truck coasted, losing speed as we passed it.

"This is a small provincial park," Zak said, checking the map on his phone. "There are a few hiking trails, but this isn't where your parents died."

"I know."

The pressure in my chest increased. We were still coasting, my foot hovering over the pedal. The highway curved, and another small parking lot for hikers came into view on the left. Just beyond it, a dirt road peeled sharply away from the main route, disappearing into the trees.

I slammed the brakes.

Zak jerked forward, his seatbelt locking, and Ríkr slid off the console and crashed ferret-face first into the dashboard. Tires squealing, the truck skidded across the pavement—then hit gravel as I steered off the highway.

The side road bent in a tight U-turn, and rocks spit from the tires as I forced the truck around the bend too fast. The road straightened out, running parallel to the highway, and the G-force inside the cab dissipated.

"Holy shit," Zak ground out, clutching the handle above his door. He twisted around, checking on his vargs in the box, then thumped back into his seat. "What the hell was that, Saber?"

I am also curious. Ríkr's flat, displeased voice preceded him as he climbed onto the console again, his fur standing on end. *What is it you are doing?*

"I don't know." My heart pounded painfully against my ribs, but not because I'd almost rolled the truck.

Ah, of course, Ríkr muttered. *Perfectly sensible.*

"This is a service road," Zak pointed out angrily, "and it's taking us in the wrong direction."

"I know that."

"Then turn around—without almost killing us this time."

I squeezed the wheel, staring at the road following the mountainside. My heart was still slamming against my ribcage, that pressure inside me intensifying with each beat.

"This isn't a sightseeing trip," he growled. "And there's nothing out here except fae that will try to eat us."

"There is."

"What?"

"There *is* something out here." My voice was a hushed whisper. "I think I've been this way before."

I could feel both fae and druid staring at me.

"You've been here before?" Zak asked. "This exact road?"

"I think so."

"With your parents?"

"Yes."

He checked his map. "Their bodies were found thirty kilometers north of here."

I breathed through my nose, trying to soothe the pressure in my chest. "I know it doesn't make sense, but this ... it's familiar. Really familiar."

Again, I could feel him studying me.

Finally, he said, "Then let's see where the road leads."

A tight smile pulled at my lips. "I wasn't waiting for your permission. I'm driving, remember?"

He muttered something under his breath, and the only word I caught was "mistake."

The truck vibrated across the rough gravel road for over a kilometer, heading back the way we'd come. The forest leaned in so close that branches slapped against the side panels.

My foot found the brake again, and I brought the truck to a gentle stop. Just ahead, the road forked, one branch curving southwest to follow the river, the other bending southeast.

I closed my eyes and let off the brake. The truck rolled forward. In my gut, I felt a pull to the left, the sensation of the turn etched deep into my memory. Opening my eyes again, I accelerated down the southeast branch with growing confidence. The road bent into a tight turn, doubling back on itself to take us northeast—and it began to ascend.

The truck roared, its powerful engine working to keep us moving as the road grew uncomfortably steep. Zak was gripping the handle above his door again, his jaw tight. For every hundred meters of road we drove, we gained fifty meters in altitude. We were climbing the mountain.

We met another tight U-turn, doubling back. Climbing higher. Another tight turn. Now we were heading east— crossing the mountain ridge. Leaving the canyon behind.

Are you certain about this, dove? Ríkr asked.

I nodded, vibrating in my seat with something strangely close to excitement. I didn't know where we were or where we would end up, but I knew this route. I knew it in my bones.

The road zigzagged over the peak, then turned north in a slow descent. I couldn't see anything but the road and the forest, barely held back by the hard-packed gravel, but I assumed we were descending into a valley between mountain peaks.

For three kilometers, we drove through dense forest, farther and farther from any sign of civilization. Ruts in the dirt suggested large vehicles occasionally passed—mining or forestry operations, I'd guess—and occasional gaps in the foliage revealed terrifyingly steep drops mere feet from the truck's tires.

The road doubled back again to continue the descent, and as we approached another tight U-turn, I slowed the truck. My heart was beating hard.

I slowed even more, the U-turn dead ahead. The truck crawled forward.

"Saber," Zak said tightly.

My foot fluttered over the gas.

"Saber, *turn*."

I let the truck roll off the road and straight into the wall of greenery. Zak made a strangled noise as foliage hit the vehicle, leaves covering the windshield in an opaque screen. Branches snapped as the bumper flattened shrubs, the suspension bouncing.

One—two—three seconds—

We burst through the wall of shrubbery. An overgrown track stretched away in a gently curving line, dappled sunlight speckling the mossy dirt.

"Shit," Zak said on an explosive exhale. "You do realize that could've been a cliff for all you knew?"

I flashed him a mean little grin. "I didn't think the notorious Crystal Druid scared this easily."

"Neither did I," he growled, "but that was before I let you drive."

Ríkr shook his whole body, his white fur fluffed unhappily. *May I request our next activity involve a deathly skirmish or some other more pleasant activity?*

"You two are wimps," I told them, urging the truck along the dirt track. The terrain was worse than the gravel road, and we bounced in our seats as the tires bumped over rocks and tree roots. "It wasn't that bad."

Zak shook his head. "Have you figured out where we're going yet?"

"No. But …" A shiver ran through me. "But we're almost there."

My limbs quivered with eagerness. Just ahead, the dense wall of trees broke. Sunlight gleamed. An open space.

We rolled out of the shadows and into a sunlit meadow.

I stopped the truck, clutching the steering wheel and staring out the windshield, lightheaded and barely breathing. Then I shoved the gearshift into park and flung my door open, not bothering to shut off the engine.

My legs disappeared into thigh-high grass as my feet touched the ground. Energy rushed through me in a welcoming wave, and my entire body flushed with warmth. I knew this feeling. I knew this energy.

The meadow stretched away, swaths of long grass rippling like waves in the breeze. Stalks of purple wildflowers swayed with them, sparrows darting among the green. Mountains rose on all sides, sweeping into the distance and blanketed in old, quiet forests. A sparkling creek ran down the east side of the meadow before zagging across it. Scattered white clouds cast soft shadows over the landscape.

I turned.

There. Right there, a dozen yards from the truck with a path of large stepping-stones leading toward it. A log house with a wide front porch and big windows pointed southeast across the meadow. Vines covered one side, the front flowerbeds overgrown with weeds. But it was otherwise the same.

My home. I was home.

I continued to spin, finding the tree where I used to play, my old swing hanging from its thick boughs. The huge garden where we'd grown all our vegetables. The well for our water. Dad's workshop.

The truck's door thudded shut, and I felt Zak's presence drawing closer—but I didn't want to share this moment with anyone. My feet moved, slowly at first, then faster and faster until I was sprinting through the grass, leaving him and the truck and the fae behind. The creek beckoned, and I ran to the edge of the water.

There I stopped, hands clasped against my chest to hold my overflowing heart together.

A few yards away, a large, red plastic bucket sat on a fat tree stump at the creek's edge. It was faded and spattered with mud from heavy rain, but it hadn't toppled. I walked over to it. Scummy water filled it halfway, but I could see the rocks in the bottom that had kept it standing for the past eighteen years.

I grasped the edges of the bucket and heaved it off the stump, then I sat. The stump seemed strangely small. My feet rested easily on the ground, but I remembered my toes barely scuffing the pebbly creek shore.

Sitting in my dad's favorite fishing spot beside his fish bucket, I watched the water flow past. My ears strained for sounds I would never hear again. My father's excited whoop as he reeled in a big salmon. My mother calling us in for dinner.

I felt like I'd stepped back in time—but there was nothing here except ghosts.

The creek blurred as tears filled my eyes, and I bent forward, burying my face in my hands.

I was a grown woman who'd survived eighteen years without her parents.

I was a terrified child whose mom and dad had never come back for her.

It took a long time for the tears to exhaust themselves. Aching from the sobs that had shaken my body, I wiped my face. This time, when I looked across the meadow, I wasn't a child who had finally returned home.

I was the daughter of the Meadowlark Druid, wondering who my mother had really been.

Small wings beating, Ríkr dove out of the sky in the form of a white jay and perched on my father's red bucket. He canted a pale azure eye at me.

You found your home, he observed somberly. *Is this what you needed?*

I didn't answer, uncertain what to say. Uncertain of what I felt.

"Are you sure this is your home?"

Stones crunched as Zak stepped onto the damp bank of the burbling creek, his two vargs ranging out behind him, only their heads and shoulders visible above the long grass. To his casual black t-shirt and dark jeans, he'd added a combat belt loaded with alchemy potions in small, test-tube-like vials. Leather bracers embedded with crystals covered his wrists, a tangle of larger crystals hung around his neck on cords, and his ten-inch knife was strapped to his thigh.

"Are you sure?" he repeated, surveying the meadow. "This is definitely where you lived as a child?"

Irritation sparked through my grief. "I'm positive. Do you think I'm making it up?"

"No." He pivoted to look back across the meadow. "Are you certain your mother was a druid?"

"Yes," I snapped. "Unless the Tempest Druid is a pathological liar who somehow knew I wasn't aware that my own mother was a druid, then I'm certain. What's your problem?"

"We're in Hell's Gate."

"Obviously. So what?"

"There's only one druid to ever claim a territory in Hell's Gate, and it wasn't your mother." His green eyes turned to me, sharp and strangely wary. "It was the Hellsgate Druid, the dominant druid in the lower mainland before the Wolfsbane took over, and the only druid crazy enough—or powerful enough—to hold a territory here."

My skin prickled all over with a sudden chill. "What are you saying?"

"I'm saying"—his gaze rose to the house in the distance—"I think your father was a druid too."

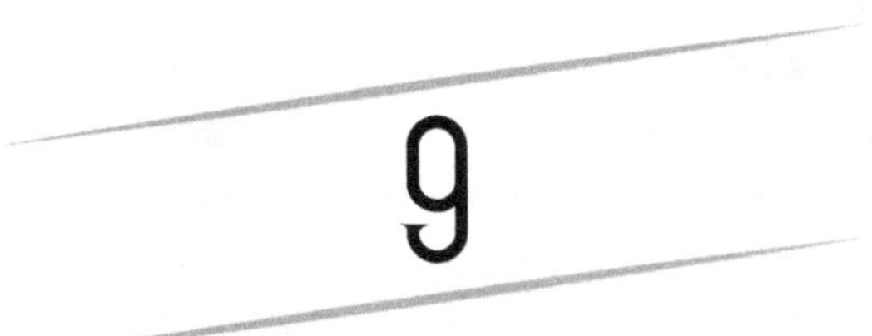

9

"MY FATHER?" I repeated blankly.

An interesting theory. Rík fluffed his feathers. *You assume this because the Hellsgate Druid was known to make his territory here?*

Zak nodded. "The Meadowlark Druid, with a water nymph for her partner, couldn't have survived here long-term on her own. But obviously Mairead was surviving just fine since she lived here with Saber. If Killian was a druid as well, that means *two* druids were holding this territory—and that makes more sense than the Hellsgate Druid being some kind of prodigy."

I wrapped my arms around myself, shivering.

If he was the consort of a powerful being inclined toward bloodshed, Rík mused, *then they would have been a daunting pair—one who excelled in defensive enchantments and one who excelled in battle.*

Shaking off my shock, I shoved to my feet. "Look, there's no proof my dad was a druid. The Hellsgate Druid might've been someone else. Maybe he let my parents live here. It could be anything."

"Did your father have a familiar?" Zak asked.

"He … yes." I squinted, thinking back. "But I didn't really know that fae. He didn't spend time with me like Ellanira—the water nymph. Dad always said I could get to know his familiar when I was older."

"Do you know what happened to your parents' familiars or why they weren't able to save your parents?"

"I've always assumed they were dead. Ellanira went with my parents to search for the hiker, and since she never came back …" I rubbed my forehead. "I don't know about my father's familiar. Like I said, I didn't interact with him much … but I'm pretty sure he's dead too."

I didn't know why I was convinced he was dead, but I felt the certainty in my gut.

Ríkr pondered my words. *That your father's companion was not suitable company for a child is, in my opinion, further evidence that he was of a powerful and aggressive nature. It seems logical that your father was also a druid and consort to a formidable warrior.*

"It's not logical at all!" I countered angrily. "It's just conjecture. Give me one fact to support this insane theory."

Zak was silent for a moment. "The Hellsgate Druid died the same summer your parents died. Is that enough of a fact?"

"How do you know when the Hellsgate Druid died?"

"Bane told me."

I pivoted to face Zak. He was gazing into the distance, a muscle ticking in his cheek.

"How did Bane know the Hellsgate Druid?" I demanded.

"The Hellsgate Druid challenged him once, and Bane was gloating that the only druid on the west coast who'd had the balls to challenge him had gotten himself killed like a fool. I remember it being late summer, eighteen years ago."

My father and the Hellsgate Druid had died at the same time, and my little family had lived in the Hellsgate Druid's territory. How could that be a coincidence? I couldn't come up with a plausible denial, and it shook me to my core. First my magic. Then my mother. Now my father.

Nothing was what I'd believed. Everything I'd grown up knowing was wrong, and the last remaining pillar of familiarity inside me had crumbled away.

"What's wrong?" Zak asked.

I shot him a glare. "Oh, nothing. Just absorbing the fact that I had no idea who my parents were."

"So what?"

"What do you mean, *so what?*"

"Why does it matter? What seven-year-old understands their parents anyway? You're getting answers. Isn't that what you wanted?"

"This isn't what I wanted!"

"Why the hell not?" he snapped.

I squeezed my hands into fists. "Because if they were both druids, then they knew how dangerous this place is. And they knew how dangerous it would be to go searching for a lost hiker. They should've been smart and strong and capable, and instead they got themselves killed, leaving their seven-year-old daughter alone, not even knowing what she was."

"They didn't know they would die."

"They risked their lives for a complete stranger." My breathing roughened. "How could they take that risk when they'd done *nothing* to make sure I'd be okay? Why did they choose some hiker over me?"

His voice sharpened. "They made a mistake, Saber."

"They shouldn't have—"

"They fucked up!" He flung a hand out angrily. "Everyone fucks up! Are you completely incapable of forgiving people for making mistakes?"

I rocked back on my heels, startled by his anger, then bared my teeth. "Some things are unforgivable. You should know all about that."

"I'm not talking about us," he growled. "I'm talking about your parents. Why are you trying to destroy what you have left of them?"

"I'm not—"

"Just forgive them! Keep cherishing your memories! For fuck's sake, do you enjoy being as miserable as fucking possible?"

I slammed my palms into his chest, shoving him back. "What's your goddamn problem, Zak? Why are you freaking out on me?"

"Because you interpret everything everyone does as a personal attack! You got seven years with your parents—"

"Seven? I should've had—"

"Well, that's what you got," he cut in, green eyes blazing. "So quit trying to ruin it all with your twisted blame game."

"Fuck you!" I yelled. "You don't get it!"

"Don't I?" He stepped back in, right in my face. "Bane murdered my parents in front of me, so I think I know what I'm talking about!"

I reeled back as though he'd hit me.

He hung where he was for a second, then jerked away with a muttered curse.

"I thought …" My voice cracked. "I thought you didn't remember your parents."

"That's my only memory of them."

"Just that one?" I tried to imagine my only recollection of my mom and dad being their violent deaths at the hands of the man who'd … "Bane abducted you?"

He glanced at me, his face stony, then strode away.

I jogged to his side, stretching my legs to match his pace. "Zak?"

"It's a custom among dark-magic practitioners," he said flatly. "They don't want to deal with finding partners or pregnancy or infants, so they 'choose' their apprentices by stealing kids."

I swallowed the sickness in the back of my throat. "How old were you?"

"Not sure. Around five."

"And … that's all you remember? Bane killing them?"

He extended his stride even more, as though if he walked fast enough, he could leave it all behind. "I remember my mother screaming. *Ni, Andrii, vin hoche zabrati Zaharia.*"

The melodic language flowed easily off his tongue, delivered in a dry recitation.

"Was that … Ukrainian?" I asked hesitantly.

He didn't answer, and as I strode alongside him, memories flitted through me. Hearing his voice for the first time, a faint accent thickening his vowels. The way his pupils had dilated with fear-fueled adrenaline when Bane's voice had boomed through the floor of the gambling den. The burning hope in his eyes when we'd made our plans to murder our guardians.

For the first time since he'd thrown my broken river-stone pendant at my feet, I thought maybe that desperate, dangerous, hopeful teenage boy hadn't played me. Maybe he hadn't pretended.

Because I couldn't imagine this adult version craving anything less than the utter destruction of his druid master.

We walked across the meadow in silence. As we neared the truck, I angled toward the cabin. Together, we halted in front of the porch steps.

I understood why my coming here and finding this lost connection to my parents had unraveled his cool control—because he would never get an experience like this for himself. His parents had been reduced to a single, horrific memory, and there was nothing for him to find, no connection to rebuild years later. He would never have what I had now.

Maybe that was the whole reason he'd agreed to help me this morning.

With heavy steps, I ascended onto the porch. The cabin's door loomed, familiar yet strangely terrifying. My heart retracted inside my chest to escape the coming grief.

Swallowing my hesitation, I reached for the door handle.

Saber!

My hand jerked at Ríkr's sharp, urgent call. The soft, powerful tide of earthly energy drifting across the land shuddered in warning.

At the far end of the meadow, the trees shook. A flock of birds took flight with harsh warning cries. Zak's shaggy black vargs sprinted through the grass toward us, and Ríkr flew after them, wings beating.

Saber, go!

The soft energy of my home twisted with something dark and ferocious.

Zak and I moved at the same time: he launched toward the truck and I leaped off the porch in one bound. He reached the truck first, racing around the bumper to the driver's side. As I threw myself into the passenger seat, he cranked the ignition. Shifting into gear, he slammed the gas. The wheels spun, the back end fishtailing as the nose aligned with the overgrown track that had led us here.

I twisted in my seat. The vargs were running all out toward us. Ríkr swept ahead of them, feathers flashing.

Across the meadow, something pushed through the trees.

Something enormous.

A head, a neck. Two legs, then two more. The creature's body had the texture of rough tree bark and the shape of a limber greyhound with a long, lizard-like tail. Its slim head was reptilian, a crest of thick branches protruding from its forehead like horns.

It turned its head toward us, then coiled its long legs and launched into a charge, its huge stride eating up the distance in seconds.

10

THE TRUCK BOUNCED VIOLENTLY over the uneven track. Going faster would risk debilitating damage to the vehicle. Forest enveloped us, cutting off my view of the meadow—and the beast chasing us down.

"What is it?" I gasped. "Where did it come from?"

Zak didn't take his eyes off the track, fighting the steering wheel to keep us from veering into a tree trunk. "A lesser woodland dragon. And it sensed us."

"What—" I broke off as Ríkr shimmered through the truck's roof and landed on the console. The two vargs appeared on the track behind us, their top speed faster than the truck could travel over the rough terrain. Behind them, the woodland dragon closed in.

It was larger than the truck. Larger than Balligor, the kelpie that'd almost killed me and Zak.

"Faster!" I yelled.

But we couldn't go any faster on the uneven track.

The vargs split, diving into the underbrush, and the dragon loomed behind us, its mouth opening to reveal rows of curved black fangs.

Zak shoved something into my shoulder. "Throw this out the window!"

I snatched the test-tube-shaped vial from his hand, barely glimpsing its iron-gray contents. With no time to roll down the window, I opened the door, clinging to the seat with one hand, and hurled the vial at the beast.

The vial shattered against the dragon's leg, releasing a puff of gray mist. The dragon stumbled, and an ear-splitting roar erupted from its throat.

I yanked the door shut and spun in my seat to face forward—right as the truck hit the wall of foliage hiding the track. We smashed through it and the wheels skidded as they met loose gravel. Zak spun the wheel, turning us onto the road. Bursting out of the trees, the two vargs leaped into the box as Zak floored the gas.

The engine roared as we gained speed—and altitude. We had to cross the mountain to make it back to the highway where the truck could really accelerate.

As we sped away from my parents' property, the dragon shoved through the foliage. It shook itself, one leg glistening with Zak's potion, then launched after us, head low for speed.

And it was *fast*.

"Another potion?" I asked tersely.

"If the iron poison isn't working, nothing I have on me will slow it down."

"It's gaining on us."

His jaw tightened. He let off the gas, and I realized he was going to stop the truck. Better to face the dragon than have it attack the moving vehicle.

Ríkr unfurled his wings. *Keep going.*

My heart jumped. "Ríkr—"

He sprang toward the back of the truck. His feathered form shimmered through the glass, and as he hurtled toward the oncoming dragon, blue light flashed over his small body.

The swirl of light met the dragon, and ice exploded outward—huge pillars of shining crystal shooting in every direction in a starburst that filled the road and tore into the surrounding trees.

Zak punched the gas and the truck zoomed forward.

"Stop!" I clutched my seat, twisting around backward. "We're not leaving him!"

"He said to keep going."

"I don't care!"

I grabbed the passenger door handle, prepared to jump out of the moving vehicle. Cursing, Zak hit the brakes. We skidded to a stop, and I flung the door open. Leaping out, I ran to the back of the truck.

The starburst of ice shattered in a snowy cloud, and the dragon lunged free, frost covering its body. It roared furiously as it turned on the spot, the white mist swirling around its legs. The fog parted.

Ríkr stood near the dragon's front feet—and he'd taken his humanoid form. His black and white garments rippled around him, his silvery-white hair flowing down his back. The short, sharp antlers rising above his head gleamed like pure gold.

He lifted his hand, and a long spear of ice coalesced in his palm. He drew his arm back and hurled it.

The spear struck the fae where its neck joined its body—and exploded into another icy starburst, tearing through the dragon's thick, wood-like hide.

"Ori fortis fiam."

The strange Latin words rumbled from Zak as he walked past me, his vargs flanking him. Two of the crystals on his chest were glowing. He pulled the cork out of a vial with his teeth, then dumped the contents into his mouth. Tossing the bottle aside, he curled his fingers. Amber light sparked over them.

Striding toward the dragon, he extended his other hand, his forearm marred with pink scars. A black rune flared over the back of his hand. Black lines twisted up his arm, pulsing with magic—and from his palm, darkness expanded and solidified into a gleaming ebony sword.

Shadows rippling off his weapon, the Crystal Druid launched into the fae battle.

I watched him with my heart in my throat and my switchblade clutched in my hand. The tiny blade was so inadequate it was almost funny. I was so inadequate it was unbearable.

Zak swept his black blade out, sending a cascade of darkness into the dragon. Ríkr, almost invisible in the frozen mist, flung an ice spear that exploded into six-foot shards upon impact with the dragon's side. The vargs darted around the dragon's back legs, harrying and distracting it.

The temperature was dropping. Frost coated the trees, and frozen specks of moisture sparkled in the air. Ríkr's wintry power was sweeping outward, and the stronger it grew, the larger his explosions of ice.

But his power wasn't all I could feel. Zak's druidic presence, that aura of cool command, pulsed through the earth. The soft energy of the forest and the ferocious power of the dragon dissipated, overtaken by the Crystal Druid.

I hadn't sensed that when Zak had fought the kelpie or the Dullahan, but I could now. I didn't understand what it meant, but I felt his presence as though he were as huge and pervasive as the forest around us.

Dodging the dragon's snapping jaws, Zak slashed its leg. As it roared, an orb of crackling purple energy appeared in his hand. He flung it into the dragon's other foreleg. From its opposite flank, Ríkr encased both its back legs in ice.

Bellowing furiously, the dragon twisted, fangs glistening as it went for Zak again. A rune on his forearm flashed, and the dragon's snout smashed into an invisible barrier just above the druid. The air rippled, revealing a transparent dome arched over him, then the spell shattered into silver glitter that danced in the air.

As the dragon recoiled from the sudden impact, an ice spear struck the back of its head. Icicles as thick as tree trunks burst off it, and the dragon's jaw hit the ground, its head dragged down by the weight.

Leaping forward, Zak grabbed the dragon by a thick horn and pointed his blade at the beast's large, sap-colored eye.

"You have a choice." With his voice, the aura of command he radiated into the earth thickened. "Swear a debt to us, or perish."

The dragon's tail lashed, scattering broken chunks of ice. Ríkr, an ice spear held casually in one hand, waited several yards behind Zak.

The fae beast held still, considering the offer—then flung its head up, the ice shattering off it. Its body swelled, leaf buds sprouting over its bark-like skin. It reared up, loosing a hungry roar.

Zak shifted backward until he was almost level with Ríkr. They gazed at the roaring dragon, neither moving.

Cold magic buzzed across my senses, and a fourth power joined the maelstrom.

A massive eagle plunged out of the sky. Her black wings slashed downward, and as shadowy blades launched at the dragon's back, Ríkr swept his spear out like a scepter. Blue light shone across the ground beneath the dragon in a looping pattern.

Ice burst up from the glowing spell, encasing the dragon an instant before the shadow blades struck. Shadow met ice, and the ice shattered—exploding the dragon with it. Fractured shards and torn chunks of flesh flew everywhere.

The black eagle swept to the ground, shadows swirling around her, and when she landed, she had taken the form of a beautiful, sensual woman. Her raven hair flowed down her back in loose waves, her flawless body draped in exotic black garments speckled with sparkling emeralds.

She faced Ríkr, ten long paces between them. The ice spear in his hand glistened, and the aggressive black headpiece covering his forehead gave his flawless face a malevolent cast. Frost thickened on every surface in sight, the temperature sinking lower—but at the same time, the surrounding shadows pulsed like dark sludge, pushing themselves out of nooks and crevices.

The tension between the two fae crackled in the air, their competing power sizzling.

Ríkr's lips curved up into the slightest smile—then blue light washed over him. His ice spear disappeared and he melted back into the shape of a small jay. Wings flashing, he swept away from Lallakai and landed on the truck's tailgate beside me.

The Night Eagle watched him with narrowed eyes and a mocking smile.

A few steps away from her, Zak opened his fingers. The black magic banding his arm shrank into the rune on the back of his hand, and his ebony sword rippled away like flames in the wind.

Lallakai turned to her consort, that smile still playing over her full red lips. "My druid," she purred. "I left you for but a few days, not expecting you to test your new power so recklessly."

Zak flexed his arm, the black rune still marking his hand. "That wasn't specifically my intent."

Saber, Ríkr murmured, his telepathic voice soft so no one else would overhear. *We have drawn much attention. We must retreat from this place.*

My gaze turned back to my unseen childhood home. *But I haven't—*

I know, dove, but more of my kin will seek out this unleashing of power. Let us journey onward with haste and return when stealth is once again a possibility.

I bit my lower lip, then nodded and turned back to Zak and Lallakai. She was holding Zak's right wrist as she studied the black rune, which had faded to a murky gray. She slid one hand caressingly up his forearm to his elbow.

"Mm," she crooned. "It is taking well. How do you fare?"

"It feels like my arm is filled with icy needles," he replied without emotion.

"Your body will adapt." She stroked the scars on his forearm. "This power suits you, my druid."

He pulled his arm away. "It's difficult to control."

"I will ensure you master it."

"Zak," I called.

He stepped away from Lallakai, and as he turned to me, the Night Eagle's emerald eyes flashed across my face. I couldn't interpret her expression. It wasn't anger or hostility, but it still sent a warning prickle down my spine.

"We should leave," I said. "Ríkr thinks more fae will show up."

Nodding, he strode toward the truck. His vargs skulked out of the trees and trotted after him. As he passed me, heading for the passenger door, I brushed my fingers across the back of his hand.

The black rune had faded from sight, but I still felt a prickle of dark, dangerous power just under his skin.

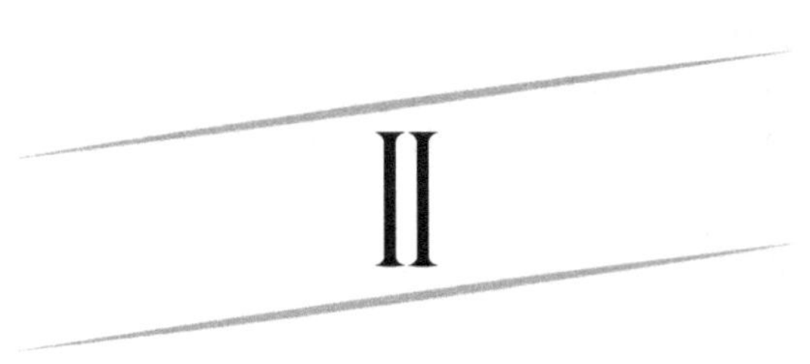

BACK ON THE HIGHWAY, I turned the truck north, continuing deeper into Hell's Gate. The mountains pressed in close on either side of the canyon, steeper and wilder than before. Forest gave way to sharp slopes of barren rock, so steep they'd been covered with steel mesh to prevent slides and debris on the road.

When we'd reached the highway, I'd had the choice of turning south to flee Hell's Gate or heading north to visit the spot where my parents had died. Leaving would've been the safe, smart choice, but I wasn't ready to go back—to abandon these threads of my past just when I was starting to discover them.

The place where they'd died was thirty kilometers away— plenty far enough from the site of the dragon's demise that we should be safe. Fae might be powerful and magical, but few could travel a hundred kilometers per hour down a highway.

Zak hadn't protested my choice of direction, and I kept half an eye on him as I drove. Every minute or so, he flexed his right arm, fingers opening and closing. Did his flesh still feel like it was full of needles? He hadn't had that shadowy black sword when we'd fought Balligor and the Dullahan. It had to be a new acquisition.

My gaze flicked to the rearview mirror. Ríkr, in the form of a white ferret, lounged on the backseat a few feet away from a black eagle, slightly larger than average and with gleaming emerald eyes.

I decided my questions about Zak's new fae-magic weapon could wait for a more private moment.

The miles sped past, all signs of civilization disappearing—until we rounded a bend and a large red sign appeared on the side of the road. I squinted as we zoomed toward it.

"'Hell's Gate, ten minutes ahead,'" I read, my brow furrowed.

"The tourist trap," Zak remarked dryly.

"Why is this area named after a tourist trap?"

"It isn't." He pulled out his phone and opened the map we'd been following before my sudden detour. "Hell's Gate was a landmark first, and mythics adopted its name for the entire area. *Then* humans turned the original landmark into an overpriced sightseeing spot."

"Have you been there?"

"No."

I drummed two fingers on the wheel. "Do you think they sell food along with the overpriced view?"

"Food?"

"It's almost noon and we've only had a muffin each."

"They probably have something edible to wring a few more bucks out of visitors. Isn't that how tourist traps work?"

"I don't know. I've never done touristy things."

"Me neither."

We glanced at each other, then I hastily refocused on the road.

The highway wound along the mountainside for another ten kilometers, periodic signs encouraging us onward to "Hell's Gate." Finally, a small building, painted the same shade of red as the signs, appeared on the left side of the road. I slowed the truck and turned into a narrow parking lot with a few other vehicles. As I cut the engine and pulled the keys out of the ignition, Zak plucked them from my hand, then opened his door. Sound rushed in—the deep roar of flowing water.

I climbed out, and energy rose through me. It was a disconcerting mix of the steady energy of the forest and mountains and the profoundly powerful rush of the massive river carving its way through the canyon.

Ríkr hopped out just before I closed the truck's door. He peered around, whiskers twitching, then transformed into a jay again.

I will survey the area, he informed me as he took flight. *Do not tarry.*

With a sweep of black wings, Lallakai launched out of the truck from the other side. She spiraled into the air, and the two contrasting birds drifted in opposite directions on the currents.

Taking Ríkr's advice, I strode to the building in search of food. Inside, I found a lobby with a ticket counter, the walls covered in signs and infographics about the canyon. An older woman, sitting behind the counter, looked up from her computer with a smile.

"Welcome!" she said pleasantly. "Two adult tickets for you? That'll be sixty dollars."

Sixty dollars? For *what?*

Zak leaned close to me, and his warm breath teased my ear as he whispered with a hint of amusement, "Right into the trap."

I elbowed him away and asked the clerk, "Do you sell food here?"

"Oh yes, we have a variety of snacks in the gift shop, and our café is—"

"Where?"

"Visiting our facilities requires a ticket." She smiled again, her finger poised expectantly over the till. "That will be sixty dollars."

Scowling, I reached for my pocket, but Zak stepped in front of me, a black wallet in his hand. He plucked out three twenties and handed them over. The clerk rang up the transaction, passed him tickets and a receipt, then waved us through the barrier and into the building.

Zak held his hand out as though inviting me to take it—but there was a mocking tilt to his eyebrows. Lifting my chin, I marched past him. Why he seemed to think getting gouged sixty bucks just for the privilege of buying food was amusing, I didn't know.

At the back of the small building, the wall opened into an outdoor platform perched on the canyon's sheer face. The far side of the gorge was a precipitous, forested slope. Waiting on the platform, a red airtram hung from a thick metal cable, windows lining its sides and the door open to reveal space for twenty passengers. No one else waited at the small ticket barrier.

Footsteps scuffed the floor as Zak joined me.

"So that's what the tickets are for," he observed, still sounding inexplicably amused. "I hope you aren't scared of heights."

"Welcome to Hell's Gate!" a young man in a red golf shirt with "Hell's Gate Airtram" embroidered on the breast pocket exclaimed, hastening through a side door. "Climb aboard! I'll join you in a moment."

Determinedly ignoring Zak, I stepped up into the airtram. The cabin swayed as I moved to the front window. Following, Zak took the spot right beside me, closer than necessary.

"Are we stopping at the souvenir shop too?" he asked, a smirk lingering on his lips.

Irritated, I leaned into his chest—and using our bodies to hide it, I slid my switchblade from my pocket. Without extending the blade, I tapped the end against his inner thigh.

"How long," I asked in an undertone, "will it take you to bleed out if I slice open your femoral artery?"

He leaned down, bringing our faces close. "About a minute."

"You'll pass out in half that."

"Thirty seconds is enough to take you down with me."

My eyelids lowered halfway. "Take me down how?"

"Should I answer that? I don't want to rile you up in public."

I slid the retracted switchblade up his thigh until it met the fly of his jeans. "Who's riled up?"

The warmth of his hand settled on my hip, fingers pressing into my skin through my pants. "You tell me."

I opened my mouth, but I couldn't speak. He was gazing down at me with those intense green eyes, and I couldn't think. I shouldn't have leaned into him. I shouldn't have brought our bodies together like this, the hard muscle of his chest, his heat radiating into me.

Even though I loathed everything about him, I hadn't forgotten how he'd pinned me to the wall outside the stable and kissed me—and how it had felt. But that had been before I'd realized who he was.

"Hey folks! Ready to go?"

I jerked away from Zak. Two steps into the tram, the operator hesitated at the sight of us, then smiled professionally and launched into his welcome speech. I turned to the window.

Berating myself for letting Zak get the upper hand when I'd been threatening him, I missed whatever the operator did next. The tram glided away from the platform—and out over the wide, rushing river hundreds of feet below. The tram dropped steeply, running along a cable that spanned the canyon and connected at a point on the far side, where a second platform awaited us.

"… was discovered by the explorer Sam Fraser," our guide was saying, cheerfully unaffected by the silent tension between his two passengers. "As you can see below, the walls of the canyon drastically narrow in this spot, forcing 750 million liters of water through a gap only 30 meters wide."

I peered downward. Steep cliffs closed in on the river, more than halving its width, and water tore through the gap with frothing, churning violence. The tram ride might've been overpriced, but I couldn't deny that the view was exhilarating.

"The river here is twice as deep as it is wide," the operator continued. "More water flows through that gap than Niagara Falls, and it's moving at almost seven meters per second. In the early eighteen hundreds …"

While the man talked, my gaze slid across the window to Zak's reflection. He was gazing at the canyon, calm and expressionless.

Our eyes met in the glass, then he turned his back on the view, facing the operator instead. "How familiar are you with this area?"

"I live in Hope," the man replied.

"What's the hiking like around here?"

I stiffened at his question, watching him with narrowed eyes.

"In the canyon?" The operator shrugged. "Not much. There are some trails near the old Alexandra Bridge, but you'd be better off heading down to Hope. The terrain there is more forgiving."

"So the mountains are too rough for hiking?"

"Yeah. I mean, the hardcore hikers still try." He eyed Zak's biceps as though assessing how hardcore he might be. "But it's dangerous, man. I don't recommend it."

"How dangerous?"

"People die. Two or three a year."

"In the canyon?"

"And the surrounding area." The man waved upstream. "It's wild out there, and there are only a few maintained trails. People fall or twist their ankles or whatever. They can't walk, and they die of exposure or animal attacks."

"Animals?" I repeated quietly.

"Yeah. Earlier this month, a guy was found torn up by something. It was … yeah. You don't want to know."

I crossed my arms. "What don't we want to know?"

He glanced at me uncomfortably, then shrugged again. "I heard the kid's ribcage was torn open and all his organs were eaten. Gruesome stuff. I'm betting a cougar—"

"Just his organs?" Zak interrupted. "Nothing else?"

"I don't know, man. I didn't ask for details."

"Where did it happen?"

"North of here, I heard. I'm not sure where." He grimaced. "Look, this is all gossip, okay? Not much exciting happens in small towns, so people talk. But still, hiking is dangerous. Head down to Hope instead."

The tram glided to the lower platform, and the operator pulled the door open. I hopped down. Several buildings, including the promised café, a gift shop, and a "fudge factory," bordered a large observation deck, as well as a steel suspension bridge that stretched across the canyon. A few couples and several families, all carrying cameras, wandered along the platform.

I hesitated, aware of our goal, then veered toward the bridge. Might as well take a quick look, right?

If Zak smirked at me again, I was going to punch him.

My shoes clanged against open steel grating, and I could see straight through it to the frothing water over a hundred feet below. Midway along the bridge, I leaned over the chest-high railing to look down at the water surging through the narrow canyon walls in an endless torrent. The roar filled my entire body, and I breathed in the river's violent energy, feeling it course through me.

"Intense, isn't it?"

I looked up to find Zak walking toward me, his expression neutral with no sign of a mocking smirk.

"Is it even possible to get used to this kind of energy," I asked, glancing back at the water, "or will it always feel like I'm vibrating inside?"

"You get a bit numb to it, but living close to this river wouldn't be comfortable."

As he leaned on the railing beside me, I studied him. He'd removed his combat gear, but there was no hiding the tattoos on his forearms—the ones ruined by scars, and the ones newly filled with magical fae gifts.

I nodded toward his right hand, where the black rune had appeared. "Did Lallakai give you a weapon?"

His expression closed, and he turned to face the river. "Yes."

"I thought you were trying to gain new fae gifts *without* relying on her."

"That was my plan, but fighting Balligor and then the Dullahan made me rethink things."

"Why?"

"Lacking any lethal magic seemed like a bad idea. Take the lesser dragon, for example." His jaw flexed. "It's a shame we had to kill it."

"Do you have a soft spot for murderous beasts?"

He snorted. "No, but if we'd controlled our auras better, it wouldn't have shown up to hunt us and it'd still be alive."

"Our auras?"

"Curious about druidry now?"

"No," I snapped.

He braced his elbows on the railing. "Why are you so opposed to being a druid? Hasn't learning more about your parents changed your mind?"

"Why would it? They died because they were druids." I scraped the toe of my hiking boot over the grate. "All I've ever known is being in someone else's power—my aunt's, the MPD's, my parole supervisor's. Being a druid will put me at the mercy of every semi-powerful fae that crosses my path. I'll never be free."

"Putting yourself in Ríkr's power isn't freedom either. It's self-imposed helplessness."

My molars ground together.

"You'll be a terrible witch with a switchblade and no power to accomplish the things you want. Forever."

"I accomplish things just fine," I snarled.

"Like intimidating farmers who mistreat their livestock? Cutting turtles free from fishing nets?" He turned to face me. "Will you be satisfied with a small life and small victories?"

"Fuck you." I shoved away from the railing.

He caught my elbow and spun me back to him. Before I could tear away, he gripped my upper arms, holding me in place.

"How deep does your thirst for justice run?" he rumbled.

"Not deep enough, or I would've already gutted you." I jerked against his hold. "Let me go."

"What about the hiker? The one the tram operator said had his ribcage pried open and his organs eaten?"

I curled my upper lip. "My 'thirst for justice' doesn't apply to idiots who put themselves in harm's way."

"Not even innocent idiots who don't know fae exist?" His gaze bored into me. "What about your parents, who weren't idiots and died exactly the same way?"

I went rigid.

"It was in the MPD report," he continued grimly. "It's not a common way to kill. Most fae either eat meat—all the meat—or feed by consuming their victim's energy, not their body. I wasn't going to tell you the details of your parents' deaths, but their killer is probably the same fae that killed the hiker."

The fae that had killed my mom and dad had ripped open their chests and devoured their organs? And that same fae was still here and still killing?

I placed my hands on Zak's chest and pushed back. He allowed me to open a gap between us but didn't release me.

"Are you sure," he asked quietly, intensely, "you want to be a powerless witch?"

His words vibrated inside me, twisting with the violent energy emanating from the river below. Just like a decade ago, when he'd known what I'd meant when I'd asked if he ever thought about killing "them," I knew what he was asking me.

Did I want to be a powerless witch?

Or did I want to butcher the fae who'd killed my parents?

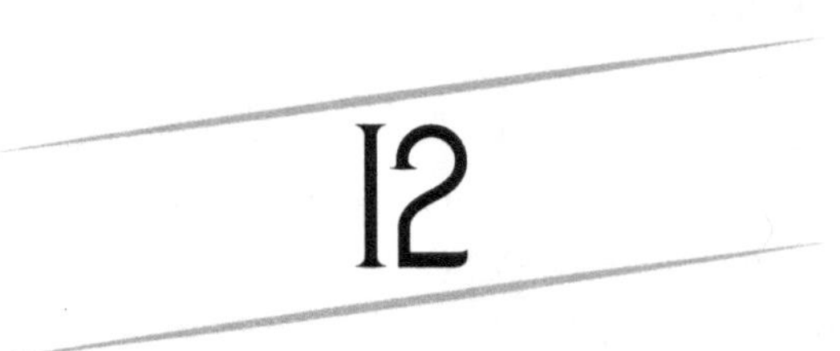

12

"THERE'S NOTHING HERE." I paced back and forth across the rocky terrain, then checked the GPS coordinates on my phone. This was it. This was the spot.

The place where my parents had died.

Faint signs that a trail had once existed here marked the ground, but nature had reclaimed it. We'd hiked for two hours to reach this spot, and though I was in excellent shape, the brutal trek over uneven ground had left my thighs, calves, and ankles aching.

Rugged trees towered around me, a mountain slope rising endlessly in the east. There was nothing special about the spot— no unique rock formations, no change in the landscape, not even a creek where my parents might have stopped to rest. Just old forest, a near-invisible trail that hadn't been used in at least a decade, and a forest floor of brown pine needles, soft green moss, lush ferns, and the rotting trunks of fallen ancients.

Strangely, I couldn't detect any fae. Throughout our hike, I'd glimpsed fae every few minutes: darting pixies, almost invisible; white-antlered bucks in small herds; well-disguised forest sprites, their branch- and leaf-covered bodies difficult to spot in the foliage; a handful of stocky hobs; smaller brownies; and countless other fae I had no names for, from woodland animals with jewel-like fae eyes to strange creatures I'd never seen before.

Though they'd shown up to observe us, none had approached. Maybe they weren't the kinds of fae to attack druids, or maybe they didn't want to tangle with Lallakai. Either way, after near-constant witnesses to our passage, this area being devoid of fae was ominous.

As I paced another circle, a white jay ghosted through the trees on silent wings.

What have you discovered? Ríkr asked, landing on a branch a few feet above me.

"Nothing," I answered irritably.

Not that I was surprised. It'd been eighteen years since my parents had died—which made me wonder for the hundredth time why I'd dragged us all out here. Had I expected to find a fae altar on which my parents had been mercilessly sacrificed?

I gazed around, trying to imagine the scene. Had my parents sensed the coming attack? What about Ellanira, my mother's water nymph partner? Had they fought back, or had the ambush been too sudden? Where had they fallen? Where had their blood fed the earth?

My imaginings went darker and uglier, and I dug the heel of my hand into my eye to push the thoughts away.

Ríkr flew down to land on my shoulder. *You seek a connection to something lost, dove. There is no shame in such a desire.*

"There's no logic in it either."

The earth remembers all life that touches it. A thousand lives have left a thousand signatures in this spot, including your parents.

"But how can I tell what marks were theirs?"

After this long, it is impossible. He slanted a pale eye toward me. *But it matters not. All you need to know is that they touched this place. That is the connection you seek.*

Crouching, I rested my fingertips on the ground and let the forest's energy drift through me. My parents had felt that energy too. They'd walked here, and they'd died here. I felt slightly closer to them even as the chasm between us yawned wider than a galaxy.

My thigh muscles throbbed, reminding me how tired they were, and I dropped to sit on my butt. Dislodged from his perch, Ríkr fluttered down to the moss and transformed into a ferret. He seemed to be favoring his smallest forms lately.

I patted him on the head with one finger. "Why don't you use your true form? You don't need to hide it anymore."

He scuttled out of the reach of my hand, then sat back on his tiny haunches. *For the same reason I did not take that form for the past seven years. I do not wish for my kin to detect me.*

"You're hiding from other fae?"

With uncompromising dedication. His ears shifted back. *Or rather, I used to be uncompromising. In my commitment to concealment, I had deeply bound my power, and even at the expense of your safety, I did not reconsider my stance. It was only after that foul kelpie struck me down and you set off alone to challenge the Dullahan that I realized my injudicious obstinacy.*

I wished he had a human face I could read to better interpret his tone. "So after that, you 'unbound' your power?"

I did. He shook himself, short fur rippling down his back. *And it took Lallakai but a brief interlude to detect the change in me and concoct her ambush.*

An ambush she'd used to force Ríkr to reveal his true power.

"So she knows now, but you're still hiding from other fae?" I asked.

I am attempting so, with a great deal less effectiveness. I dare not fully bind my power again with the Night Eagle so close and hungry.

"Hungry?"

His look, even in ferret form, gave me the impression of an arched eyebrow. *To add a second druid to her menagerie.*

I snorted. "Like that would ever happen."

"Would it not?"

The purring voice drifted out of the trees, then Lallakai sauntered into view, her hips swaying with each seductive step. I rose to my feet as she ambled toward me, a sprig of wildflowers pinched between her long, delicate fingers.

Her gaze flicked dismissively over Ríkr, barely ankle-high in his current form, then settled on me. "Will you choose a cowardly fae with broken power as your master out of loyalty? Where was his loyalty when he was draining you like a *draugr* at your throat?"

"Why would I choose *you*?" I sneered at her. "Even Zak doesn't trust you."

She twirled the flowers, pleased with my response. "He swore his life to me in exchange for my help in killing his druid master. What is that if not trust?"

My eyes widened. *She* had helped Zak kill Bane?

"He may rebel, as strong-willed men do," she continued in a sultry croon, "but when his need overcomes his pride, it is to *me* he turns."

Tightness gripped my chest at the double meaning in her words.

"I am his mistress and his champion—and I will be for the rest of his life." Her tongue slipped between her lips, dragging across soft red skin. "As for you, well, I am considering you as a second consort, but at current, I am unconvinced you would be worth the trouble."

"I'll never be your consort," I spat.

"If you want him, then you'll become mine as well."

"In what twisted reality would I ever want him?"

I didn't realize how near she'd drifted until her knuckles brushed across my cheek. She tucked the sprig of flowers behind my ear.

"Why, in the very same reality where your aura curdles with jealous fury at the mere suggestion that I have lain with him in the throes of carnal pleasure." She leaned in, bringing our faces indecently close. "To be clear, darling druid, it was more than a suggestion."

I slapped her arm away, my other hand pulling out my switchblade—but before I could do anything more, the temperature dropped warningly and Ríkr landed on my shoulder, back in jay form.

You have made your offer, Lady of Shadow. Wintry power shivered through his voice. *I am obligated to allow nothing more.*

Lallakai stepped back, one hand sweeping locks of her flowing hair off her shoulder. "Your manners are impeccable, Lord of Winter. Though, since you are incapable of killing me to protect your claim on her, you have little choice but to obey decorum"— her eyes gleamed dangerously—"and hope I do the same."

Seething, I pulled the flowers from my hair. "Where's Zak? He's taking way too long."

Shadows rippled across her. "He comes now."

With the last word, she swirled into darkness that reformed as an eagle. Wings beating, she swept up into the trees and vanished from sight.

A moment later, Zak appeared on the near-invisible trail, striding toward me with his vargs flanking him. His dark hair was mussed from running his hand through it, his damp t-shirt clinging to his muscular chest and perspiration dotting his forehead.

I watched him approach, trying not to imagine Lallakai's creamy skin and voluptuous curves pressed to his naked body—and completely failing. My stomach twisted with nausea.

"I had to hike half a kilometer to find a high spot," he said, "but I finally got reception. What's wrong?"

He fired the last part in a sharper tone, his mouth creasing into a frown as he took in my expression—whatever it was.

Shaking myself, I waved off his question. "Nothing. Did Morris reply?"

Zak nodded. "I downloaded all the attachments, but I haven't looked at them yet."

Ríkr took flight from my shoulder and the vargs dispersed among the trees as Zak and I sat side by side on a fallen log. He tapped on his screen, opening documents, and I struggled not to think about everything else Lallakai had said and implied.

She'd called Ríkr's power broken.

She'd suggested I was jealous of her and Zak's relationship.

She'd claimed that she'd helped Zak kill Bane.

Setting aside the completely ludicrous idea that I'd be jealous of Zak's bond with his fae mistress, I considered the implications of her helping him murder Bane. Had he been considering a consort offer from her at the same time we'd been making our shared murder plans? If he'd had her, why had he needed my pendant? Had he actually attempted to kill Bane that night, or had he planned to do something else with the river stone's enchantment?

Had it all been a deception? Had he ever—

"Are you listening?"

Zak's deep voice punctured my thoughts, and I jolted. "Huh?"

"What's the matter?"

"Nothing. What were you saying?"

He gave me a clear "I'm not convinced" look, then focused on his phone screen. "Kit said fifty-four people have died in hiking accidents in this area over the past twenty years. About a quarter were mythics. He's going to check for older cases to see if there are more."

"Fifty-four," I muttered darkly.

"He sent me the MPD reports for the past three years of deaths, including the hiker from earlier this month. All of them are flagged as potential fae killings, but the MPD doesn't do much when it comes to fae. They're considered a force of nature, and it's up to individual mythics to stay out of their way."

"That's fine for chance encounters with violent fae," I said. "But what about fae who actively hunt humans? That's not a 'force of nature' scenario anymore. Tornadoes and wildfires don't deliberately target people."

"The MPD will occasionally put bounties on fae, but only druids—and black witches, to a lesser degree—can hunt a fae that doesn't want to be found." He tilted his screen toward me. "This is the hiker who died earlier this month. He was a mythic—an aeromage."

A photo filled the screen. The man—no, boy—couldn't have been older than eighteen, with a baby-smooth jawline and a big smile. He was decked out in hiking gear and posing beside a girl of the same age.

Sharp edges stirred in my chest, grinding against each other. I'd claimed not to care if a stupid hiker was dead, but seeing the boy's face—his sunny, optimistic smile—I couldn't help the cold fury building under my ribs. Fae didn't need to kill humans, and they weren't animals incapable of distinguishing humans from their usual prey. If fae made no distinction, it was because they didn't want to—because they enjoyed hunting and killing more intelligent prey.

And this boy had been a mage, making him a more interesting quarry.

Zak flipped to the next report, and together we reviewed the details. Of the nine deaths, four victims had been human. They'd gone missing in the wilderness and their bodies had been discovered days or weeks later, eaten by animals.

The other five victims had been mythics, and their bodies had been found with their ribcages pried open and their organs devoured. No other flesh had been eaten, not even by the usual forest scavengers.

Holding Zak's phone, I flipped between reports, studying the photos of the mythics' bodies. The snapped bones and gore barely registered as I compared them.

"Did you notice this?" I asked, pointing at a picture of the most recent hiker. "The bodies haven't been touched by anything, but ..."

My finger tapped a spot on the photo, and Zak leaned close to peer at it. "You mean the seedlings?"

I nodded. Sprouting from the corpse's chest cavity were a handful of young, leafy trees about six inches tall. I flipped to the other photos. Each mythic's body had seedlings growing from the shattered, empty torso, their sizes varying depending on how long the body had gone undiscovered.

"There are no seedlings growing around the bodies," Zak observed. "Only inside them, where the fae consumed their organs."

"Was it the same for my parents?"

He slid the phone from my hand and sorted through the files he'd collected. I didn't try to peek as he opened the report on my parents.

"Yes," he murmured. "It's the same for your parents' bodies—and that can't be a coincidence."

My fingers curled into fists. "What does it mean?"

"I don't know, but it's clear this fae is targeting mythics specifically." He locked his phone screen. "What do you want to do?"

I knew exactly what I *wanted* to do: find that fae and cut out its heart so it would never kill another person.

Exhaling slowly, I pulled out my switchblade and pressed the trigger. Zak watched the four inches of black steel pop out with silent wariness.

"This is all I have." My throat was tight, turning my voice husky. "And it isn't enough. I know that. I didn't come here to hunt a fae predator. I came to learn about my parents."

Zak watched me mutely, but I didn't need him to speak. His voice already echoed in my head, asking if I would be satisfied living a small life with small victories. As a powerless witch, I couldn't hunt a fae predator. I might have helped kill the

Dullahan, but the luck that had gotten me through that encounter wouldn't save me again.

"So," I concluded, each word paining me, "the real question is, what do *you* want to do?"

Because he was the one with power, not me. He was the one who could take action and achieve victory over his enemies.

"Hm." He considered me for a long moment. "I figured you'd charge in fearlessly like you usually do."

I scowled. "I'm not delusional. I know perfectly well that my switchblade isn't the solution to every problem."

"Yet you still attempt to stab everything in your path."

"If I had a bigger knife, I'd use that instead."

He leaned in, bringing his face closer, our shoulders pressing together. "Then why don't you get a bigger knife? Magical blades work much better on magical beings."

I pressed the switch on my knife and the blade snapped back in. "But at what cost? What did you trade for your new shadow sword, Zak?"

His eyes held mine, then he pushed to his feet and stretched his back, muscles bunching in his arms.

"Now that Lallakai is here, very few fae will be brave enough to bother us—unless there's a greater dragon nearby." He glanced at the sky, fluffy white clouds dotting the blue. "The aeromage hiker died three kilometers northeast of here. We have time to check it out before dark."

I didn't move from the log. "Why?"

"Why what?"

"Why are you willing to do this? It's my vendetta, not yours."

He flexed his right hand, the scars on his forearm tautening. "That fae will keep killing if no one stops it, and I don't like innocent people dying either."

"That doesn't sound like the kind of thing a notorious rogue would say. I thought you've killed so many people that you don't even know the number."

"I have, and I don't."

"What do you really want out of this?" Standing, I stepped aggressively close. "Because if you're offering for my sake, you should know it won't change anything between us."

He snorted. "I'm not delusional either."

"Then why?"

"Because I feel like it."

"Bullshit," I accused. "Tell me why."

A corner of his mouth curved up at my hot glower. "Do you want to go or not?"

I bared my teeth at him.

A magnanimous offer, Crystal Druid. Ríkr flew out of the trees like a pale phantom and landed on my shoulder again. *But your dubious benevolence aside, we have lingered in these woods too long already. It is well past time to retreat from Hell's Gate.*

I shook my head. "I want to go back to my parents' property. I didn't get to go inside the house."

We can return another day for unhurried exploration. Presently, we need to retreat.

"Do we? Zak said there shouldn't be any fae around here strong enough to risk ticking off Lallakai."

He underestimates the eminence of the fae within these lands. Venturing farther is a perilous gamble with no gain. You have sought your parents' place of life and of death. Let us return now, whole and victorious.

I bit the inside of my cheek. "What about the fae who killed them?"

The white jay shuffled sideways on my shoulder, debating his response. *Dove, there is a crossroads to the northeast—one of great significance. Where power lives, powerful beings gather. We must go no closer.*

A crossroads?

I peered disbelievingly at Ríkr. We'd been wandering Hell's Gate for the better part of a day, and only *now* was he revealing his familiarity with this area? Only *now* was he revealing that he'd known a crossroads existed here?

Anger surged through me, and I jerked my shoulder, forcing him to take flight. He landed on a nearby branch. I glared at him, furious and hurt that, even after I'd told him how important trust was between us, he continued to be secretive.

I turned away from him. "The spot where the aeromage died isn't that much farther. Let's check it out, Zak."

Ríkr's gaze pressed into my back, but he said nothing.

13

A THREE-KILOMETER HIKE on an easy, level trail usually took me under thirty minutes. A three-kilometer hike on a nonexistent trail in rugged mountains, at high altitude and with a vertical gain of over three hundred meters, took us almost two hours.

Breathing hard, I gulped down several mouthfuls of cool liquid from my water bottle, glad I'd had the foresight to grab a few basic hiking supplies before leaving the rescue this morning. Several yards ahead of me, Zak had a hand braced on a boulder as he stretched his thighs. At least I wasn't the only one out of breath.

The terrain here was rockier than the spot where my parents had died, with more stone outcrops and jagged cliff faces than forest. We were near the summit of a mountain, and the late afternoon air was cool. I peered at the sky, judging the angle of the sun peeking through the scattered clouds. It wouldn't set until after nine p.m., but we had a four- to five-hour trek to the truck. If we took too long here, we wouldn't make it back before dark.

I gulped down another mouthful of water, then clipped the bottle onto a belt loop of my jeans. "This is it, right?"

"Yeah." Dropping his foot to the ground, Zak rolled his shoulders. "I'm not looking forward to hiking back again."

Neither was I. "Makes you miss Tilliag, huh?

Zak grunted.

"Where is he?"

"Doing whatever horse fae like to do. I didn't ask."

I frowned. "Has he paid off his debt to you?"

"Not yet, but our agreement wasn't for consecutive days of service. Just ninety-nine days. He shows up when I call for him."

Interesting. I'd never considered a fae agreement like that.

As though summoned by my thought of fae agreements, a white jay swooped down and landed on a boulder to my left. Ríkr's pale azure eyes surveyed the scene, but he didn't comment on the unremarkable stretch of mountainside. He'd said little since I'd decided to ignore his warnings about traveling closer to the crossroads.

I couldn't see the other fae in our group. The vargs had wandered ahead, their tireless trot eating up the miles, and Lallakai soared in broad circles around us, occasionally coasting on air currents where we could see her before drifting out of sight again. Like the last spot, there were no fae here, and aside from a few birdcalls in the distance, I hadn't noticed any signs of wildlife.

Chewing the inside of my cheek, I focused on the landscape. Stretches of exposed rock rose steeply on my left, and on my right, the ground sloped down toward a dense cluster of red alders, easily identified by their mottled ash-gray bark.

The photos of the aeromage's body had shown a woodier spot, so I veered into the sparse grass, heading for the small grove. The trees were pushing a hundred feet tall, their maximum size if I remembered correctly, and I was surprised to see them growing at this altitude. They were more common in moist areas or the margins of wetlands, not a dry, windswept slope.

Footfalls crunched behind me as Zak followed. I went one way and he went the other. We circled the clump of trees, meeting on the other side, then we both stepped between trunks. I wove through the trees, fallen leaves rustling underfoot, with no real idea of what I was searching for.

"Saber."

At Zak's quiet call, I hurried to join him. He was crouched in the middle of the grove, where an eight-foot-wide gap was free of trees and foliage. I squatted beside him, my stare fixed on the ground. Six seedlings the circumference of my pinky finger, each with a dozen healthy green leaves, were growing in a small, perfect ring.

"A circle," I muttered.

"Fae favor circles in their magic," Zak said quietly. "They represent continuance, containment, and sometimes ingress."

My gaze flicked to the circular tattoos on his forearm. "Ingress?"

"Doorways. Usually to their realm." He leaned over the seedlings. "I don't think that's what this is, though."

"Then what is it?"

"No idea, but this is probably where the aeromage died. Was he a sacrifice for the seedlings? That might explain why the killer has been targeting mythics. It wanted more powerful sacrifices than regular humans."

High overhead, the alders' leaves rustled, but the breeze didn't reach us at ground level.

"Why would the aeromage come in here?" I asked, lowering my voice to a whisper even though there was no need for quiet. "Or was he moved here?"

"Or chased?"

I glanced around at the tightly packed trunks. "Does that mean the killer is small? The woodland dragon would never fit in here."

"*Lesser* woodland dragon," Zak corrected. "Real dragons are much larger."

"What makes a 'real' dragon more real than the woodland dragon?"

"You'll know what I mean if you ever meet one."

Refocusing, I brushed fallen leaves away to expose the ground, wondering if any other clues about the killer fae had survived. Another gust of wind stirred the trees, their trunks groaning. The foot-tall seedlings seemed to shiver in answer.

"What now?" I asked.

"Alder trees don't live long enough to house dryads, and I haven't noticed any other fae around here that we could question." His eyes glazed as he focused beyond the mundane landscape. "Which is unusual, now that I think about it."

Unmoving, he seemed to listen, then he rose cautiously to his feet. Without looking my way, he flicked his hand in a small gesture.

Obeying his silent command, I got to my feet. Gooseflesh prickled my bare arms as the trees rustled and groaned in the wind—but I couldn't feel any wind.

The quiet but immense energy of the mountain shifted as dark malevolence threaded it.

Saber.

Ríkr's voice slid softly into my mind, a faint whisper as he attempted to reach me without drawing attention to it. My hand instinctively sought my pocket with my switchblade.

Saber, get out.

At his whispered warning, I squinted my eyes, refocusing them on the fae demesne. Mist rose around us, and the ashy bark of the alders morphed to black, with iridescent red streaks wherever the bark was damaged. Their leaves shone silver.

When I looked into the ethereal realm, trees usually turned semitransparent.

These remained solid.

Zak's fingers closed around mine—and I shivered as cool, steady energy flowed from his touch. It emanated out of him, blanketing the growing malevolence in the grove.

He pulled me with him toward the wall of trees. Turning sideways, he stepped between trunks. I slid in after him. Had the trees been this close together before? I didn't remember needing to squeeze between them.

We zigzagged through the grove as the leaves rustled overhead louder and louder. Urgency rose in me, and I hastened after Zak, right on his heels. He pushed between two trunks, his shirt catching on the bark. Golden sunlight beckoned a few yards ahead, and a pale shadow moved across it—a white coyote pacing back and forth just beyond the trees.

Zak stopped.

Leaning into his back, I looked over his shoulder. Ash-gray bark formed a near-solid wall of trunks and branches ahead of us. The gaps were too small for us to fit. We'd have to try another route.

I turned—and found another unpassable barrier of trees. There was no path behind us. The route we'd used to reach this spot had vanished.

The trees leaned in. Whispering leaves and groaning wood filled my ears, and I pressed against Zak. The gap we stood in was shrinking. Bark caught on my clothing as I shifted.

"Zak," I whispered.

He stretched out his right hand. "Get ready."

"For what?"

A black rune bled across the back of his hand, then inky lines spread from it, coiling up his arm. "Angry trees."

Shadows spilled out from his palm, and that ebony blade took shape in his grip. He lifted the curved sword and brought it down on the branches filling the gap in front of us. The fae blade sliced through the living wood as though the tree were a clay sculpture.

Rage boiled up from the earth, and a soundless roar of lethal intent flooded the grove.

Zak leaped into the opening, sword slashing, and I rushed after him. The trees shuddered, branches weaving, their roots vibrating beneath the rocky soil. I could see them moving now—the trunks closing in around us like hundred-foot-tall soldiers encircling an enemy.

With a flash of his blade, Zak hacked straight through a trunk. The tree tipped, slamming into its neighbors, but the grove was so dense that the tree didn't fall. Cutting down the trees wouldn't open a gap for us.

Bark pushed into my back, shoving me into Zak. I gasped as the pressure increased, compressing us together. Zak's sword arm was pinned down. He couldn't cut the trees.

Magenta light ignited on his left forearm, glowing from one of his tattoos. It rushed outward into a shimmering dome, enclosing us—then exploded outward. Trunks shattered and wood splinters flew as the force blew everything back.

Grabbing my hand, Zak raced through the new breach in our wooden prison. The trees roared, the sound of leaves, bark, branches, and wood thundering in my head. We launched out of the grove and into the sunlight.

And the trees reached after us, branches snapping at our backs.

Ríkr sprang toward the grove. His teeth snapped down on the nearest branch snaking toward my leg. Ice raced along the bough and erupted into a massive starburst of gleaming crystals twenty feet tall. The alders caught in the cluster of icy spires groaned.

We fled thirty feet from the trees before Zak halted. Breathing fast, I turned to stare at the alders. Their crowns swayed furiously, as though a great beast were violently shaking the trunks—but the trees themselves were the beasts.

Ríkr trotted to join us, his ears angled back toward the grove. *I take no pleasure in my rightful assessment, dove, but there is naught to be found here but peril and d—*

With a violent shudder and booming crack, the rocky ground around us split open. Thick, twisted tree roots tore out of the dirt like tentacles, and their spear-like points flashed at their target.

Crunch.

The sound hit me like a blow—the crack of snapping bones and the wet *gluck* of tearing flesh. Then it hit me again and again as second, third, and fourth roots ripped through a living body.

Ríkr's body.

The white coyote jolted as the spearing roots pierced him one after another. Red blood drenched his fur. They'd struck him from every side—his left flank, right shoulder, straight up through his belly. And the fourth had launched out of the ground directly in front of him and torn through the center of his chest, shattering ribs and organs before bursting out of his back just to the left of his spine.

I stared at the bloody body of my familiar for one sickening heartbeat before my horrified scream rang out.

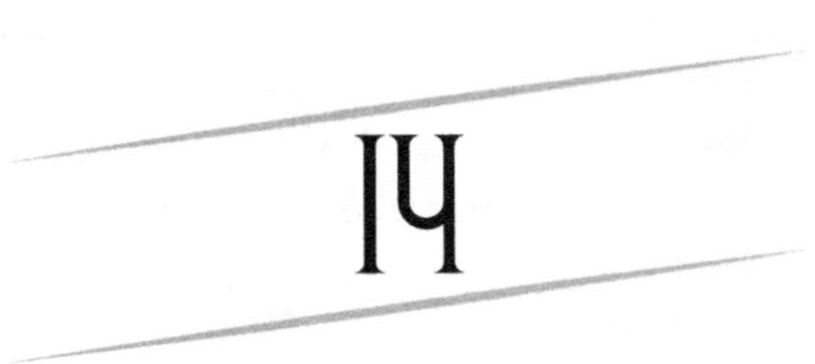

AS I SCREAMED, more roots tore from the ground and shot for my chest.

Amber light flashed. A glowing line of magic snapped around my middle and yanked me backward. The attacking roots shot through the space where I'd been.

I fell back into Zak, his arm closing around my middle as he retreated, his black sword in his other hand.

Power sizzled in the air.

A black eagle with a twelve-foot wingspan plunged out of the sky. Lallakai swept over the alder grove, and darkness poured from her wings like a heavy black fog. It pooled over the trees, and they shuddered from within the dark, eerie cloud. The silhouettes of their quaking leaves went still. The groaning of enraged wood quieted, and the murderous intent tainting the earth dissipated.

She swooped down to land, and as she furled her wings, the cloud of darkness drifted away to nothing. The alders remained inanimate, the roots that had been attacking us now stiff, twisted caricatures—including the ones that had speared Ríkr.

I tore free from Zak's arm and ran to the coyote. I dropped to my knees beside him. His unseeing eyes were hazed with white.

"Ríkr?" I whispered, my hands trembling as I gently touched his snout. No breath passed his nose or mouth. "*Ríkr?*"

Zak appeared beside me, still holding his ebony sword. Setting the dark blade against the nearest root, he cut through it. I supported Ríkr as Zak severed the roots, and when no more wooden spears held him up, I lay him gently on the ground.

"Ríkr?" I tried again. He'd survived terrible injuries once before. Balligor had nearly bitten him in half—but puncture wounds and broken bones were far more survivable than a spear through the chest.

"An unfortunate end." Lallakai had taken her humanoid form, and her bare feet were silent on the rocky ground as she stopped beside Zak and gazed down at the lifeless fae. "Rather pathetic, but unfortunate nonetheless."

"Lallakai," Zak snapped angrily.

My anguish crystallized into hard, pulsing rage.

I pushed to my feet. My hand floated to my pocket. Vaguely, I remembered telling Zak that I knew my switchblade was useless against fae opponents. Just as vaguely, I didn't care.

Every particle of my being wanted to kill that bitch for disparaging Ríkr.

Every torn shred of my heart wanted her dead for insulting him.

And every iota of untapped magic in my body would make it happen.

My knife was in my hand, and the mountain's energy screamed with me as I launched myself at Lallakai.

Zak grabbed me around the middle. He hauled me back, and I screamed even more furiously. Twisting in his grasp, I thrust the knife at his throat, stopping it an instant before it touched his skin.

"Let me go," I hissed.

"Saber …" His green eyes were wide, but not with fear. With astonishment. "You just took control of the whole mountainside."

I didn't understand and I didn't care. "*Let me go.*"

His arm loosened—then his attention jerked to something behind me, and shock rippled over his face again.

A wave of freezing cold hit my back, rushing outward.

Shoving away from Zak, I spun around.

Ríkr's body lay on its side where I had left it—and a ring of frost was expanding around him. His staring eyes glowed azure, and strange markings flared above and below his left eye. The coiling, spiraling design raced down his face and along his neck, then over his shoulder and down his left foreleg to his paw.

The pattern flared with rippling blue power, and the temperature dropped. Frost covered the roots protruding from his body, then thickened into jagged ice. Frozen moisture sparkled in the air. Shimmers of blue power ran across his fur.

Fine lines spiderwebbed across the white ice coating the roots—then the ice disintegrated into sparkling dust, the frozen roots crumbling with it. Light danced over his wounds as though he were bleeding arctic blue fire.

He moved.

Slowly, he rolled onto his stomach and rose on four paws, legs braced wide. His eyes glowed unseeingly as magic shimmered across him.

He no longer resembled a coyote. His form was still canid, but now it looked more like a white wolf crossed with a long-legged hunting hound—and larger than both. Short, sharp antlers that gleamed like gold rose above his forehead between his furred ears.

The blue markings running down his left side dimmed, as did the magic leaking from his wounds. Where the magic had shone, unblemished fur replaced his injuries. Even the blood had vanished.

Last to fade was the eerie glow lighting up his eyes from within. The magic dissipated, and his pupilless blue irises reappeared.

The wolfish hound swiveled his ears—then shook his entire body like a wet dog after a bath.

I inhaled, air rushing into my desperate lungs, and realized I hadn't breathed since turning to see the magic lighting up his body. It hadn't been long—maybe twenty seconds—but it felt like an eternity.

"Ríkr?" I croaked.

He turned to me, his short antlers shining in the sunlight.

Did you fear I had perished, dove? he asked with mild surprise. *I am moved by your concern, but as I already warned you …*

His pale stare shifted to Lallakai, and his voice sharpened into blades of ice.

I am very difficult to kill.

THE FRONT DESK CLERK of the small hotel smiled expectantly at me.

"You only have *one* room?" I repeated, trying not to snap. "Why is this whole town booked up?"

"There's a mountain biking competition tomorrow." She gave a slight, apologetic shrug. "Someone canceled their reservation twenty minutes ago, which is the only reason we have a vacancy."

I rubbed my hand over my face. "What kind of room is it?"

"A single queen bed with a lovely view of the mountains."

"Can I get a cot?"

"They're all in use."

Jaw flexing, I glanced over my shoulder. Zak's truck was idling in the drop-off zone, waiting for me. This was the fourth hotel we'd tried, and one room was better than no room.

"I'll take it," I said, pulling out my wallet and handing over my credit card. She entered my information, keyed a pair of cards for the door, and handed me a bundle with my receipt.

"Checkout is at eleven tomorrow," she told me pleasantly. "Enjoy your stay in Hope."

I trudged across the lobby and back outside. Yanking the truck's passenger door open, I climbed in.

"They had one room," I told Zak as I thumped back in my seat. "I booked it, but it's not ideal."

Zak shifted into drive. "How 'not ideal'?"

"One bed."

I expected him to smirk tauntingly, but he merely grimaced. We were both exhausted.

The parking lot was packed, and Zak had to circle the building to find a spot. Twisting around to grab my things from the rear seat, I felt a quiet rush of relief to see Ríkr alive and unharmed. He'd traded his majestic wolfhound form for a comparatively tiny ferret, and as I stretched for my sweater, he hopped onto my arm and scuttled up to my shoulder.

Juggling my sweater, empty water bottle, and a ferret, I hopped out of the truck and slammed the door. Zak was waiting for me with his black backpack slung over his shoulder. *He* had overnight supplies. I should've at least brought a change of clothes for this little adventure.

As he strode toward the hotel, his vargs trotted in the opposite direction, invisible to humans and off to explore the town. Hope was nestled at the mouth of the Fraser Canyon, far enough from the wilderness that we weren't likely to be followed by any stubborn, druid-hungry fae, but better to keep an eye out for trouble.

That's what I assumed Lallakai was up to as well. The black eagle was impossible to see in the dark, and I hadn't spotted her since returning to the truck and starting the hour-long drive out of Hell's Gate.

Our room was on the main floor, and I took the lead, following the door numbers to 122. With a swipe of the key card, I opened the door and elbowed the nearest light switch.

A reasonably spacious bathroom beckoned to my right, a closet on the left. The queen-sized bed filled most of the room, facing a small flat-screen TV on a desk. An uncomfortable-looking armchair sat beside the window. Even if the hotel had provided a cot, it wouldn't have fit.

Maybe I should sleep in the truck.

Zak kicked off his shoes. "Do you want the shower first?"

"No, you can have it."

He headed straight into the bathroom, not bothering to check out the rest of the room. As the door locked behind him, I walked to the bed and sat on the edge. Ríkr jumped off my shoulder and walked across the comforter, whiskers twitching.

The moment the shower started, the muffled rush of water audible through the wall, I turned to him.

"Start talking, Ríkr," I ordered.

He looked over his shoulder at me. *Upon which topic shall we converse?*

"Don't play dumb. You promised to explain everything, and this is the best chance we'll get to talk without an audience." I waved at the bathroom in emphasis. "So *explain.*"

He turned to face me and sat, his small ears perked attentively.

"Wait." I pursed my lips. "Transform first. I want to do this face to face—your real face, not your beady-eyed weasel face."

He leaned back, affronted. *My what?*

Though he'd been in animal form for every conversation we'd ever had, this one was different. I wanted to see his expressions and watch his mouth as he spoke.

I folded my arms. "We don't have time to argue, Ríkr. Just do it."

Though a wholesome sentiment, it would be ill-advised for me to—

"*Ríkr.*"

His back arched at my tone, then relaxed again. He hopped off the bed—and blinding blue light burst off him. A blast of icy air hit me, and the temperature plunged. I squinted, trying to force my vision back, but everything had turned white.

Actually … everything *was* white.

A thick layer of frost covered every surface in the room. Crystalline fractals sparkled across the desk and TV screen. Tiny, delicate icicles dripped from the light fixture on the ceiling. A coarse layer of frozen snow coated the bedcovers and armchair—and me.

My breath rushed out in a puff of foggy air as I studied the creature who brought winter with him wherever he appeared.

Ríkr's true form resembled a human man, but his otherworldliness radiated from every molecule of his being. It wasn't merely his impossible beauty, enhanced by his sculpted cheekbones, narrow nose, and delicate mouth. Nor was it his smooth, pale skin, as flawless as a marble statue. Nor his pure white hair, so colorless it had a blueish tinge like shadows on snow, hanging down to the small of his back and bound near the bottom with a golden tie.

No, it was the delicate, prong-shaped golden antlers rising above his head that truly revealed his nature. It was the impossible luminescence of his pale azure eyes, framed by thick white eyelashes. It was the stripe of alien markings that ran from his left temple down to his jaw, then continued over his throat and along the side of his neck to disappear beneath the collar of the white cloak he wore, the heavy fabric glimmering as though it too was coated in frost.

Those markings were identical to the ones that had glowed down his left side when he'd healed his wounds—or come back to life. I wasn't sure which.

My gaze traveled down, his open cloak revealing garments that mixed white and black fabrics with gold accents and embroidery, then moved back up to study the unfamiliar face of the fae whose company I'd kept for the past seven years.

His pupilless eyes gleamed with the vibrancy all fae possessed, and the delicate markings running down from his temple shared the same blue iridescence. Covering his forehead, a metallic black headpiece with aggressive lines mimicked the shape of a crown and accentuated the angles of his features.

I let out a long breath, another puff of white accompanying it, then glanced around the newly winterized hotel room.

"I did warn you," he murmured.

I shivered at the sound of his voice in my ears instead of in my head—or maybe I was shivering from the intense chill in the air. "Was it necessary to freeze the room?"

"An unfortunate side effect, dove." His lips curved in a smile that was equal parts composed and teasing—a perfect match to a tone I'd heard every day for years. "Taking this form requires me to exert a fair amount of power. Which, coincidentally, allows other fae the opportunity to detect my presence."

I peered up into his face—he was over six feet tall, and though androgynously beautiful, also distinctly masculine. Lips pursed, I stretched my arm out, hesitated, then poked his stomach. His abdomen was firm with taut musculature beneath his garments.

"Uncertain if I am a phantom?" he asked with amusement.

"Just checking," I muttered, leaning back. "Now, start talking."

15

"FIRST," I ADDED, "explain how you're still alive. I thought for sure you were dead."

"I am difficult to kill." The small, teasing smile lingered on his lips. "It is a particular magic of mine and the sole reason I have survived a multitude of attacks intended to end me."

"Are you some sort of fae pariah?"

His smile widened, showing a hint of white teeth. "I am deeply detested by a great many of my kin, and in the past, entire courts swore to destroy me by any means."

"Why do you sound proud of that fact?"

"Would you not be flattered as well? Their loathing is a commendation of my achievements."

Shaking my head, I propped my feet on the bed's low footboard. Melting frost chilled my heels. "Who are you? *What* are you?"

"Currently, I am Ríkr, and this identity has defined me for …" He paused to think. "Perhaps a millennium, as humans know time."

My mouth went dry. "How old are you?"

"That is an inconsequential question, dove. I am ageless."

Ageless … meaning *immortal*. I massaged my temples to calm the panicky feeling gathering in the back of my head. An immortal fae. Speaking with a being who'd been alive and walking the world since at least the Middle Ages was disconcerting enough, but I was also questioning my assessment of his power. From my vague understanding, only the most powerful fae were immortal—the so-called "fae lords."

Which would explain why Lallakai had called Ríkr the Lord of Winter.

He shook out his wide sleeves. "As for my past self, I am forgotten by all but my most dedicated enemies, and it would be safer for us if I remained a dormant shadow in my kin's collective memory. That is why I've prioritized this deception above all else."

"You promised to tell me."

"And I shall, but my history is a long, pitiful tale. With our limited time, allow me to summarize. I once thought myself unassailable, but as the arrogant often do, I lost everything I believed would forever be mine. I was weak, hunted, hated, and as the Lady of Shadow so kindly described me, broken."

He spoke of his downfall with smooth, unflinching simplicity, but maybe that was no surprise. He'd had a very long time to accept it.

"In this diminished state, I am vulnerable." He spread his arms, his cloak sweeping out. "If I were a truly weak creature, I could go unnoticed. If I were truly powerful, I could go unchallenged. Instead, I am neither, and any creature of greater magic would happily devour what power I have."

"So you're hiding from all fae, not just your old enemies." Hot anger simmered inside me. "Why didn't you tell me? I would've kept your secret."

"Perhaps." His eyes met mine, arctic and ancient. "But I have zealously guarded my survival for years beyond your comprehension. I had no reason to risk it on a druid I have known for but a blink of time."

I leaned back, unsure what to feel. On one hand, his logic made sense. On the other hand, I felt dismissed, as unimportant to his immortal life as an ant scurrying across the path where he walked.

"But," I said slowly, thoughts churning, "you did take that risk. You revealed yourself to Lallakai to protect me. Why?"

He folded his hands into the opposite sleeves of his cloak. "Seven years ago, I was lurking about the mountain forests, far closer to human civilization than I should have been, when I felt the most unexpected thing: the potent call of a druid's energy. The nearer I drew, the stronger the waves of rage, regret, bitterness, and hatred became, all softened by bright threads of relief and hope."

That had been my first day out of prison, and I'd been a complete mess—ecstatic to finally be free of the concrete box that had held me for three years but cracking under the strain of fury and anguish over everything that I'd lost in those same years.

"I finally found the source: a dark-haired girl striding the forest paths like a queen surveying her new kingdom."

"I don't remember striding around like a queen," I muttered.

"Druidic instinct, dove." His mouth curved. "Your kind are very territorial."

I grimaced.

"That day, I could not have anticipated our unusual alliance. I told you that feeding upon your druid power benefitted me. I confess I minimized my profit. Seven years ago, I would have struggled to take this form. Through you, I have recovered threads of who I once was. I have found strength again."

My throat tightened as I gazed up at his beautifully inhuman face.

"Thus," he said softly, "when the Night Eagle threatened your life, I could not abandon you. What an unappreciative and ungracious act that would have been."

"But I didn't know I was helping you recover your power. I didn't know you *had* any power. I wouldn't have seen it as a betrayal."

"I would have." He stepped back, his cloak shimmering faintly. "I am not a benevolent creature, dove. I care little for the lives of humans, witches, or even druids. Had our first encounter gone differently, I would have devoured you in whole."

I blinked at his unapologetic confession.

"But neither am I without compassion or integrity. You have been my ally these past seven years, and I will be your ally in turn, even should that mean risks taken and wounds inflicted."

Even if it meant endangering his ageless existence for a human who'd be gone in "a blink of time."

The air left my lungs on a shaky exhale. "Shit," I said unsteadily, rubbing my hands over my face. "You're making it really hard to be mad at you, Ríkr."

"Am I?"

"You lied to me for seven years."

"I did. Am I despicable?"

"No, you're—" I looked up and saw his expression. My mouth twisted in a scowl. "Oh, shut up."

"But you bid me to speak."

I groaned. "How can an immortal fae lord be this childish?"

"Childish? I am supremely august. Imperial, even. In fact, I would say I am exceptionally imposing."

With another groan, I flopped sideways across the foot of the bed. Ríkr leaned over me, his long hair slipping off his shoulder, each strand gleaming like a thread of spun silver.

"It is odd to me," he murmured, "feeling the power well within you when I have consumed it for so long. Do you still wish me to devour it and reduce you to a near-human state?"

"Isn't that what *you* want? To keep feeding off me?"

His thick lashes lowered partway over his iridescent eyes. "Your growing power intrigues me. I can benefit from it in other ways should you become my consort."

Uncomfortable with him leaning over me, I sat up and swung my legs off the bed, facing him. "What other ways?"

"The ways of druids, dove. As I said, our bond would be one of mutual empowerment."

I bit my lower lip. "Do you think I should become a proper druid?"

"If that is your desire. Now that you feel the power growing within you, can you willingly give it up?"

"I don't feel any different." I shrugged. "Whatever druid power is, it doesn't seem very useful. Sharp blades are much simpler. Speaking of which ..." My eyebrows lifted. "What's up with Zak's new sword?"

"A gift from his mistress—a dangerous one. Not all fae magic is suitable for a human body to wield, even an experienced druid." He lifted his hand, palm facing upward, and blue light swirled over his fingers, a frigid chill emanating off it. "The gift I would give you is more suited to an untried druid, but still deadly."

My eyes widened. "A gift for me? You mean a fae rune?"

"For when you accept my offer and become my consort."

"Are you trying to bribe me?"

"Have I succeeded?"

I pushed off the bed and stood, unintentionally putting myself inches away from the fae. I looked up into his flawless face. "How about you give me your gift now? As an incentive."

His lips curved, and he closed his fingers, snuffing out the blue glow. "You would need, at the very least, marginal control of your druidic power first."

I scowled.

"A druid teacher would be preferable," he added, "but if you desire it, I can instruct you."

"You can?"

"Who do you think first taught your bumbling ancestors how to weave their power with the great energies of the earth? No master druid is as adept as my kin and me." He leaned in, his pupilless eyes filling my vision. "We can grow our strength together, Saber. You need not be powerless, and you need not fear every beast who hungers for your essence."

My heart thudded.

"Or …" His hand brushed across my throat, then curled over the back of my neck. "Shall I devour your power and all its vibrant potential right now?"

A chill washed over me from his touch. My head spun with indecision.

"*Or*"—Zak's low rasp sounded right beside me—"you can take your hand off her, Lord of Winter."

Another hand, shockingly warm, closed around my upper arm. Zak stood beside me, his hair dripping from the shower. He wore a pair of jeans and nothing else. His right hand was half raised in readiness, the black rune of his sword staining his skin as he prepared to summon the weapon.

Ríkr turned his cool gaze on Zak. "Your input is not needed, druid."

I jerked away from both their hands, stepping sideways along the foot of the bed. "Stay out of my business, Zak."

He didn't shift out of his defensive stance. "Don't accept his offer until you understand it, Saber. You've been a druid for a week. You have no idea what he really wants from you."

"I know what he wants," I snarled, my temper flaring. "It's you I don't get. Helping me for no reason, following me, protecting me, blabbing about me to Morris. What do *you* want, Zak?"

He said nothing, but something in his green eyes pushed me back a step.

Ríkr's lips curved into a slight smile, then blue light swirled across him. The temperature plunged all over again as his form shrank, and in a rush of cool air, he swept out feathered wings. The white jay soared toward the wall.

"Where are you going?" I called after him.

He vanished through the wall, and I heard his reply in my head. *Your meager room is crowded enough without my presence.* A moment passed, then his voice, more distant, floated back to me.

Unless you wish me to return and guard your virtue for the night.

If he heard the foul-mouthed retort I threw back at him, he didn't comment.

I STOOD IN THE SHOWER, hot water pouring over me, but no amount of relaxing steam could calm the maelstrom of worries overflowing in my head.

Ríkr's story kept pushing to the forefront of my thoughts. He'd been hiding for centuries, but he'd risked exposure to save me. The trees that had attacked us today had targeted him first, even though all three of us had been in striking range. If he'd been any other fae—one without his ability to recover from horrific wounds—he would have died.

And it would have been my fault.

I'd brought him out here. I'd ignored his warnings about the dangers of Hell's Gate and deliberately gone against his recommendation to travel no farther. The result? All three of us had nearly died from attacking *trees*.

I tipped my face into the water. Ríkr and Zak both wanted me to embrace my druid power. Ríkr, because the more powerful I was, the less of a burden I was. We could grow together, like he'd said. And Zak … I didn't know why he was so bent on me becoming a proper druid, and he wasn't sharing his thoughts on the matter.

Either way, they were both taking big risks. And I, powerless and weaponless, was leading them from one danger to another without taking any responsibility for our safety. I wanted to know about my parents. I wanted to see our old home. I wanted to investigate their deaths.

Me, me, me. My wants, while they risked their lives to protect me.

I disgusted myself.

Turning, I let the water sluice over my back. Ríkr had convincing reasons to stick with me, but Zak didn't. I didn't understand why he was here. Morris had told him where to find me after I'd left the precinct yesterday, but why did Zak care where I wandered? Why had he taken me home, slept in his truck, or gone with me on this pointless trek into danger? A guilty conscience didn't explain this level of interference in my life.

I shut off the shower and climbed out. Wrapping myself in a white towel, I gave the square of folded gray fabric on the vanity a mean look. It was a t-shirt. *Zak's* t-shirt. As I'd headed for the bathroom for my turn in the shower, he'd pulled it out of his backpack and thrown it at me.

Catching it automatically, I'd given him a blank look.

"You don't have a change of clothes," he'd said neutrally. "Or were you planning to sleep naked?"

It'd been tempting, so tempting, to pull my knife and see whether my inexplicable resistance to killing him had weakened.

Growling under my breath, I dried off, tossed the towel in the bathtub, and picked up the shirt. When I shook it out, a hint of pine scent teased my nose. My scowl deepened as I pulled it over my head and poked my arms through the sleeves. The hem fell just past my butt.

I put my underwear back on, because no way was I going back out there without underwear, then twisted my damp hair into a bun on top of my head. I didn't have a hairbrush either.

A white bathrobe hung on the back of the door. It was scratchy and threadbare, but I pulled it on anyway. After knotting the tie, I left the bathroom.

Zak was reclined across the far side of the bed, reading something on his phone. He'd put on a t-shirt, but it'd scrunched up his torso when he'd lain down, revealing the black waistband of his boxers and a few inches of taut skin. He looked rumpled, comfortable, and tired.

I marched to the bed. He glanced at me, weariness creasing his forehead.

"Tomorrow." I cleared my throat. "I want to visit my parents' old house. Then … go home."

"What about the fae that killed them?"

"I'm not powerful enough to kill a fae like that. When I am, I'll hunt it."

"What if *I* want to hunt it?"

"Then you're an idiot."

His eyebrows arched.

"You only want to kill that fae because of me," I growled. "And that's stupid. Completely stupid. It won't change anything between us. I won't forgive you. I won't hate you any less. You'll be risking your life for *nothing*."

He returned his attention to his phone. "Not nothing."

"Then for *what*? Tell me why you're helping me. Tell me why you're here. Tell me *something*." When he didn't answer,

I spat a string of curses at him. "You're doing this on purpose! You get off on antagonizing me, don't you? That's what this fucking is—you torturing me."

"Not even close."

My voice rose with impotent, frustrated fury. "I told you I hate you. Being around you *hurts*. Seeing you reminds me of everything I forgot, and I have to relive it over and over. Why don't you get that? Why don't you *go*?"

This time, when he looked up from his phone, his gaze was sharp. "Everything you forgot?"

My anger faltered. *That* was what had gotten his attention? I'd never explained my memory loss to him. I hadn't wanted him to know yet another way I was dysfunctional—but now I wanted to wipe that neutral expression off his face.

I let out a low, harsh laugh. "Everything, you bastard. I forgot *everything*. Dissociative amnesia caused by trauma. You might know what trauma I'm talking about—or did you not notice that night how my aunt beat me half to death?"

His eyes widened, his calm demeanor cracking.

"I forgot you. All I remembered was that there'd been a boy—a faceless, nameless boy. That's why I didn't recognize you. I didn't *know* you. You didn't even exist in my memory until I saw that scar on your hand."

A strange, morose elation rose through me at the way his face was paling.

"That's when you remembered me?" he asked quietly.

"That's when I remembered you," I echoed. "I remembered all your lies, how you used me, how you betrayed me. How you threw the only thing I had left of my parents at my feet and walked away like I was *nothing*."

I spat the last word, my trembling hands clenched at my sides.

He'd gone completely still, gazing at me without blinking, his face distinctly pale. His chest rose and fell, then his stony countenance broke.

A short sound crackled from his throat—a laugh. Another clipped bark of laughter. He tipped his head back, and the room filled with the coldest, most bitter laugh I'd ever heard. The sound pummeled me like blows, and I recoiled from him.

"Well, fuck me," he rasped, choking back his dark humor. "Ten years being haunted by you. Ten *fucking* years, and you'd forgotten everything."

Another rough laugh shook him as he shoved off the bed. Jamming his phone in his pocket, he strode across the room. As he passed me, he slowed, his hard, hateful green eyes slashing across me.

"I guess we're more even than I thought."

He kept walking. The door clacked open, then slammed shut.

I slowly turned, staring at the empty room, everything inside me frozen in shock. His bitter laughter echoed in my ears, his cutting stare engraved into the back of my eyes. The silence in the room felt airless and oppressive.

What the hell had just happened?

***

HIS BACKPACK WAS GONE. He'd taken it with him. I hadn't seen him grab it, but it was no longer in the room.

In the middle of the bed, I had curled into a tight ball with the covers pulled up to my chin. Wearing his shirt. His pine scent filling my nose. My unblinking eyes staring at nothing. Fatigue ached through my limbs, making my body feel ten times heavier.

Ten years, he'd said. I'd haunted him for ten years. What had he meant?

I kept seeing that look he'd given me as he'd walked away. Even though I hated him so much I could barely breathe through it, it'd somehow never occurred to me that he might hate me too. He was the betrayer. He was the deceiver. Why had that hard bitterness in his eyes looked so much like hatred?

Why did I care?

I didn't. I did not care—but no matter how many times I repeated that mantra, my lips moving in a silent whisper, the hollowness in my chest didn't change. Where was the grinding, razor-sharp rage?

The room was so quiet. So empty. I could hear the faint rumble of the elevator down the hall, the muffled sound of a TV from a nearby room, the whoosh of traffic on the street outside.

I couldn't stop smelling his pine scent on the shirt I wore. I couldn't get it out of my head.

Hugging the pillow to my chest, I buried my face in it, filling my nose with the hotel's laundry detergent fragrance and trying to shut off my brain. Physical exhaustion won out over mental turmoil, and I drifted into a restless sleep.

A clatter from across the room trickled into my awareness. I struggled toward wakefulness as quiet, muffled sounds moved closer. The blankets covering me shifted, then a hand prodded my shoulder.

"Move over." Zak's low, rumbling voice broke the quiet hold of night. "You're in the middle of the bed."

I unclamped my arms from the pillow I was hugging and twisted to squint into the darkness. His silhouette stood at the edge of the bed, leaning over me.

"You left," I whispered.

"I needed air."

"But you took your backpack."

He huffed quietly. "Yeah, so you wouldn't snoop through my shit again. Are you going to move?"

I shuffled over, and he flipped the covers back. The mattress dipped as he lay down on his side, facing away from me.

Huddled between cold sheets, I stared at the dark shape of his head resting on the second pillow. With his return, my hollow chest had filled with sharp, hot edges. They sliced me, stinging and burning, but it felt so much better than emptiness.

My hand slid across the sheets. I touched the center of his back between his shoulder blades. His breath caught, muscles tensing.

I retracted my hand. "I didn't think you would come back."

"Would you have preferred I didn't?"

I flinched at his quiet question. I had no response. I didn't know anymore. What did I want?

Silence crept over the room. My hand rested on the sheet, still stretched toward him, an inch from his body. The boy who'd betrayed me. Now he was a man who plagued me, provoked me. Who hurt me and helped me. A man who wanted something from me, and I had no idea what.

What did *I* want?

My fingers curled, nails dragging across the sheets. With my other arm, I pushed myself forward, shuffling across the mattress until I was as close as I could get without our bodies making contact. Close enough that I could hear the quiet sound of his breathing—but I didn't touch him. He didn't want me to touch him.

But he was here. He'd come back.

And somehow, that was enough.

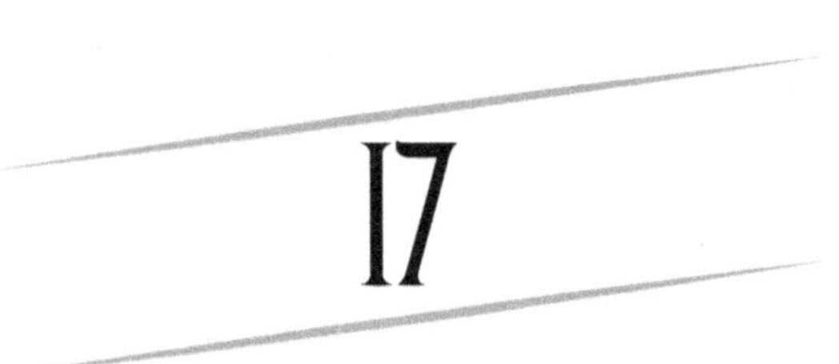

IN THE BATHROOM, I flattened my bangs. I'd had to wet them, then blow-dry them before they would lie flat. The rest of my scraggily, finger-combed hair was wrestled into a high ponytail, my mouth rinsed with mouthwash, and the minuscule hotel deodorant applied. I'd dressed in yesterday's pants and bra, but I was still wearing Zak's t-shirt.

Steeling myself, I marched out of the bathroom.

Zak was sitting on the edge of the bed, tiredly rubbing his face with one hand. His hair was rumpled, his shirt wrinkled, and he was wearing boxers but no pants. His jeans were haphazardly slung across the armchair, his backpack resting on the seat.

I cleared my throat. He turned to peer blearily at me.

"I'm going to visit the meadow again before I go back to Coquitlam. If you ..." My voice caught, and I cleared my throat again. "What are you going to do?"

He squinted at me, then scrubbed his face a second time. "Are you inviting me to go with you?"

"No, I'm just checking. What your plans are."

"By inviting me."

"I'm not *inviting you*."

"Then how are you planning to get there?"

"Huh?"

"The truck is mine."

I opened my mouth, then snapped it shut and folded my arms. "Are you coming or not?"

He looked away, his hands pressed to the mattress. As the silence stretched, as he considered how to answer, tension ratcheted through my body, winding my muscles tighter and tighter. Would he say no? Was he done with me, ready to give up on whatever it was he wanted? Had he come back for the night, only to leave in the morning?

"Fine."

I started. "What?"

"Fine," he repeated heavily, pushing to his feet. "I'll come with you."

But. I could hear a "but" hovering at the end of his statement. But what? But that was it? But he was leaving afterward?

I opened my mouth, but I couldn't make myself ask what came after that unspoken "but."

An hour later, I was back behind the wheel of his truck, the tires rumbling along the gravel road toward the hidden meadow. The silence in the cab was oppressive, and I usually enjoyed quiet.

My gaze slid sideways. Zak sat in the passenger seat, head tilted back and eyes closed, somehow attempting to nap despite the rough ride. The vargs were riding in the box, and Lallakai flew high above, a dark spot against the low, rain-heavy clouds.

Ríkr also kept watch from the sky. Before Zak had woken up, I'd discussed my plans with the fae. He'd agreed that, as long as we were quick and didn't go any farther into Hell's Gate than my childhood home, we should be safe enough. But we couldn't stay for long.

I parted my lips. It took me two tries to force myself to speak.

"Zak."

He grunted, not opening his eyes.

"What you said last night …"

He cracked one eye to look at me. "If you want to talk about last night, then we talk about everything. Are you ready for that?"

Everything? A shudder ran through me.

He watched me clutch the steering wheel, vibrating with tension, then closed his eyes again. "Didn't think so."

Letting up on the gas as the road sloped down toward the hidden meadow's valley, I stole a glance at him. His dark hair, the angle of his face, the sweeping line of his cheekbone. He looked so much like he had a decade ago.

"Does it bother you?" I asked. "That I had amnesia?"

With a rough exhale, he sat up in his seat. His eyes turned to me, the vibrant green of his irises darker and colder than they'd been yesterday.

"Part of me is glad you were spared from the memories." His expression was cold like his eyes. "The other part of me is pissed that you got off so easy."

"Easy? I had it *easy*? I went to prison!"

"And then you got to get a normal job and volunteer at a rescue and do things you enjoy. Sounds pretty fucking nice."

"Whatever happy little life you're imagining for me, it wasn't even close," I snarled. "What about you? Once you killed Bane, you were free to do whatever you wanted."

"Free? Is that what you think the life of a rogue is like?"

"You made yourself a wanted rogue."

"Yeah," he snapped, "because of *you*."

My head whipped toward him, my eyes wide and teeth bared with enraged disbelief that he was blaming his entire life on me.

He swore. "I didn't mean—*watch the road!*"

I jolted back toward the windshield—and slammed the brakes. The truck skidded across gravel, the back end fishtailing as we slid to a stop in the middle of the road.

Six feet in front of the bumper were the remains of the lesser woodland dragon we'd killed yesterday—but it no longer looked like a dragon's corpse. Its flesh had hardened into solid wood, and its enormous torso resembled a tree trunk, thick branches replacing its ribs. Its shape had roughened, its head no more than a lump of timber, features indistinguishable. To anyone who hadn't witnessed the dragon's death, its remains would look like a recently fallen tree.

I cut the engine and pushed my door open. Zak climbed out too, and we met in front of the truck.

Though the rest of the dragon's body seemed undisturbed, its torso was different. Had its ribs bent open like that as it had morphed into wood?

Together, Zak and I circled the torso to stand near the broken base of the "log." The chest cavity was empty, and in the middle, a perfect circle of tree seedlings had sprouted, a finger length tall, each with two small leaves.

"This," I said slowly, "looks just like the seedlings in the alder grove where the aeromage hiker died. Did they come from the woodland dragon?"

"I don't think so." Zak stepped closer, peering at the newly sprouted trees. "I think the seedlings were planted here—and the fae who did it doesn't need to kill its victims itself. It just wants the corpses."

"Wants the corpses for what?"

"Remember the alders that attacked us? This might be how they were made. The fae uses some kind of ritual involving a body and a circle of seeds to create animated plant life."

I studied the seedlings. "I don't think those are alder seedlings."

"Maybe the fae can grow its special trees from any seed."

My gaze moved across the dense woods surrounding the road. Forest blanketed these mountains. There were millions of trees. How many had this fae planted?

Zak straightened. "My question now is whether the fae responsible for these seedlings is the same fae killing hikers. Or does the tree-planting fae make use of any body it comes across?"

"If they are the same fae, that means the one that killed my parents was here in the last twenty-four hours."

We exchanged a terse look, then he stepped back. "Let's keep moving."

Back in the truck, I steered partway off the road, branches scraping against the vehicle's side, and squeezed past the dragon's woody remains.

It wasn't far to the hidden property, and ten minutes later, I parked in the same spot, breathing deep to steady myself. This time, I didn't experience a burst of happiness and excitement to balance my grief.

As we climbed out of the truck, two raptors spiraled down from the sky, one black, one white. Lallakai landed on the roof of the truck and Ríkr changed forms in midair to land on my shoulder as a white jay.

The black eagle watched his every move, her emerald eyes calculating. She'd been scrutinizing him since he'd recovered from his near-death yesterday.

"Did you see the dead woodland dragon?" I asked him.

He canted his head. *I approached from the south after surveying the valley. Is something amiss?*

"There's a circle of tree seedlings growing in it, just like in the alder grove where the aeromage—"

A circle of seedlings? he cut in sharply. *You saw this in the alder grove as well?*

"Yes, I—I forgot to tell you, I guess. All the bodies of this fae predator have had—"

The dragon's body grows trees? His small claws pricked my shoulder through my shirt. *Are you certain?*

"Yes, we saw them. We think—"

I must see this. He launched off my shoulder. *Visit your childhood home quickly, Saber. If the bringer of trees is this close, we must flee.*

"Flee?" I repeated, but he was already sweeping away, wings beating urgently. It wouldn't take him long to reach the dragon's body, see the seedlings, and return. I had ten minutes, at best.

"Go," Zak said, reaching into his truck. He pulled out his alchemy combat belt. "I'll wait out here."

I looked from him to the house and back, then ran to the cabin and up the three steps onto the front porch. Only as I was grabbing the handle did I realize I needed my lock-picking kit, which I hadn't brought with me—but the knob turned under my hand, grinding with rust. My parents had rarely locked it, probably since our property was so remote and well-hidden.

The door opened, the creaking hinges resisting the motion they hadn't performed in eighteen years. I stepped across the threshold, my heart thumping in my throat.

An open kitchen and living room filled the small main space. A hallway led to two bedrooms and a bathroom. Everything was covered in dust. Cobwebs in the corners. Damage from rodents.

A stack of books sat on the coffee table. A small pile of dirty breakfast dishes waited beside the sink from our last morning before my parents had set out for the ill-fated rescue of an already dead hiker. A set of wooden horses, carved in loving detail by my father, were scattered in front of the fireplace where I'd left them.

I could hear my mother's voice chiding me to tidy up my toys. Throat closing, I swallowed my grief. I didn't have time to get lost in memories.

I hurried to the fireplace. On the mantle were framed photos, the glass covered in dust, but I knew which one I wanted—a heavy ash frame stained a dark brown, carved with leaves. Scooping it up, I left the kitchen. I passed a small bedroom with a child-sized bed and a comforter embroidered with roses, then veered into my parents' room.

Their king-sized bed was large enough to accommodate my father's height, the bedcovers hastily made. A change of clothes was thrown over the rocking chair by the window, my mom's favorite red shirt lying on top. Spare hiking gear spilled out from the open closet.

I walked to my father's nightstand, opened the drawers, and dug through a random assortment of his belongings. I wasn't searching for anything in particular—just something that would provide the answers they'd never had a chance to give me.

Circling the bed, I opened my mother's nightstand drawers and found a similar jumble of items: reading glasses, a notepad with a few reminders jotted in it, an old watch that didn't work, a sleep mask, vanilla-scented lotion, and a handful of hair ties with strands of black hair knotted around them. In the bottom drawer was a jewelry box large enough for a dozen small pieces or a few larger necklaces. I almost didn't open it. I didn't wear jewelry, and I didn't remember my mother wearing any either. But out of curiosity, I popped the lid up.

A tangle of leather ties filled it, braided and pristine. They were the same leather ties I'd worn around my neck for my entire childhood—the ones that had held my river-stone pendant. Any time the tie had shown signs of wear or weakness, my mom had replaced it. This was her collection of spares.

My fingers trembling, I lifted them out. Something inside the box clattered.

Lying in the bottom, unattached to a tie, was a river stone the size of the end of my thumb. A familiar rune was etched in its face.

I stared down at it, not breathing. If my parents had wanted to keep me hidden—especially in the middle of Hell's Gate—it made sense that they would have kept a spare pendant in case something happened to the original.

My fingertips brushed the cool surface of the stone.

"Saber!"

Zak's muffled shout almost didn't reach me at the back of the cabin, but I caught the urgency in it.

I grabbed the river stone, leaving the jewelry box on my mom's nightstand. Clutching it and the picture frame, I sprinted through the house and out the door.

My stride stuttered. I stumbled to a halt so fast I had to grab the porch railing to stop myself from falling.

A golden-green haze hung over the meadow, as though we were simultaneously immersed in sunlight and olive-tinted fog. The faint breeze tasted like sweet, crushed leaves, and humid summer warmth hung in the air—far warmer than it'd been minutes ago.

Zak stood ten feet in front of the house, facing the hazy meadow. He was fully geared—his alchemy belt, potions and spells hanging from it; a knife strapped to his thigh; bracers around his wrists. His vargs flanked him, their hackles raised.

At my stumbling appearance, he glanced back at me. His green eyes were vibrant, iridescent, almost glowing, and a tattoo-like pattern of feathers ran down his arms.

Lallakai was possessing him.

"Zak?" I gasped.

He faced the meadow again. "Get ready."

My heart thumped hard against my ribs. I set the picture frame and river stone on the porch railing and rushed down the steps. Pulling out my switchblade, I stopped beside him so that we faced the meadow shoulder to shoulder.

"What's happening?" I asked.

Two of the gem-like pendants hanging around his neck were glowing. He extended his right hand from his side, the black rune appearing on his skin as he answered.

"The Forest Lord is here."

18

Standing rigidly beside Zak, I didn't dare call for him. If this "Forest Lord" was that close, I could give away Ríkr's presence or location.

The gold-green haze filling the valley deepened. The quiet, impassive energy of the mountain was shifting, sharpening, filling with … something. I didn't know what I was sensing, except that it was powerful.

One moment, the fog was empty. Then I blinked, and the fae was there.

Thirty feet away, he stood as still as an immoveable red cedar. Elegant, silk-like robes draped his slender frame in shades of brown, green, and gold, and his long, pine-green hair was braided over one shoulder. A circlet of woven branches with spring buds wrapped around his forehead, above pupilless eyes the color of sunlight, and ivory deer antlers rose a foot above his head.

The atmosphere thickened with his power, sweet and cloying in my lungs.

"Is that him?" I whispered, my fingers tightening around my useless switchblade. "The fae who makes the seedlings grow?"

Was I looking at the fae who had butchered my parents, split open their chests, scooped out their organs, and planted trees in their bodies?

The Forest Lord tilted his head slightly.

Stinging pain cut across my ankles. Thorny vines had sprouted from the ground and were spinning around my lower legs. They swept up my body impossibly fast, the cordons thickening and coiling arms sprouting every six inches to bind me tighter. I writhed, the thorns scraping me.

Snarls erupted close by. Vines had captured the vargs where they stood. Zak was trapped too, his arms ensnared, a thorny vine wrapping around his throat.

He held perfectly still in their grasp, and I stopped struggling as the pain in my scraped skin burned hotter and hotter. Were the thorns toxic? My lungs heaved as the pain worsened. Definitely toxic.

The Forest Lord moved toward us, his steps smooth, gliding, leisurely. His sickly-sweet power filled the air like a warm cloud.

He halted ten feet away, his sunlight eyes moving from Zak to me, then back to Zak.

"Tell me," the fae said, his voice low, smooth, and poised, "where is the Winter King?"

"I don't know a fae by that title," Zak replied neutrally.

The vines around him cinched tight, jerking his limbs. Blood trickled down his throat where the thorns pierced his skin.

"He is near," the fae stated. "Does he accompany you?"

"I already said I don't know the Winter King."

"What of the Lady concealed inside you?" The Forest Lord canted his head in the opposite direction—and the vines pulled tighter around Zak. His breath hissed out through his clenched teeth. "Does *she* know?"

The feather markings running down Zak's arms blurred—and phantom wings swept off him. Slashes of dark power erupted from their shadowy feathers, severing the vines ensnaring him.

He stepped out of the torn vines, his black sword swirling into existence in his hand. Power rippled off it, and the dark wings arched off his back.

"The Night Eagle has nothing to tell you," Zak said in a quiet, impartial tone. "If you want us to leave your forest, we'll go immediately."

The Forest Lord studied him with those unblinking yellow eyes.

New vines sprang up from the ground around Zak's feet, but he leaped away before they could trap him. He whipped his sword outward, and a dark crescent of power flashed toward the Forest Lord.

The golden glow in the meadow brightened, and the shadowy attack faded before it could touch him.

Zak thrust his other arm into the air. Black magic swirled around his wrist, gathering in his hand, and he brought it down sharply, pointing at the Forest Lord ten feet away. A spear of black power—the same lethal shadow spear Lallakai had used to skewer Balligor—launched from his fingers.

Golden light flashed—and the shadow magic disappeared.

The bright haze intensified. As the glow swept across the meadow, the wings arching from Zak's back fizzled away. His sword lost solidity, turning semitransparent, then disappeared too, as though washed away by the sunny glow.

Vines ripped out of the earth. Even faster than before, they spun around Zak, lifting him off the ground as they locked tight around his body, binding his limbs.

The Forest Lord closed the distance until he stood directly in front of the druid. His hand closed around Zak's throat. The fae's flesh shimmered faintly, then he sank his fingers *into* Zak's neck and pulled. Shadows rippled across Zak, drawn out of him. The darkness solidified into Lallakai's womanly form.

The Forest Lord dragged her out of Zak by her throat. Her emerald eyes blazed—and she lunged at him, slashing with her talons, black magic rippling in their wake. Power collided, then exploded in a twisting mass of golden light and dark shadow.

Wind and debris tore across me. I cringed, unable to shield my face, more thorns scraping my skin as the gusts made the vines sway. The fog intensified. Another explosion of wind, dirt, and light assaulted me.

Then it stopped.

The golden radiance died, and I squinted through the dusty haze.

Lallakai was sprawled on her back, her raven hair tumbled across the ground. Slashing wounds scored her pale skin, leaking blood. The Forest Lord stood over her, untouched. It didn't even look like he'd moved.

She rose into a crouch at his feet. Her blood dripped into the long grass.

"I have no interest in you," the Forest Lord intoned. "I will spare you and your druids if you tell me: Where is the Winter King?"

"You cannot find him yourself?" A taunting note slipped into her throaty voice. "Then I will enlighten you. He is here."

"Where—"

Pale blue light flared in a circular pattern beneath the Forest Lord's feet—then burst upward into a towering spire of ice, engulfing the fae.

Cold blasted out from the frozen starburst, and as flurries of snow danced violently on the wind, Lallakai launched for Zak. Slender shadow blades cut through the vines holding him. As his feet dropped to the ground, she cast the same blades at me. I stumbled, my feet freed, and yanked the vines off my body, burning scrapes lacerating my fingers from the thorns.

Golden-green light ignited inside the huge ice spire. The luminescence flared even brighter, and loud cracks shook the ice. It broke apart, crumbling to the ground.

The Forest Lord stood in the center of the melting ice, faint light radiating off his skin. He looked up.

The white hawk diving from the overcast sky transformed, and a beastly wolfhound slammed down on top of the Forest Lord in a rush of sparkling snow.

Lallakai cut the two vargs free, and they bolted toward the truck. Zak grabbed my wrist and ran after them. Lallakai didn't run, but she backed away, her focus locked on the two fae lords.

The Forest Lord was moving—his feet dancing lithely across the ground. The wolfhound, his golden antlers gleaming, attacked with ruthless aggression, teeth snapping at the Forest Lord's flesh.

We reached the truck and I seized the handle. Rίkr had wanted to flee from this fae. His power was diminished. He couldn't win this fight, and his only chance was to escape—

which meant I had to escape too. The only reason he'd attacked was to buy me time to get away.

But as I yanked the door open, Zak's fingers bit down on my hand so hard that I hissed in pain. I jerked toward him, then froze when I saw the thick, woody vines encasing the truck's front tires. Wriggling sprouts crawled out of the wheel wells, and the tire let out a high-pitched wheeze as it deflated.

The Forest Lord had destroyed our only means of escape. We couldn't outrun him on foot; the entire forest was his domain.

I spun back to the meadow, panic rushing through me.

Golden-green light swirled around the Forest Lord like an incessant breeze, and around Ríkr, a sphere of arctic cold turned the air to crystals and the ground to frost. As the wolfhound lunged for the fae, their power collided.

Ríkr snapped his jaws at the Forest Lord's arm, but a thick, sword-like branch appeared in his hand. He swept it out, and the wolfhound's teeth crunched down on it instead. Ice burst over the wooden blade, and it shattered.

They lunged back and forth, the Forest Lord circling within the same ten square feet. Plants and vines erupted all around him, blocking Ríkr's attacks and trying to strike or entangle him. But the spinning cold around the wolfhound was so intense that the plants froze and crumbled. Everything Ríkr bit down on turned to ice and shattered.

I stood beside Zak, my heart lodged in my throat. Lallakai waited half a dozen steps in front of us, blood running down her exposed skin.

The Forest Lord pivoted, dodging another attack from the wolfhound. His hand snapped up. The earth shook, then tore open. Tree saplings, leafless and pointed like spears, shot out of the ground so fast and strong that they pierced Ríkr's wintry sphere.

They plunged into his body.

Ice rushed out from him, coating the saplings. They shattered andRíkr dropped to the ground, staggering for balance. His eyes glowed blue, and swirling markings lit his canine face and rushed down his left side. The same azure light glowed from his wounds, and the dripping blood stopped. His injuries vanished.

"Do you think you can defeat me in such a weak form, Arawn?" The Forest Lord curled his fingers, and a new double-edged sword grew out of his palm like a tree branch, but with an edge sharper than wood should've been able to hold. "As though such a paltry ambush could harm me."

The wolfhound opened its jaws in a fang-filled grin. *It was worth an attempt, was it not, Luthyr?*

A blue glow ignited over Ríkr. Snow and ice crystals rushed outward as his humanoid form appeared, standing in the center of a frozen circle twelve feet across. The markings on his face shimmered faintly.

Luthyr's sunlit eyes drifted down the other fae and back up again. "Long I have waited for our final encounter."

"What a tragedy, my fair Lord of Summer, for I have never once yearned to see you again."

"You know you will perish by my hand. It is why you hid yourself so cunningly." The humid power saturating the meadow deepened. "And now, after all this time, you come into my forest, into my power, and challenge me. Your arrogance cost you Annwn, and now it will cost you your life."

The ring of frost around Ríkr continued to spread. "Then you must be pleased, Luthyr, to finally discharge this long-drawn duty and return to the Summer Court."

"As flippant as always, Arawn, but your hubris is again misplaced." Luthyr lifted his sword, pointing it at Ríkr. "I have waited seasons beyond count for a sign of your presence. Do you think, in that time, I would not have devised a way to kill The Undying?"

With no more warning than that, he sprang at Ríkr.

A spear of ice formed in Ríkr's hand, and he thrust it into the oncoming fae. Their power met in a concussive burst of opposing magic. The air boomed and wind gusted, swirling violently and whipping dust and snow into a spiral around the two fae.

This wasn't a battle between a forest fae and a shapeshifter. It was a collision between Summer and Winter.

Ice spires erupted in crooked, frozen towers. Plants tore up from the ground as flashes of golden warmth—summer sunlight—blazed through the ice. The wind howled as the temperature flashed hot and cold over and over, and within the maelstrom, the two fae sought to kill each other.

But it wasn't an even match.

Luthyr's sword ran through Ríkr's shoulder before it shattered from the cold. The Lord of Summer grew another one from his palm in an instant and slashed again. Ríkr's ice spears melted before striking Luthyr's body. His wintry sphere of cold was shrinking, his explosive spires of ice collapsing faster.

The wooden sword opened his thigh. Another slice tore across his side.

Plants poked up through the ground around Ríkr's feet, his freezing power no longer killing them instantly. They tangled around his ankles—and Luthyr thrust his sword, throwing his whole weight behind the strike.

I choked on a scream as the blade plunged straight through Ríkr's heart.

Ríkr's limbs seized, his head falling forward. Holding the blade, Ríkr's torso skewered on it, Luthyr curled his fingers like claws and rammed his entire hand into Ríkr's chest. Ribs snapped, the horrific sound filling the meadow's summer-calm air.

I lunged forward, no idea how I could help—but if I could buy Ríkr even a moment of distraction, then I'd risk it all. Catching my elbow, Zak hauled me back into his chest, clamping his arms around me in a vise-like grip. The harder I struggled, the tighter he held me until I could scarcely breathe.

Ríkr's eyes blazed with light. The markings on his face lit up, and his left arm rose, the sleeve of his cloak sliding up to reveal his forearm, the markings running all the way down his hand and along his first two fingers.

He raised his palm to Luthyr's face, and ice exploded outward, encasing the fae in a frozen tidal wave.

Ríkr stumbled back a step, then sank to one knee. The markings on his left side flared brighter. The sword sticking out of his chest—out of his heart—frosted over, then shattered to dust. Blue light rippled from his wounds like fire.

From within the wave of ice encasing the Summer Lord, a faint gold light appeared. It brightened, expanding. Deep cracking sounds echoed from within the ice. The jagged shape shuddered, and with a sharp hiss, it disintegrated into a wave of steam.

Luthyr appeared again, unharmed. Not even disheveled. He stood over Ríkr, who was still down on one knee as though bowing before the Summer Lord.

His expression as unfeeling as the arctic tundra, Ríkr pressed his hand to his chest. His other wounds had vanished, but blue light was still rippling over his brutalized sternum and broken ribs.

"Your fall from the throne was satisfying." Seedlings sprouted from the ground in a circle around Luthyr. "But I find no gratification in victory over such a weak and pitiful foe."

The seedlings rose around the Summer Lord, thickening into saplings.

"Farewell, Arawn of Annwn, the long-forgotten Winter King."

The young trees rushed upward, growing with impossible speed, then pulled inward. Luthyr disappeared as the trunks twisted around him, fusing together. Their rapid growth slowed, and where the Summer Lord and the circle of young trees had been, a single trunk had formed. Large, five-lobed leaves opened on its spreading branches until, finally, it stilled.

A mature maple, its broad boughs filled with healthy green leaves, stood tall in the meadow where no tree had ever grown before.

19

"RÍKR!"

Tearing away from Zak, I sprinted toward the fae. He rose to his full height, and as he turned to face me, the magic glowing over his chest finally faded. Unblemished skin peeked through his torn clothing.

I slid to a stop in front of him. "Are you okay?"

"I am most wounded."

I blinked at him, then narrowed my eyes angrily. "Are you hurt or not?"

Ríkr tapped his undamaged chest. "As you can see, my magic again defies certain death."

"Does the Lord of Summer believe he fatally wounded you?" Lallakai strode toward us, none of her usual sensuality in her walk. Blood still ran from her wounds. "Or did he intend only to defeat you, not kill you?"

Ríkr tucked his hands in the opposite sleeves of his cloak. "It is difficult to say, but in either case, he seems to believe his mission was accomplished." He nodded toward the truck. "Can it be repaired? I doubt Luthyr will return promptly, but it would not be wise to linger in his forest."

The three of us turned to the vehicle. Zak was already crouched beside the deflated tire, his knife in his hand as he cut through the tough vines wrapped around it. I hastened toward him, the two fae following.

"It doesn't look like there's any damage to the engine," Zak told us, "but I need to cut off the vines and swap the tire. It'll take a few minutes."

"Can I help?" I asked.

"Your knife isn't big enough. And no fae assistance," he added, grunting as he snapped a vine on his blade. "The last thing we need is a severed brake line."

"I will refrain," Ríkr drawled.

Lallakai crossed her arms, heedless of her injuries. "Arawn of Annwn, The Undying." Her gaze slid over Ríkr. "The Winter King. I did not suspect, even for a moment, that would be your true identity." Her upper lip curled. "How far you have fallen indeed."

"A pale shadow of glory, am I not?" he agreed. "Once, you would have cowered at my mere presence." A chill washed through the air. "Though I could *make* you cower, Night Eagle, should I desire it."

She lifted her chin. "Me, cower before the pitiful dregs of a fallen king?"

The temperature dropped further, and the markings down his face shimmered. "Or I could simply shatter you into a thousand shards of ice and be done with your specious contempt."

I wrapped my fingers around his cool wrist. "As much as I'd enjoy that, I also want to know what's going on. Who was that fae? How do you two know each other?"

"And"—Zak pushed to his feet, his ten-inch knife in hand—"how long did you know he was in this area? Because I don't remember you mentioning that Hell's Gate is ruled by a fae lord who's out for your blood."

Lallakai added nothing, but expectation weighed on her silence.

Ríkr sighed. "Then we may as well find some comfortable seating, for it is a long tale."

EVEN IF THERE'D BEEN somewhere comfortable to sit, I wouldn't have been able to relax—not with the scratches all over me stinging like acid. Whatever toxin had coated the thorns of those vines was excruciatingly long-lasting.

I sat with my knees pulled up to my chest, my back resting against the rear tire of the truck. A few feet away, Zak was under the truck, only his legs sticking out. He'd lifted it with the jack from his roadside kit, and he was sawing at the vines tangled around the tire and axle. Though we all wanted to get out of Hell's Gate as quickly as possible, we had no way to speed the process.

Lallakai knelt in the grass, her hands resting on her lap as she waited. The vargs were lying a short distance away, and judging by the way they were panting, they were hurting from the thorns too.

Ríkr sat across from me, his cloak spread out behind him. His golden antlers gleamed in the overcast afternoon light. "Are you all agreed that you wish to hear the long, tedious tale and not a more entertaining and timely summary?"

"The whole thing," I told him firmly.

"As you wish." He breathed in, and when he spoke again, his lightly amused tone had deepened with somberness. "Long ago, there existed two Winter Courts that battled for supremacy over the land known as Annwn. The king of one court, known as Arawn, was powerful and ambitious, but despite both, he could not defeat his rival, the king of the opposing court, Hafgan."

"Are you going to tell the whole story in the third person?" I asked. "We already know you're Arawn."

His teasing smile ghosted over his lips. "It sounds much better this way. As I was tastefully recounting, Arawn was indisputably more gifted than Hafgan in both magic and cunning, yet he could not defeat his rival. Hafgan possessed a unique power, one that made him impossible to slay. Arawn struck him down time and time again, but he would not die."

I frowned. Hadn't Luthyr called Ríkr "The Undying"?

"One fair night, after yet another frustrating failure to end Hafgan, Arawn was hunting in the mortal realm in the form of a winter hound when he encountered a human hunter—a druid."

With a scuffling sound, Zak slid out from under the truck, eyebrows raised curiously as he gave Ríkr his full attention.

"The druid, mistaking Arawn for a mere beast, attempted to steal his kill. When Arawn revealed himself, the druid knew he would suffer dire consequences for his disrespect. However, Arawn generously offered the druid a bargain."

"I feel like this is a very subjective retelling," Zak observed dryly.

Ríkr's smile reappeared before he resumed his grave tone. "Arawn suggested to the druid that they exchange places. For one year and one day, the druid would live as Arawn and find a way to defeat Hafgan. While he made this attempt, Arawn would live as the druid."

Zak idly spun his ten-inch knife in his hand. "And what was the penalty for failure?"

"That is not important to this tale," Ríkr baldly evaded. "The druid agreed, for he was no mere druid. He was Pwyll, Prince of Dyfed, the mortal kingdom that mirrored Annwn."

"A druid prince?" I murmured, impressed.

Lallakai made a small, thoughtful hum. "It was common in the days of old for mythics to rise into positions of great power among humans."

"Very much so," Ríkr agreed. "Thusly, Arawn shifted into the form of Pwyll, then cast his magic upon Pwyll to give the druid his own form. They set out to live each other's lives for a year and a day—Arawn to rule the mortal kingdom of Dyfed, and Pwyll to rule Arawn's Winter Court in Annwn."

"That's it?" I interjected. "Arawn just—I mean, *you* just turned him into your doppelganger and tossed him into the fae demesne?"

"Generous," Zak added with a snort.

"Well …" Ríkr gave a small shrug. "I also gifted him several powerful enchantments, but I was attempting to keep this tale somewhat concise."

I closed my mouth, resisting the urge to ask more questions.

"For one year, Arawn and Pwyll lived as the other—and with remarkable success, I must say. Pwyll diligently applied himself to his task, and just before their bargain expired, he slew Hafgan."

"How?" I asked.

Ríkr ignored my question. "As Hafgan's life faded, Arawn appeared and consumed the unique gift of his hated rival, thus becoming as unkillable as Hafgan had been. And so Arawn ascended as the sole Winter King, ruler of his court and all of Annwn, and The Undying."

Incredulity sharpened my voice. "You *stole* Hafgan's power?"

"It is a gift many of my deadlier kin possess. Some may steal power, while others may steal magical gifts upon the deaths of their enemies. It is how we grow so powerful." He slanted a look at Lallakai. "Is it not, Lady of Shadow?"

She shot him a venomous look, and I guessed it wasn't an ability she possessed—at least, not the magical gifts part.

"How does Luthyr play into this story?" Zak asked, lying back. He scooted under the truck again. "And the Summer Court?"

Ríkr braced one hand on the ground behind him, getting more comfortable. "Jubilant with victory, Arawn lavishly rewarded Pwyll, and though they returned to their rightful places in their own realms, they remained warm companions. Arawn sent gifts to Pwyll, and they met every winter to hunt wild boars in the far, snowy reaches of Dyfed.

"However, Arawn's attention upon the druid prince—soon to become King of Dyfed—did not go unnoticed. Rhiannon, a Lady of Summer with great might and vigor, appeared to Pwyll and seduced him with her many irresistible wiles. He became her consort, she his queen, and together, they raised a son."

My mouth fell open. "A son?"

"A druid child," Ríkr added amusedly, "but humans in that age enjoyed their subterfuges surrounding parentage. Rhiannon was the Queen of Dyfed, so of course she claimed the child as her blood.

"To Arawn's sorrow, Pwyll passed from life. His heir, Pryderi, ascended the throne, and Arawn treated the son as he had the father, offering gifts and friendship. But this did not suit Rhiannon's ambitions, for Arawn bolstered Pryderi's resistance to her influence, just as he had supported Pwyll. Pryderi would not bend to her will and ambitions any more than his father had.

"Then came the day Rhiannon met another druid, one by the name of Gwydion. Gifted in magic as well as druidry, he was everything Pryderi was not—markedly powerful, exceptionally shrewd, and above all, fiercely ambitious."

Zak threw a handful of severed vines out from under the truck. "Gwydion was a di-mythic? What was his second class?"

"Earth magery. A deadly combination."

I wondered if it was as deadly as Zak's di-mythic combination of druidry and Arcana.

"Gwydion was most impressive—for a human." Ríkr's tone lost inflection, becoming more detached. "He lured Pryderi into a duel, and against the more powerful druid, Pryderi perished."

My breath caught.

"Enraged at this ill-concealed murder, Arawn struck against Gwydion, but he did not realize the depth of treachery he faced, for Rhiannon had conspired with Gwydion to set an inescapable ambush for the Winter King. In his desire to avenge the son of his beloved Pwyll, and in his arrogant belief that he was unassailable, Arawn fell into their trap."

"The Battle of Trees," Lallakai murmured. "The Winter King lost to a forest army."

Ríkr didn't acknowledge her statement. "Gwydion, Rhiannon, and her Summer Court waylaid Arawn. Leading the attack was Rhiannon's boldest and most loyal lord, Luthyr of the Forest, who gives life and will to trees so they might do his bidding." He tilted his head back, gazing at the overcast sky. "Arawn was soundly defeated, his wintry magic overwhelmed, his power broken, and his kingdom lost."

Quiet slipped over our small group, disturbed only by the rasp of Zak's knife on the vines tangled over the truck's underbelly.

Ríkr let out a soft breath. "Rhiannon swept into Annwn with her victorious entourage, and the Summer Court claimed the land that had once been Arawn's. But Rhiannon was not wholly satisfied, for Arawn, though defeated, had survived. He was The Undying, and even with nothing else to his name, he could not be killed. To ensure he would never return to challenge her, she set her loyal warrior Luthyr to the task of finding and slaying Arawn."

His voice was slowing, the words coming with longer pauses. "Forgotten by all but Rhiannon and Luthyr, Arawn fled farther and farther from his homeland. The Forest Lord hunted him relentlessly, year upon year … century upon century … appearing whenever Arawn gathered any power with which he might rebuild."

Again, Ríkr paused, his flawless countenance ancient and otherworldly.

"Eventually," he continued, "Arawn lost all hope of reclaiming his throne. He found a crossroads and fled to the land across the sea. There he hid, binding the dredges of his power so tight and so deep that when Luthyr followed, he could not detect any sign of the fallen Winter King. Stymied in his hunt, Luthyr settled near the crossroads, and there he waited, the ever-patient hunter, for the day his prey would reveal himself once more. And Arawn … Arawn disappeared into obscurity, never to reclaim his lost glory."

I absorbed his story, sifting through the details as sympathy weighed on me. With a quiet scuff, Zak sat up, his green eyes surveying Ríkr. Even Lallakai had no scathing remarks to make.

"The crossroads to the northeast," I murmured. "That's the one you used when you first came to North America, isn't it? You knew Luthyr was in Hell's Gate. That's why you didn't want to come here."

His eyes, solemn and unreadable, turned to me.

"For fuck's sake, Ríkr!" I burst out, leaning forward and planting my palms on the ground. "Why didn't you say anything? Why risk a confrontation with Luthyr over me?"

He tipped his head back again, and when he spoke, his voice still held that unhurried storytelling tone. "For over a hundred years, Arawn wandered the new world, adrift in hopeless despair. Then, one quiet summer morn, he encountered a druid—a fair maiden of fierce yet naïve power. Unknowingly, she struck a tacit bargain with the Winter King, and in payment, he consumed her druidic power."

Eyes gleaming faintly, he looked back at me. "He consumed her power that day, and every day that followed, for seven years. With each turn of the moon, his broken strength grew, and though he stayed hidden, and though he held to his disguise, he remembered more of what he'd lost—and what he wished to recover. He began to think that, one day, perhaps he *could* escape his past and begin again."

I knew all about wanting to start over.

"Though in different ways," he said, his voice sliding into a more conversational cadence, "I was as crippled as you were the day we met, dove. Your gift to me was the breath of a new life, and even at the prospect of entering Luthyr's domain, I could not deny you something so close to your heart."

I swallowed against the lump in my throat.

"I must confess," he added with an unhappy twist of his mouth, "that I suffer still from my own arrogance. I thought we would slip through Luthyr's territory without drawing his notice, but I overestimated my ability to hide my increased power and underestimated his commitment to my death. Again." He ran his thumb down his jaw. "You would think, after a thousand years, I'd have learned better. A shortcoming of my kind, I must assume."

"A shortcoming of *yours*," Lallakai corrected, smiling cattily. "The older you are, the less adaptable you become."

"I fear you are correct."

Lallakai blinked, surprised he'd agreed with her.

I scrubbed my hand over my face, then regretted it as all the scratches on my palm flared with stinging pain. "Still, Ríkr. You could have said something. You could've warned us about Luthyr."

Had he kept silent out of long habit? Or had he realized that the "bringer of trees" had killed my parents? If Ríkr hadn't come to North America, Luthyr wouldn't have followed him, and my parents wouldn't have died by his hand.

But Ríkr and Luthyr had settled here long before my parents had even been born, so I could hardly blame him.

I pushed to my feet. "How about we get the hell out of here before Luthyr figures out you're alive? If he wants to kill you that badly, he'll probably come back to make sure you actually died."

Ríkr smiled faintly. "I heartily approve of this plan."

I hadn't been able to help Zak clear the vines from under the truck, but I knew how to change a tire. I hauled the full-sized spare out of the box and helped him swap it for the deflated one.

With a grunt of effort, I shoved the ruined tire into the box. When I turned, I noticed Ríkr and Lallakai gazing at each other with an odd intensity—a look I recognized as silent communication. Anxiety sparked in my gut, fizzling uncomfortably.

Zak pulled the lowered jack from under the truck, all four tires solid and vine-free. "Ready?"

"Yes," I said, dragging my attention away from Ríkr.

Lallakai rose to her feet. Her wounds had finally stopped bleeding, and she seemed unconcerned by the streaks of blood all over her. "The Winter King and I will fly. I want to ensure Luthyr makes no attempt to block us."

"You two," Ríkr added emphatically, "will travel directly out of Hell's Gate."

"The town we stayed in last night should be far enough." Zak tossed the jack into the truck's box. "Saber and I need to clean up and treat our injuries."

"Then await us there," Lallakai said with a graceful nod.

Ríkr gave me a flourishing bow worthy of any royal court, his cloak swirling around him. "Safe journey, dove."

Rolling my eyes, I climbed into the truck. I'd fetched my framed photograph and the river stone from the porch, the latter stashed in my pocket. Assuming it worked like the last one, it wouldn't have any effect unless it was touching my skin—though who knew if it had any magic left after nearly two decades. I settled the frame on my lap as Zak buckled in and started the engine. The suspension bobbed as the vargs jumped into the box, then we were rolling forward, leaving my childhood home behind.

I glanced at the side-view mirror. Ríkr and Lallakai were speaking again, and to my surprise, he dipped his head in a nod that appeared genuinely respectful.

The anxious feeling of dread simmering in my gut inexplicably deepened, and I had the feeling I was overlooking something.

Shadows whirled across Lallakai's body as she shrank into the form of a black eagle. Wings flashing, she took flight. Ríkr glanced over his shoulder, looking back at Luthyr's maple tree, then an azure glow washed over him as he changed forms too.

The truck bounced around a curve in the overgrown track, and I lost sight of him.

BY SOME MIRACLE, the same room in the same little hotel in Hope was available again.

As I tossed my phone, wallet, and water bottle on the bed, I realized I hadn't asked the front desk clerk if there was a second vacancy so Zak and I wouldn't have to share a room. Well, too late now.

The door thumped behind me, and Zak walked in carrying his backpack in one hand. He set it on the bed and unzipped it. "Turn on a light."

The heavy drapes were pulled shut, blocking the gloomy late afternoon light. I turned on the nearest lamp, and its soft orange glow washed across the room, dim and moody. He pulled out his alchemy kit, which I knew from experience doubled as a first aid kit. Flipping it open, he selected a jar of translucent white cream.

"Come on," he said, heading for the bathroom.

I followed him into the small space, only a few feet between the counter and the tub. Turning on the sink faucet, he soaked a washcloth, wrung it out, then tossed it to me.

"Clean your cuts," he told me. "Then apply a thin layer of the cream. It'll take away the sting."

"Do you know what toxin was in those thorns?" I asked, pressing the cloth to my scraped fingers. The cold soothed the sting even without the ointment.

"Some sort of irritant." He wet a second washcloth. "If it was anything worse, we'd know it by now."

He wiped the scrapes on his hands clean, and I followed suit, scrubbing my fingers first, then working up my wrists. Aside from the occasional deeper slice, the scratches weren't as bad as the pain had made me believe.

"Ríkr seems to care about you."

I looked up.

Zak glanced my way, his washcloth stained with spots of blood. "I thought he was an opportunistic leech, but I think he cares, as much as a fae that old can care about anything but his own power."

"That was almost a nice apology for misjudging him," I replied in a clipped tone. "Until the last part."

"The last part is a fact. He hid from Luthyr for over a millennium, and that's just the most recent part of his existence. How can any human's life matter that much in comparison?" He shrugged. "I'm not trying to belittle your relationship, but that perspective matters."

I scrubbed my arm harder than necessary. "I think that makes it more meaningful that he cares enough to risk his life for me."

"It is meaningful," he agreed quietly.

I stole a glance at him in the mirror. "Would Lallakai risk her life for you?"

"The way Ríkr did? No."

Silence fell. Pulling my shirt up halfway, I cleaned a shallow slice across my stomach. Zak finished his arms, then without any apparent self-consciousness, pulled his shirt off with one hand. Naked from the waist up, he started scrubbing the cuts on his torso.

I angled away from him. The bathroom suddenly felt much smaller.

Working around my shirt—or rather, the t-shirt I'd borrowed from him—I took care of the few scratches on my upper body, then frowned at my legs. My ankles were scratched to hell, and my calves weren't much better.

I undid my fly, pushed my jeans off, and tossed them out of the bathroom. They landed with an odd clatter. Had I just thrown my phone? No, I'd left it on the bed.

Making a note to investigate when I was done, I bent down and scrubbed at my ankle. The angle wasn't working, so I tried awkwardly propping my foot on the counter. It wasn't much better.

Zak plucked the cloth from my hand. "Sit."

"What? Why?"

"You aren't cleaning those cuts well enough."

"They're hard to reach," I growled.

"Obviously. That's why I'm offering to help."

Irritation flashed through me, but he had a point. I boosted myself onto the cold countertop as Zak rinsed out my cloth. When he turned back to me, I stuck my bare leg out.

He wrapped a hand around my calf, then began scrubbing the scrapes on my ankle. I gritted my teeth at the deep sting.

I'd made them worse with my pointless struggles. Everything I'd done had been pointless.

"I'm completely helpless."

The words slipped out before I could stop them, and I grimaced.

"At the moment?" Zak asked, my knee resting in the crook of his elbow. "Or in general?"

"At the moment, I could break your stupid jaw. But I meant in general."

"We were all helpless against Luthyr." He ran the cloth up my calf. "Even Lallakai got nowhere. Her shadow magic isn't much use against his sun magic."

That explained why she'd lost so badly.

"But if you don't like it," Zak added, "learn to use druid magic."

"How would that help? Druid energy doesn't *do* anything."

He lowered my leg and I stuck out the other one. I winced as he started on a scrape above my anklebone.

"Energy is everything for fae," he said. "Why do you think they take druids as consorts?"

"To feed off us."

"We're way more useful than just as a snack bar." He worked the cloth up my leg, ignoring my quiet hisses of pain. "We can make fae more powerful. We can also make them weaker."

My eyes widened. "What?"

"Did you feel how the energy in the meadow changed as Ríkr and Luthyr were battling? Whoever controlled the meadow had the advantage, and Ríkr couldn't manage it. Luthyr's control over his territory is too strong."

When Ríkr had first attacked, the ring of frost around him had been spreading, but once he and Luthyr had begun to fight in earnest, the cloying summer sweetness saturating the meadow had increased. And Ríkr's ice had melted faster and faster.

"Fae draw power from the earth," Zak continued, "and the more influence they have over the energies around them, the faster they can draw on that power. It's the reason only weak fae tolerate the polluted energy of cities. They don't need much power."

Zak lowered my leg. Turning to face me, he tossed the washcloth in the sink. "A druid's ability to influence natural energies allows them to create an advantage for their consorts. Learn how, and you can amplify Ríkr's power while simultaneously weakening your enemies."

Mutual empowerment. That was how Ríkr had described our potential relationship as master and consort.

I doubted any advantage would've helped Ríkr win against Luthyr, but could I have helped Ríkr stand his ground? Was I hamstringing not only myself but Ríkr too by refusing to learn anything about my druid powers? Would I be more of an asset as his druid ally than a druidic "snack bar"?

I jumped at the cool touch of ointment on my leg. Zak slathered a line of cream across a cut on my calf. His touch moved upward, dabbing at a scrape just above my knee. I watched him, my gaze drifting from his hand to his strong forearm to his sculpted bicep. Then it roved across his bare chest and the hard planes of his pectorals before trailing down to the ridges of lean abdominal muscles.

His hand drifted up my thigh, his fingers leaving a streak of ointment across my skin.

I looked up and our eyes met, electric tension firing through my nerves. His green irises were dark with a glint of challenge I remembered well.

"Don't even think about it," I growled—but my heart rate picked up even as I spoke, the warmth of his hand on my skin consuming my awareness.

His fingers curled around my thigh, digging in. "You already did."

"I was thinking about what it'd be like to gut you," I lied.

"And what would it be like?"

"Gratifying." My voice came out low and husky. "But I don't have my knife."

"That's a shame."

"Are you volunteering as my victim?"

His other hand, warm and strong, curled around my other thigh. "Depends how literally you mean it."

My chest rose and fell as slow heat uncoiled in my center. "I hate you."

Was I reminding him or me?

"I know." His hands slid up to my underwear, then over my hips. "I don't think I hate you."

"You don't *think*?"

"Sometimes I do. Sometimes I really fucking hate you." He leaned in, and my face tipped up, staying oriented to his as though we were locked in orbit. "But only sometimes."

My fingers clutched the counter in a death grip, fighting the urge to reach for him, to put my hands on him the way he had his hands on me—like he had no intention of ever letting go.

"Why do you sometimes hate me?"

"Because …" His mouth drew closer, almost touching mine. "Because you remind me of a past I can't change. Because I keep making stupid fucking choices around you. Because you push me away and pull me back and hate me and want me, and I can't figure you out."

My head spun with everything he'd thrown at me, and I latched onto the simplest one. "Who said I want you?"

He pulled on my hips, sliding my ass across the counter until I was pressed against him. Heat surged up into my core and ricocheted back down. My breath caught, my skin flushing, my lips parting.

His fingers dug in. He drew me harder into his hips, rubbing against me, and the friction of his jeans through the thin fabric of my underwear sent pleasure spiking through me. I bit down on my lower lip, stifling a gasp.

His eyes burned into mine as he watched my reaction.

My breath came faster than it should have. Why was I thinking about him shoving me into the stable wall and kissing me hard enough to bruise? Why was I thinking about his mouth and what it'd feel like to have it on mine again?

My fingers uncurled from the counter.

"Oh, am I interrupting?"

At the purring question, Zak stepped back sharply, his hands leaving me.

Lallakai stood in the bathroom doorway, arms crossed, hip cocked, and full lips turned up in a sultry smile. Cuts still marred her skin, but she'd washed off the blood.

"Don't let me stop you," she added.

His mouth twisted. Picking up the ointment jar, he pushed it into my hands. "Finish treating your cuts."

With that, he strode for the door. Instead of moving out of his way, Lallakai turned sideways, forcing him to sidestep through the gap. As he brushed past her, her tongue ran across her lower lip, and her bright eyes turned to me.

Sitting rigidly on the counter, I kept my expression coldly neutral.

With a smile, she pulled the door shut. It clacked, and I was alone in the bathroom.

Zak's confession about sometimes hating me replayed in my head. His confession about dwelling on the past. About making stupid decisions. About not being able to figure me out— though that last part was fine, because I couldn't figure him out either. What did he want from me?

It took only a couple of minutes to smear the cream over all my scrapes, then I capped the jar and opened the door. My pants were lying in the entryway, and I hastily pulled them on before entering the bed side of the room.

Zak and Lallakai stood three feet apart. Her emerald eyes were glinting and he was outright glaring. The intensity between them suggested a heated discussion I couldn't hear.

Frowning, I surveyed the room. The moment I realized Ríkr wasn't present, the trepidation lingering in my gut flared to life again, adrenaline rushing through me.

"Where's Ríkr?" I demanded, a sharp edge of alarm in my voice.

Lallakai stepped back from Zak. Her suddenly neutral expression only fueled my apprehension.

"Where is he?" I fired at her.

"The Winter King is not returning with us." She swept her hair off her shoulder. "He bid me to tell you that he has chosen to stay behind, and you are not to enter Hell's Gate in search of him."

My feeling of dread crystalized into fear. "He *stayed behind*? Why?"

The Night Eagle considered me, then let out a quiet breath.

"Because he is dying, and he does not wish you to perish with him."

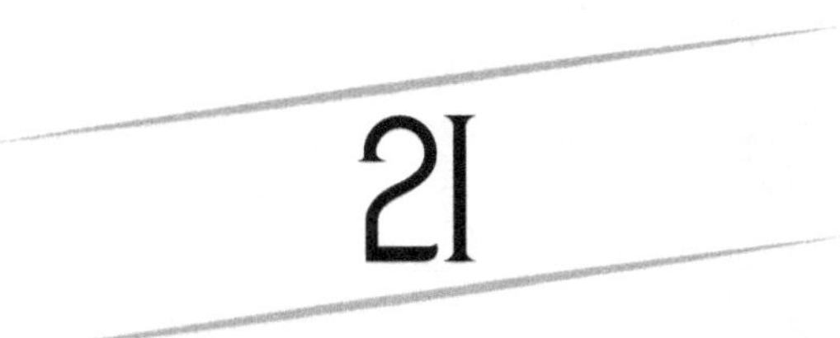

"SABER!"

"I'm going back!" I yelled over my shoulder as I ran for the hotel room door. "Don't try to stop me!"

Zak caught my arm, spinning me back toward him. "He doesn't want you there."

"Too bad for him!" I wrenched on my arm, teeth bared. "I'm not leaving him to die. That proud idiot should've come with us, even if he was wounded!"

Lallakai twirled a lock of hair around her finger. "Luthyr wants Arawn to perish alone, without a single witness to his death, as a final insult. But he is still monitoring Arawn's presence in his territory. If Arawn attempts to flee Hell's Gate, Luthyr will intercept him immediately."

"Ríkr is protecting you," Zak added.

"I don't care!" Tearing my arm free, I shoved him away. "If he's dying, then there's probably nothing I can do, but I'm going anyway. He's my best friend."

I faltered at my own words. My best friend? Ríkr? I'd always thought of him as my familiar and a companion, but maybe that had been my own insecurity lying to me. He'd always been so flippant about our relationship—saying he only kept me company out of boredom—but now that he'd demonstrated how much I meant to him, I couldn't deny he was my closest friend.

"I don't expect you to understand." Remembering my phone and wallet, I hastened back to the bed to grab them, then held my hand out to Zak. "Let me borrow your truck."

His green stare bored into me. Slowly, as though debating every movement, he reached into his pocket and pulled out his keys. He held them above my waiting palm but didn't release them.

His fist clenched around the keys, knuckles turning white. Eyes sliding closed, he exhaled through his nose, his jaw tight.

He opened his eyes. "I'll drive."

I rocked back on my heels. Was this what he'd meant about making stupid decisions around me? I shook my head. "You don't have to—"

"I know," he snapped, shoving the keys back into his pocket. "But maybe I can help. I—"

"You will not." Lallakai appeared beside him, her usually sultry expression hard. "Setting foot in Luthyr's domain again is too dangerous. I cannot protect you from him."

"Luthyr isn't interested in us, and there's a chance I can help Ríkr. I'm not a healer, but I know a lot of alchemic remedies."

"Alchemy will not save him."

"I can still—"

"You will *not*."

He sucked in a breath, air hissing through his clenched teeth. "I'm not your property."

Her eyes blazed. "I give you more leeway than you deserve. I let you do as you please so long as it doesn't endanger you, but this is too far. You will not go back to Hell's Gate."

Zak looked at Lallakai—just looked at her—then turned to the bed. He zipped up his backpack and slung it over his bare shoulder.

"Zak," Lallakai snarled.

"Come on, Saber. Let's go."

"*Zakariya.*"

"Are you going to possess me, Lallakai?" His voice was quiet, dangerous. "Do you think I was bluffing when I promised to sever our bond if you ever forced your will on me again?"

Her fingers curled into tight fists.

He waited, then grabbed my hand and strode for the door, leaving Lallakai standing alone in the center of the room, trembling with fury.

A **BOLD SUNSET** bathed the mountains as the truck raced along the gravel road, back to my parents' property for the third time. I gripped my seat, mentally urging the vehicle to move faster. I knew why Zak had insisted on driving; I would've gone way too fast.

Were we already too late?

Zak had slowed us down by insisting we stop for "a few" supplies. In the outdoor sports store, he'd stocked up on extra clothing, as well as warm jackets, flashlights, a battery-powered lantern, sleeping bags, and a dozen other assorted camping items. Then he'd dragged me to the grocery store two blocks over and bought a few days' worth of nonperishable foods.

In case we needed to stay the night, he'd said.

Logically, it was smart, but I didn't care about logic. I wanted to get back to Ríkr. Would he still be in the meadow? What if he'd wandered somewhere else? What would I do when I found him? How could I help?

How could I save him?

Zak slowed the truck, then eased it off the road and onto the hidden dirt track—a more nerve-racking maneuver in the reduced light. We bounced over tree roots, and I leaned forward in my seat, eyes straining for the meadow.

The foliage parted, and the meadow appeared, awash in golden light and shadows. The overcast clouds had broken up, and the sinking sun had stained the sky in vibrant shades of orange and pink. Luthyr's maple tree was a dark silhouette against the blazing sky.

A white shape lay at the base of the maple's trunk.

My heart lurched into my throat. The truck was still moving when I unbuckled my seatbelt and threw open my door. Zak hit the brakes as I leaped out, and I ran for the tree, long grass whipping at my legs.

The white shape stirred, and the large wolfhound lifted his head. Blue eyes shone in the moonlight.

"Ríkr!" I gasped, careening toward him. I dropped to my knees and threw my arms around his furry neck.

Ah, my stubborn dove, he sighed. *I knew it unlikely you would heed my instructions.*

"Of course not, you idiot! Why didn't you tell me? You promised not to keep secrets from me anymore!"

I'm afraid I have struggled to keep that promise since making it.

I sat back on my heels, still gripping his fur with both hands. "What happened, Ríkr? Lallakai said you're dying, but you look fine."

The grass swished with approaching footsteps. Joining us, Zak sank into a crouch beside me. Ríkr glanced at the druid, then back at me.

Luthyr did not deceive when he said he had devised a way to kill me. His ears swiveled back. *You have already seen his unique magic at work in the seedlings. They consume the life-giving organs of the dead to grow into sentient life forms obedient to his will.*

"Was that why he killed my parents? To grow trees from their bodies?"

Yes. The more power the victims possessed in life, the faster the trees grow.

"What does that have to do with you?" I asked urgently.

His muzzle ridged with either anger or disgust. *When Luthyr breached my chest, he implanted magic inside me—a new form of his life-devouring seedlings, one which I cannot remove or destroy.*

"What do you mean?" I whispered, dread closing my throat.

He drew himself up, sitting on his haunches. Poking out of his fur—no, out of his *chest*—in a perfect circle were six green sprouts, but they weren't normal plants. They were made of soft light, radiant and semitransparent.

Zak swore under his breath.

"There's ..." Horror strangled my voice. "There's something inside you?"

It is quite ingenious. As soon as the seeds sprouted, they imbibed my essence, becoming part of me. Thus, my magic cannot destroy them. They feed off my power, weakening me to fuel their growth.

My legs lost strength, and I sat heavily on the ground. "Can someone else destroy them before they kill you?"

They are not killing me, dove. They are consuming me, and it cannot be undone. Luthyr's cancerous seedlings have rooted inside my very essence. They will destroy me, regardless of the magical gift of The Undying. He lay back down. *So, stubborn dove, you must now go home.*

"No."

You cannot aid me. Once I die, Luthyr will return to confirm his success. You must not be here when he does.

"*No!*" It came out in a hoarse shout. "I'm not leaving! I'm not giving up on you and going off to live my life like you never existed!"

All life ends. Even that of an undying king.

"But you want to start over." My voice broke. "You said I helped you remember that you want to live again."

He was silent for a long moment. *Your compassion sweetens this bitter day, dove. Please do not weep for me.*

Tears I hadn't noticed were streaking my cheeks. "You can't die because of me, Ríkr. I won't let you."

Not all things can be changed.

"Fuck that fatalistic bullshit!" I grabbed his sharp antler, heedless of a pointed tine piercing my palm, and forced his head up. "Think, Ríkr. You're thousands of years old. There must be *some* way to save you. Anything you can think of, no matter how unrealistic."

Only because I was looking him dead in the eye did I catch the flicker in his gaze.

There is no way, dove.

I shook my head, my grip on his antler tightening. "That was a lie. Spill it, Ríkr."

He met my glower, then puffed out a wolfish sigh. *It is nigh impossible to accomplish, unlikely to succeed even if attained, and most certainly lethal to attempt.*

"What is it? What do we need to do?"

Kill Luthyr.

Zak inhaled sharply.

In some cases—not all, Ríkr emphasized, *magic born from a being's core power will perish with its creator. However, I do not possess the strength to slay him, and an attempt will only speed my demise. My remaining time is measured by my conservation of power.*

Releasing his antler, I sat back on my heels. "Does Luthyr have any weaknesses?"

None we can exploit. In his own territory, he is unassailable.

I dug my knuckles into my forehead. "His territory … Zak, didn't you say that druids can give their consorts an advantage?"

It will not be enough, Ríkr answered without hesitation. *No druid can maintain an aura sphere significant enough to hamper Luthyr, and even if you could, he is too strong, too entrenched, and too experienced to fall in battle.*

He flattened his ears. *Dove, I am honored, but you must protect yourself. I am yet your guardian. I cannot allow you to discard your life alongside mine.*

I bit down on my inner cheek, the tang of blood on my tongue, but the pain was nothing to the slicing anguish in my chest.

"One druid can't," Zak said quietly. "But what about two?"

My head snapped toward him.

"I'm not your consort, but if Saber and I harmonized with you, we could create the advantage you need."

Saber does not have the skill, Ríkr countered.

"Raw talent can compensate for developed skill, and you know she has the power to make a difference."

A dismissive huff escaped me. "*I* have the power?"

"Your druidic energy is stronger than mine," Zak said matter-of-factly. "It's not even a contest, actually."

"What?"

Ríkr considered me. *You rival Pwyll in strength. I suspect it is due to your dual bloodline, and I understand the lengths your parents went to hide you.*

"And that's why feeding off your energy helped him so much," Zak added, a slight growl in his voice. "If we work together, we could catch Luthyr off guard."

*I still cannot kill him,*Ríkr said flatly.

Zak glanced back at his truck. "I have an idea on how to make that work too. But ..."

Hope seared my innards. "But what?"

"But we'll have to convince Lallakai to help us—and her price will be high."

22

ZAK, RÍKR, AND I RETURNED to the truck, where we found Lallakai lounging on the hood, her long legs crossed as she reclined against the windshield. She had her head propped on her hand, her expression one of boredom.

"So?" she drawled. "Have you convinced them of the futility of their return, Arawn?"

His wolfish ears flicked back. *No more than you convinced them not to return, Lady of Shadow.*

She tsked. "What is your grand scheme, then, Zak? I can see you have one."

He pulled open the door of his truck and dragged his backpack out. As he set it front-down on the hood beside Lallakai, I noticed my picture frame sitting on the dash. I'd grabbed it from the hotel room right before leaving.

My hand jumped to my pockets, and I hastily felt for the river-stone pendant—but all I found was my switchblade. I remembered the clatter of something falling when I'd tossed my pants out of the bathroom, and I muttered a curse, feeling sick. I would call the hotel later and ask them to find the river stone for me. The room was paid for until morning, so it should still be there.

Zak unzipped the small pouch I hadn't had a chance to investigate when I'd snooped through his belongings a week ago. From the compartment, he took out a flat, square object a few inches across. In the fading light, it looked black.

Turning to face me and Ríkr, he pinched two corners of the square and pulled, his arms sweeping wide. The object unfurled into billowing purple fabric—if mere fabric could ripple without wind, light streaming off it in amethyst and cobalt ribbons. Power radiated from its folds, tinging the air with a heavy, sweet tang completely different from Luthyr's aura, and I recognized its shape as a long, flowing cloak with a hood.

Ríkr backed rapidly away. Her upper lip curling in distaste, Lallakai slid off the hood, putting distance between her and the mysterious, magnificent magic Zak held.

"What is it?" I whispered, stretching a hand toward the cloak.

He swung it out of my reach. With a few quick folds, he compressed it back into a tiny square, and the indigo light washing over us died away. The sweet tang in the air faded.

"It's called the Carapace of Valdurna." He set it on the hood beside his backpack like he didn't want to hold it any longer than necessary. "It's a powerful fae relic I inherited from Bane. It can absorb all the magic around it."

"It *absorbs* magic? Like the way Ríkr drained my druid power?"

"Sort of, but much faster. If we can get this on Luthyr, it could weaken him very quickly."

"Put it on Luthyr?" I asked in confusion. "Why not put it on Ríkr so it can absorb Luthyr's spell?"

Ríkr flattened his ears. *Though the relic protects its wearer from all harm, its parasitic magic would destroy me as certainly as Luthyr's foul seeds.*

"It'll be just as dangerous for Luthyr," Zak said, turning to Lallakai. "He'll try to get it off immediately, so we don't have to worry about its defensive properties. If we attack at night, the sun aspect of his magic won't be as strong, and your shadow magic will be *much* stronger. You can ambush him in the darkness and get the Carapace on him, just for a few seconds, then escape with it. Saber and I will overwhelm his aura with ours, and Ríkr can finish him off."

Lallakai waved her hand irritably. "Handling the Carapace will drain *my* magic. I will be weakened along with Luthyr."

"Which is why you have to do it," Zak said. "You can move through the shadows to get close and escape quickly, and you have more magic to spare than Ríkr does."

Her face went colder, and she folded her arms. "It is too dangerous. Luthyr is too powerful, and if anything deviates from your flimsy plan, we will all die."

Ríkr sat on his haunches, watching them argue.

"What will it take to make you agree?" Zak asked impatiently. "What do you want?"

"I want to keep you alive, foolish druid."

"What's your price?"

"For you?" Her eyes flashed. "Obedience. When I command you, you will submit without question."

He leaned back slightly.

She swiveled to me and Ríkr. "Saber will become my second consort. And Arawn, you will share with me the power of The Undying. That is my price."

Silence answered her as the three of us stared wordlessly.

"Oh?" she mewed innocently. "You do not like my terms?"

Disgraceful, Ríkr growled, his voice thrumming with ancient power, *but I will acquiesce—on the condition you demand nothing from the two druids.*

Her eyes widened. "You agree?"

"Ríkr …" I muttered uncertainly.

I agree, he declared, a flare of blue light running over his wolfhound form. *But should you falter in your commitment even once, Lady of Shadow, our bargain is void.*

A covetous smile spread across her face. "Agreed. I will not falter, Winter King."

SITTING IN THE MIDDLE of the meadow, a warm hoodie zipped up to my chin and a battery-powered lantern beside me, I watched Zak blow onto his hands. The mountains got cold at night, even in the middle of summer.

"All right," he said in a "here we go" tone. "The two most basic druid skills are aura reflection and aura spheres. Aura reflection is minimizing and disguising your energy by matching it to the natural energies around you. If you don't practice aura reflection, your strongest emotions spread into the earthly energies, drawing unwanted attention."

I nodded. Josephine had mentioned aura reflection too, suggesting I should be using it.

"Aura spheres are the opposite, where a druid pushes their energy outward with the intent to dominate the natural energies around them. Fae can do it too, and it's how they and druids create and hold territories. We control the energies in a particular location so often that the land stays in tune with our auras, even when we aren't present."

"And that creates an advantage?"

"If the energy around a fae becomes hostile, it's like a plant that needs acidic soil trying to grow in alkaline soil. It stunts their ability to fuel their magic. Meanwhile, the fae who are close to us and attuned to our auras get a boost, because we're creating an ideal resonance for them."

I rubbed my chilled fingers together. "So I need to learn how to do this aura sphere thing."

"You can already do it. You created an aura sphere when you tried to attack Lallakai yesterday." He leaned forward, bracing his elbows on his knees. "It's like a temporary territory. You dominate the energy around you so that any fae approaching you will be at a disadvantage and your familiars will be stronger. The more powerful and disciplined the druid is, the larger and more potent their aura sphere is."

"And … I'm a strong druid." My tone was dubious.

"Without a doubt." He tapped my knee. "You have the ability. You just need to practice doing it on command."

I let out a breath. "And how do I do that?"

Simple. Ríkr, still in wolfhound form, padded toward us. *There is no need for complex instruction.*

Zak quirked an eyebrow. "It's *simple* for her to consciously tap into an ability she's only used instinctively before?"

Stopping beside me, Ríkr sat on his haunches. His pale shape glowed in the darkness—or maybe that was the translucent tendrils of Luthyr's cancerous magic peeking out of his fur.

Exceedingly simple, he declared. *You can create an aura sphere, dove. All you must do is sing.*

Zak blinked. "Sing?"

"*Sing?*" I repeated. "Come on, Ríkr. Be serious."

I am profoundly sincere. You wield your power through your voice. So it has been since we met.

"I just like to sing."

His mouth cracked open in a canine grin. *Because the act of singing connects you with your very essence. That is why it brings you peace—or, at other times, clarifies and empowers your emotions.*

I stared at him.

Try it, dove.

"Just … sing?" I glanced around. "Won't messing with aura spheres draw Luthyr's attention?"

I am certain he is monitoring me to ensure I continue to die as planned, but he will not interfere.

"How can you be sure?"

Because I know him well from our centuries of conflict. He will assume you are creating aura spheres for my benefit, and your seemingly desperate attempts to prolong my life will only feed his satisfaction at besting me.

I grimaced, unable to argue with his logic.

Now sing. With that final command, he slanted his ears lazily backward and settled in to wait.

I glanced at Zak, felt a prickle of self-consciousness, and determinedly closed my eyes. As I sat there, trying to think of a song, the familiar scent of the night-cool meadow stirred a hundred memories of my childhood. A deep sadness permeated me, building on the tragedy of this place, of my past, of the struggles and pain all three of us had faced. And the deepest anguish: the longing for my parents and my hopeless yearning to see them again.

A mournful note murmured across my lips, and I began to sing.

"*Macushla, macushla,*" I crooned, the Irish word for "darling" soft and forlorn, "*your sweet voice is calling, calling me softly, again and again.*"

I sank into the song, and the lyrics filled my mind, pushing away everything else.

"*Macushla, macushla, I hear it in vain. Macushla, macushla, your white arms are reaching, I feel them enfolding, caressing me still.*"

As the song rose through me, I rose with it, my heart riding on a wave of sorrow.

"*Fling them out from the darkness, my lost love, macushla. Let them find me and bind me again, if they will.*"

The notes thrummed in my throat, thick with emotion.

"*Macushla, macushla, your red lips are saying, that death is a dream, and love is for aye. Then awaken, macushla, awake from your dreaming. My blue-eyed macushla, awaken to stay.*"

The last note faded from my throat, and silence fell. I didn't open my eyes, my skin prickling all over.

Instead of the meadow's soft, steady power, it felt like my song was resonating through the earth itself, reflecting everything I'd poured into the lyrics. The natural energies thrummed with my voice … with my essence.

I opened my eyes, focusing on the fae demesne. The landscape shimmered into pale mist—but instead of drifting without direction, the fog was swirling in a sedate maelstrom with me at its center.

Unnerved by the sight, I hastily blinked my eyes to focus on the mundane world.

Sitting across from me, Zak's face was smooth and unreadable. Whatever his reaction to my singing had been, he'd had time to hide it.

I looked at Ríkr.

Behold, he declared. *I told you I could instruct you in druidry as well as a druid.*

"Okay," I said unsteadily, struggling to tamp down on the raw grief I'd channeled into the song. "So … this is an aura sphere? This has never happened before when I sang."

But it has, dove. You have used your voice to manipulate the energies around you to your benefit for as long as I have known you. Only now do you have enough power to sense its effect so clearly.

Zak sat forward. "Now let's see if you can repeat this without singing."

I scowled. "Oh, and you can sing better?"

"No, but that isn't what I was getting at. It could be difficult to sing and fight for your life at the same time, don't you think?"

He had a point, but my budding druid skills wouldn't matter if our plan to ambush Luthyr ended in a life or death fight—because we'd all be dead.

23

LEANING ON THE PORCH RAILING, I gazed across the meadow, the swaying grass lit by another spectacular sunset.

Zak and I had practiced aura spheres for most of the night. As dawn had broken, he'd declared me competent—then revealed the next challenge. We needed to create aura spheres at the same time, and they needed to resonate. Harmonizing our energies would double their potency.

Easier said than done.

The cabin's front door creaked, the old hinges complaining. Zak stopped beside me, his gaze on the sunset.

"As soon as it's fully dark," he rumbled, "we'll head for the crossroads."

At the crossroads, Ríkr had said, we would find Luthyr, but our plan was to lure him away from that bastion of fae magic and intense natural energy.

I studied Zak out of the corner of my eye. "Let's try one more time before we go."

His lips pressed into a thin line. "Fine. But let's do it in a fresh spot."

"Like where?"

He nodded to the far end of the meadow.

"All right. Give me a minute to check on Ríkr first."

I slipped through the door into the cabin. Zak and I had stashed our sleeping bags and gear in the living room after dozing for several hours in the shade behind the house. A white wolfhound was curled up beside my sleeping bag, his ears slanted back and eyes closed.

My throat tightened at the sight of the faintly green, translucent vines twirled and coiled around him, shifting with his slow breaths. The more of his power the ethereal plant consumed, the more it grew. Tiny, pale flower buds had formed at the ends of the tendrils, and I dreaded the moment they bloomed.

At the sound of my hiking boots on the floor, Ríkr opened his eyes. The dullness in his gaze hurt more than the sight of the deadly plant overtaking him.

"How are you doing?" I asked softly, crouching at his side.

He raised his head. Even his golden horns had faded. *Persisting, though I have certainly felt livelier.*

"Zak and I are going to try one more time at the other end of the meadow, then we'll head for the crossroads." I hesitated. "Are you strong enough to fight Luthyr?"

If Zak's plan succeeds, I can defeat him. He swiveled his ears. *If it fails, I will expend the last of my power and perish in battle, which I would prefer to idly wasting away beneath this wicked magic.*

I understood why he felt that way, but it was still difficult to hear.

My concern, should that be the outcome, is your safety. His eyes fixed on mine. *If it appears hopeless, you must flee, Saber.*

"Not happening."

What purpose is there in dying with me?

My hands curled into fists. "You survived with Luthyr hunting you for centuries, and now because of me … this is all my fault."

Your fault? Amusement tinged his voice. *Do not insult me with the ridiculous presumption that my fate was ever at the mercy of a single human's whims. My choices are my own, and I understand the consequences of each far better than you.*

His tone was gently chiding, and I bit hard on my lower lip. "But you wouldn't have done any of this if not for me."

And if not for you, I would not have made any choices at all, for I would have been too weak from lost power and dreary despair. Gathering himself, he pushed to his feet. *For mortal creatures living brief, fierce, desperate lives, death is their greatest foe. But for beings such as me, the greatest foe is atrophy—to cease living and merely exist, trapped in the passionless patterns of the long, long years.*

Blue light rippled across him, then flared blindingly. A blast of cold air frosted every surface in the cabin. Ríkr appeared in his humanoid form, but the glimmering tendrils of Luthyr's magic overshadowed his otherworldly beauty. The curling cordons looped around his arms and clung to his shoulders.

"Your life is short, dove," he murmured, "and has only just begun. Do not discard it. Now, give me your hand."

I obediently raised my arm. He took my hand with cool fingers and pushed my sleeve up to expose my wrist. In his other hand, azure light sparked between his finger and thumb. It brightened, and frigid air swept out.

The pale glow solidified into an inch-long shard of ice. He lowered it to my upturned wrist and pressed the cold crystal to my skin.

It pushed through my flesh and into my arm. A burning chill rushed through my body, raising gooseflesh across my limbs and shaking me with a bone-deep shiver. The feeling of cold in my veins faded, and a rune the same size as the ice shard glowed faintly on my skin.

"This should be sealed within a circle," he said. "Zak will make certain you are branded with a druid's ink soon, I'm sure."

A druid's ink? He had to mean the circle tattoos on Zak's forearms that held the various fae runes he'd been gifted with. I held up both wrists, one inscribed with Ríkr's invisible familiar mark and the other now stamped with this new rune.

Ríkr cupped my hand with his as though holding my palm up. "May I show you how to use it?"

I nodded.

His hand blurred, then shifted up—*into* my hand, our flesh sharing the same space. I gasped, barely managing not to recoil at the sensation of something foreign inside my skin. His wintry power washed up my arm.

"Pay attention now, dove."

He curled his fingers, bending mine at the same time, and the spot where he'd pushed the ice crystal into my wrist burned with cold. Icy blue light sparked above my palm, then rushed outward into a long line. My fingers, guided by Ríkr, closed around the shimmering glow, and it flashed white. The glow vanished and weight pulled at my arm.

I held a three-foot-long ice spear in my hand.

"It behaves similarly to the spears I favor." He lowered his hand from mine. "Do not wield it as a sword or a bludgeoning weapon; they are not intended to resist impact. Instead, treat them as disposable. Throw one, summon the next. With practice, you can control the size and shape."

I weighed it in my palm. It wasn't as heavy as it should've been given its size, and it felt uncomfortably cool but not like I was holding a block of actual ice.

"Ríkr …" I gulped. "This is …"

"Power." His lips curved up, but it wasn't his teasing smile. It was sharp, sly, ancient, frigid. "What you have long needed, dove. Should I perish tonight, I have woven this magic to survive me for several years. Use it to guard your life until you find a worthy guardian to whom you can pledge yourself as consort."

My fingers clenched around the spear. He placed his fingertips against it, and it shattered into sparkling ice dust.

"To clarify," he added, leaning close. "I do not consider Lallakai a worthy guardian."

"We agree there." I drew in a deep breath. "Ríkr, I accept your offer to become your consort."

"Ah. I am honored, dove, but I would not have your acceptance during such a period of duress. If we survive the night, you may accept then."

I rolled my eyes. "You're awfully goody-goody for a fae."

"Only within a steeply limited set of parameters. On the whole, I prefer blood altars and the merciless annihilation of my enemies." He tucked his hands into the opposite sleeves of his cloak. "Now, make your final attempt with the impatient druid waiting outside the door. He is as stubborn as you. Understanding that may help you find resonance with him."

Hastening across the room, I grabbed the door handle, then looked back. "Ríkr ... thank you."

"So daring, dove, to express thanks to my kind."

With another eye roll, I pushed through the door and closed it behind me.

Zak was leaning against the railing, facing the door as he waited. "What was all that?"

"All what?"

"The power Ríkr was throwing off. He should be conserving his strength."

My left hand closed around my right wrist. "He gave me a gift."

Zak's gaze dropped to my arm, and he reached out. Pulling my wrist up, he studied the rune, his pupils dilating and contracting as he looked at the fae magic with his other sight.

"You'll need a tattoo," he murmured.

His hands were pleasantly warm. I tugged my arm free and slid my sleeve back into place, hiding the fae rune, then strode down the porch steps. He followed.

"What's the purpose of druid tattoos?" I asked.

"They contain the magic in fae runes, keeping it from leaking through our bodies. One or two runes isn't usually a problem, but without the tattoos, they can start interfering with each other and your body."

I glanced at his hand where the black rune for his sword kept appearing, remembering how the magic spread up his arm. "Will you get a tattoo for that one?"

"Maybe. Lallakai doesn't think it will work as well if I seal it."

Silence fell between us, and I sank into my thoughts as we walked toward the far end of the meadow. I led us slightly west, where flat stones formed a pathway across the creek. We hopped from stone to stone, then continued through the long grass.

My gaze slid to Zak, studying his profile. His jaw was tense, tired lines around his mouth, his brows low over his green eyes; he seemed lost in his own grim thoughts, probably debating whether we were about to embark on a suicide mission. Our plan hinged on me and Zak creating a shared aura sphere—and we hadn't fully succeeded yet.

As we neared the tree line, I slowed my pace. "Zak, why are you doing this?"

Stirring from his thoughts, he glanced at me.

"I keep trying to guess what's motivating you," I pressed on, "but nothing makes sense. We're about to attempt to murder a *fae lord*. We're probably going to die, and even if we succeed, you're getting literally nothing out of this."

We reached the edge of the trees and walked beneath the leafy canopy. Shadows engulfed us.

I shoved a branch out of my way. "I don't know if not understanding your motivation is why I can't properly resonate my aura with yours, but we can't go up against Luthyr like this. I need answers. Why are you helping me? Why are you doing any of this?"

He grimaced.

"Just *tell me*."

"Why should I?" he growled. "I'm not made of fucking stone."

"What does that mean?"

He extended his stride as though planning to leave me behind.

Rushing forward, I swung onto his path, forcing him to stop. "Zak, I'm not trying to trap you or trick you or screw you over. I just *need to understand*. Talk to me. Please."

His eyes widened at my "please," then narrowed warily. He tried to step around me, but I grabbed his arm, got in front of him again, and seized the front of his shirt.

"Tell me why you're here!" I half shouted, unable to stand his silence. "Tell me why you're risking your life for me!"

"I can't!" he snarled.

"Why not?"

"Because *I don't have a reason.*"

I stiffened in disbelief.

"I already told you." He pushed at my hands, but I didn't let go of him. "I told you how I fucked up and lost everything and didn't know why I was getting involved with you. And that was *before* I realized who you really were."

I held on to his shirt with both hands, keeping him in place.

His eyes swept over me, burning like green fire. "And now here you are, the girl from ten years ago, hating me just like I deserve. And here I am, ten years later, hung up on you all over again. What the hell else should I do? I can't fix this. All I can do is *be here.*"

My breath rushed through my nose. "You can walk away."

"Walk away to *what*?" His mouth twisted, eyes darkening. "I have nothing left. My home, my animals, the kids—all gone, and it's so hard to care about anything. I'm just a fucking empty shell, and you—you're it. The only thing I *feel*, even if it's tearing us apart."

I stood there, his words reverberating through me. My throat moved as I swallowed. "So this isn't a remorse-fueled, fix-your-past-mistakes crusade? You aren't helping me to soothe your guilt?"

His hands closed around my wrists, my fingers still squeezing fistfuls of his shirt. "No."

Did he even feel guilt? He should. He'd betrayed me and left me to die … probably. In some way. My understanding of those events had grown fuzzy over the past few days, what I remembered conflicting with what I suspected about this man who'd crashed back into my life like a knife to the chest.

His fingers squeezed my wrists. "I can't leave you alone. If I was less selfish, I would disappear. But I won't."

My throat tightened, uncomfortable pressure shoving down on my lungs. My fingers uncurled from his shirt and I pressed them to his chest. His heart beat under my palm.

My heart was thudding, tripping, stuttering. I didn't know what to think, what to feel. All I knew was his declaration that he wouldn't leave me alone didn't fill me with fury like I would've expected. His desire to be near me, even though it hurt us both, didn't make me rage.

His heart kept beating under my hand, and I wondered if his chest ached as much as mine.

Pulling away from him, I started walking, my pace slow and uncertain. After a few seconds, he fell into step beside me, and I could feel his gaze. We didn't speak, the air between us strangely charged, emotions raw and painful memories hovering too close like phantoms walking alongside us.

We didn't need to go any farther to practice our shared aura sphere, but I was too unsettled to attempt it. He didn't suggest we stop either, so I kept striding through the forest—until we reached a gap in the foliage.

Fallen trees had torn a hole in the canopy, and the mossy trunks of ancient giants rotted on the forest floor. Standing at the edge of the clearing, I stared. What could have caused half a dozen mature trees to topple in the same spot, in the same direction, and at around the same time? And why was I breaking out in a cold sweat at the sight of it?

Zak's gaze was darting across the forest too. He seemed pale.

"What—" I began.

Saber?

My head snapped to the east, Zak mirroring me as he also heard the soft, high-pitched voice.

Saber?

A strange sensation rushed through me—warm, wild eagerness mixing with stone-cold dread like opposing storm fronts. I hovered for a moment, then stepped in the voice's direction.

Zak's hand closed over my arm, stopping me. "It could be a trap."

Saber?

As the unseen fae called to me again, I knew it wasn't a trap—because I recognized the voice beckoning me closer.

PULLING FREE FROM Zak's restraining hand, I followed the voice's call.

He trailed on my heels as we passed the unusual swath of fallen trees. Beyond them, shards of mossy stone were embedded in old trunks, jutting out of the bark like oversized shrapnel from a grenade. Beyond that, a three-foot-deep tear had opened the earth, roots poking out of the sheer sides. Beyond that, a boulder had been split clean in half as though sliced by a giant sword.

What the hell had happened here?

I stepped over a leafy fern and onto dead earth. That was the only way I could describe the sickly stench of rot that covered the clearing. Three dead larch trees stood together in the center, and everything else was rotting. Nothing grew, not even moss.

Saber.

At the edge of the clearing, a western red cedar stood like a sentinel over this pocket of death. I walked slowly toward it, my boots squelching in the decomposing muck.

Just below eye level, the cedar's bark blurred.

The trunk bulged outward in odd lumps, and a shape took form. A human-like creature stepped out of the tree, its skin the same color as the cedar's bark and its young face framed by thick, straw-like hair the same deep green of the cedar's foliage. The fae's thin, graceful limbs seemed feminine, but its body was sexless.

Large yellow-green eyes looked up at me. Mouth stretching in a smile, the dryad spread her arms as though inviting me closer. *Saber. It is you. It is you.*

Though I hadn't spoken to her in eighteen years, her name came easily to my lips. "Farana?"

You remember me. She brought her hands together in a hollow, woody clap of delight. *You have changed so much. So much. You were but a sapling when I last saw you.*

"I remember … we used to play here."

Memories rocked through me. Running around the woods, picking up leaves and twigs and bits of plant matter, then racing them over to Farana so she could tell me their names and characteristics. My talent for recognizing tree species clicked in my head.

Part of me wanted to run over and hug her—an actual living being from my past, a witness to my childhood, someone who'd known me before my life had gone to hell. But another part of me, the part drenched in nauseating anxiety, wanted to turn around and run.

I felt your energy. Farana stepped from foot to foot but didn't close the gap between us; dryads couldn't move far from their trees. *Have you finally come to claim your family's territory, Saber?*

"Claim it?"

It is yours. All yours. I missed you. I miss Killian and Mairead.

"They … they're dead."

Her happiness dimmed. *I know. I have always known. But I miss them.*

"So do I."

Then you will stay?

I opened my mouth but didn't speak. How did I tell her I had no plans to stay here?

As I hesitated, her attention flitted past my right shoulder. *You returned as well. I did not expect you. It has been so long.*

I pivoted on my heel, bringing Zak into view where he stood a few feet behind me.

"So long?" he repeated, frowning.

Many, many years. As many years as Saber.

"I've never been here before, not until a few days ago."

But I know you.

Painful tension wound through my muscles, my confusion tinged with inexplicable dread. "How do you know him, Farana?"

Do you not remember? The day, the terrible day. She pointed at the swath of decomposing ruin so encompassing that nothing could grow in it. *The day this happened.*

"I don't remember this at all." I looked back at Zak. "Do you know what she's talking about?"

His gaze ran across the destruction. "No, but …"

"But what?"

He brushed his fingers across a tree's rough bark. "It feels familiar."

The weight of dread in my gut heightened, pressing on my innards. I felt a strange familiarity too, and it wasn't Farana's presence. She wouldn't make me feel this sort of cold unease.

Shall I show you?

My attention snapped back to the dryad. "Show me?"

I can show you my memory. It is part of my magic. I am witness to all that treads upon my roots, and I do not forget.

A shiver of warning, of even deeper trepidation, ran down my spine, but I moved toward her anyway. "Yes. I'd like to see."

Zak also faced Farana. "Me too."

She stepped between us. Her small, rough hand clasped mine, the other gripping Zak's fingers. Lifting her chin, she closed her eyes and chanted softly. The alien language flowed around us, and a soft green light washed through the forest—or was it washing across my vision?

The reeking death in the clearing melted away as rich forest shimmered into view—the three larch trees alive and heavy with needle-like leaves. Moss, ferns, and low huckleberry shrubs with dark berries covered the forest floor. Everything had a faint green-gold cast, as though a soft mist filled the forest.

"Hide, Saber. Hurry!"

I jolted as my father's voice, having existed only in my memory for so long, whispered in my ear—and as he spoke, I saw him.

He stood just ahead, tall and strong, his brown hair mussed and his reddish beard trimmed close to his jaw. Beside him was a child—a girl with pin-straight, raven-black hair hanging just past her shoulders.

He pushed her away, and as she turned, blue-gray eyes in a young face passed across us. It was me, seven years old.

Her features tight with alarm, my younger self scrambled across the mossy ground. She ran to the cluster of three larch trees and squeezed into the shadowy gap between their trunks, hidden by the ferns and huckleberries growing around them.

Killian turned, facing southeast. His hands were empty and he had no druid tattoos on his inner forearms.

The sunlight streaming through the trees dimmed. In the darkness, something moved. Underbrush rustled softly. A dark shape pushed out of the foliage—first a narrow, canine snout, then a hunched, bony neck. Bulky shoulders appeared, followed by long, gangly arms.

The creature lumbered into the small clearing. It walked like a ten-foot-tall gorilla, but instead of a thick-bodied primate, it was emaciated, its ribs pressing against tight skin covered in short, ragged black fur. Jackal ears stood erect on its head, pointed toward my father, and large blood-red eyes glowed in its bestial face.

I found you.

The jackal beast's hideous voice scraped inside my skull, but Killian didn't flinch. "This territory is mine. You are not welcome here."

A cackling laugh screeched from the jackal. *Did you hear? We are not welcome.*

Another shape appeared in the gap in the underbrush where the jackal had forged a path. A man strode casually into view, even taller than Killian and thick with muscle, his broad shoulders stretching his long leather coat. His harsh features were Slavic, his hair buzzed short but his gray-streaked beard thick and untamed.

I almost didn't hear Zak's quiet, hissing intake of breath.

"We are not welcome?" the man repeated, his deep, growling voice thickened by an Eastern European accent. "Do you know who you refuse, druid?"

"It doesn't make a difference who you are," Killian replied steadily. "This is my territory."

The jackal shrieked in laughter again.

"And you intend to defend it?" the intruder asked, smirking through his beard. "You're a ballsy one."

As he spoke, the shadows beneath the trees rippled. Large wolves with red eyes prowled out of the darkness, shaggy black coats blending together until it was impossible to count them. An entire pack, their fangs flashing with silent snarls.

Killian watched the vargs, his face impassive. "Why is the Wolfsbane Druid in Hell's Gate?"

"I'm in search of a new territory," the Wolfsbane replied mockingly. "This is a nice little valley, hmm?"

"That's one way to put it." Killian raised his chin. "But as I said, it belongs to me."

And to me.

Beside Killian, the air shimmered—and a fae appeared. He came only to Killian's elbow, with tawny skin and pale gold hair that stuck out in every direction as though it'd been hacked off with a knife. Billowing black pants covered his legs, but his thin chest was bare and his wrists jangled with golden bracelets.

"I am Dex, master of fire, and I do not like you, druid trespasser." The boyish fae raised a slender hand, palm up, and curled his claw-tipped fingers. A golden spark appeared in his palm. "And I do not like your darkness, shadow-wielder."

Lifting his hand to his mouth, he blew on the spark floating above his fingers. It burst into a thousand embers that swept out to fill the clearing in an instant—and at the same time, fire flared to life all through the forest, glowing among the trees as far as the eye could see. The small flames flickered and bobbed like fireflies, chasing away the shadows.

Bane glanced around with cool interest. "Impressive, if we're comparing parlor tricks."

Dex smiled mischievously. He extended his hand, fingers positioned to snap them—but before he could, Killian placed a hand over the fae's. "Let's not start killing yet, Dex."

Bane's thick eyebrows rose.

"Wolfsbane," Killian declared coolly. "Hell's Gate belongs to me. Take your search for a territory elsewhere—immediately."

The dark druid studied his opponents, then smirked. "As you wish, Hellsgate Druid. Since I won't find a welcome from the fae here, which direction do you suggest I travel?"

"North," Killian replied without hesitation. "The south is too tame and the west is too populated. The northern wilds will suit you."

"Then I'll head that way." Still smirking, he gestured at the jackal. "Let's go."

Disappointing, the beast growled. *His flesh would be sumptuous.*

"The same can't be said of you," Dex taunted.

"*Dex,*" Killian muttered warningly, too low for Bane to hear.

With his jackal beast ambling behind him, Bane crossed the clearing, heading north. His pack of vargs followed like a swarm, snapping and snarling at one another. As the rogue and his jackal passed Killian and Dex, a cautious twenty feet between the opposing pairs, the two druids' eyes met—but neither moved to attack.

Once Bane was past him, Killian's gaze darted sideways for just a second, and Dex's fire-orange eyes did the same, both druid and fae looking at the same spot—the trio of larches where my child self was hiding.

They were protecting me. My father was letting an evil druid and his evil fae walk out of his territory because he didn't want Bane to notice me.

A few steps past Killian, Bane stopped and looked over his shoulder.

"Hurry up!" he barked, vicious impatience roughening his deep tone.

From the trampled pathway through the foliage where Bane had appeared, clopping steps crunched over the leaf litter. A brown buck plodded into sight, mundane except for the unnatural stumps of its white antlers. Its drooping head was wrapped in a leather halter, and a loaded pack was strapped over its back, heavier than any load a horse could bear.

I was so appalled that Bane had cut the antlers off the fae buck that I didn't immediately notice who walked beside it, holding its lead line.

A boy.

25

LEADING THE BUCK by a tattered rope, the boy followed Bane's path across the clearing. His dark hair was tied in a short ponytail at the back of his neck, strands hanging in his face, his head tipped down in the way of children who'd learned to avoid eye contact with adults.

He seemed clean, his clothes in reasonably good shape, his shoes sturdy. But he walked with such painful exhaustion that each step he took hurt to watch. He and the buck were on the brink of collapse.

A handful of vargs paced alongside the boy like jailers escorting a prisoner. Killian watched him approach, his horror growing by the second. As the child and the buck drew level with Killian, the boy raised his head and looked up into the face of the unfamiliar druid.

Green eyes, sunken and haunted, gazed at my father, then he stepped past Killian, following his master.

Killian stood frozen in place, barely breathing. For a second time, his gaze swung to the trees where his daughter hid, and indecision twisted his face as though he were in physical pain.

"Killian?" Dex whispered.

My father briefly touched the fae's arm, his expression shifting as he communicated something in silence. Then he turned, watching the boy follow closely on Bane's heels like a well-trained dog. They reached a dense stand of alder, a narrow path weaving through it, dotted with Dex's floating flames.

"Wolfsbane!" Killian called commandingly.

Bane, about to step onto the shadowed path, turned around. The jackal looked over its bulky, hunched shoulder, ears pricked forward. The boy halted but kept staring at the ground.

A fireball burst to life behind Bane.

Dex appeared from the flames—and scooped the boy off the ground. Fire rushed over them, and they disappeared. Another flash. Dex reappeared beside Killian, holding the boy tight in his arms. The child didn't fight the fae's hold, his eyes wide.

"What is this?" Bane boomed, fury contorting his features.

Killian drew himself up, and as he widened his stance, power rolled off him, fierce and uncompromising. "I'll allow you to walk out of my territory, but I can't allow you to take this child. A monster like you has no right to be within a thousand feet of any child."

Bane stared across the clearing for a nonplussed moment. "Are you challenging me for my apprentice?" He let out a short roar of laughter, then pushed up the sleeve of his coat, revealing the circular tattoos running down his arm. "Fine then, Hellsgate Druid. I'll enjoy killing—"

Dex snapped his fingers.

All the dancing spots of flame floating around Bane and his fae entourage exploded into howling fireballs, and the clearing filled with the dying screams of his vargs as they were consumed in an instant. The jackal reared up with a screech—and darkness swept out from him, plunging the clearing into utter blackness.

But I didn't need to see to know what happened next.

The sounds. The screams. My memory cracked open, and it all came pouring into my consciousness.

I remembered the shrieks and howls. The jackal's cackling laughter and Bane's booming voice. Explosions of fire, clouds of suffocating darkness. I remembered crouching in my hiding spot between larch trees, hands over my ears, crying silently with terror.

And I remembered Farana calling me, telling me to come to her, that she would protect me. I squeezed between the trunks, my t-shirt with its cute pattern of galloping horses catching on the bark. I fell, landing on my hands and knees, then looked up.

Pressed into a nook beside the trees, inches away, was the boy. Curled tight, arms wrapped over his head to shield it. Hiding from the battling druids and fae.

Our eyes met.

His green stare. Exhausted and terrified. Hollow and desperate. A faint, terrible spark of hope deep within them.

I looked into his face, then scrambled up and ran desperately for Farana's cedar. She appeared in the bark, her wooden arms reaching. Grabbing my shoulders, she pulled me inside the trunk, into the strange world of a dryad's inner tree.

I hadn't witnessed the rest of the violent battle. I hadn't seen Dex's explosive fire or the jackal's deadly shadow magic that had poisoned the forest itself, melting the leaves off trees and turning their bark black and toxic. I hadn't watched Killian and Bane attack each other with their fae magic.

But I was seeing it now.

And I saw when Bane added mythic sorcery to his weapons, flinging spells at Killian. And I saw the forest dying all around Dex as the jackal countered his fire attacks with dense clouds of poisonous shadow. I saw Dex's fire losing strength as Bane and his fae gained the upper hand—and took control of the dying forest's energy.

And then I saw Dex die.

It was over fast. A snap of the jackal's huge jaws. Dex didn't scream, didn't make a sound as his slender body was crushed. The jackal threw its head back. Crunching jaws. A heaving swallow. And the fire fae disappeared, splatters of his blood all that remained.

Killian faltered. He stumbled to his knees, and with a gloating grin, Bane leveled a dark fae sword at Killian's throat. He raised the weapon to deliver a lethal strike, and Killian was too slow to react, too slow to call upon a defensive spell.

"*No!*"

A blue sheen swept through the forest. The air shimmered, and the toxic cloud of death the jackal had spawned dissolved into glittering blue.

With crashing footsteps, Mairead streaked into the clearing. Bounding at her side was a blue-skinned, blue-haired water nymph. Ellanira shot ahead and blades of water rushed from her fingers, flying at Bane. He slashed them apart with his sword, retreating from Killian. Mairead knelt beside her husband while Ellanira jumped in front of them, blue magic shimmering off her hands.

"Another druid?" Bane sneered. He glanced at the jackal, its dark skin scorched and blistered from Dex's attacks, then grunted. "Hellsgate Druid, consider yourself lucky. Next time we meet, I won't stop with killing your fae."

He strode away, his sword dissolving. Crossing the decaying clearing, he grabbed the cowering boy by the arm and hauled him up. The jackal lumbered after them, a handful of surviving vargs slinking in its shadow, and with a tired grunt, the buck carrying all of Bane's supplies trotted in their wake. They disappeared into the forest gloom.

"Killian." Mairead grasped her husband's arm, her dark, windswept hair tangled across her face. "Is Dex really …"

He bowed his head, shoulders drooping forward.

"No," she whispered, her voice trembling—then she stiffened, her frightened eyes sweeping the battle zone. "Where is Saber? Where—"

Her voice cut off as I yanked my hand out of Farana's. The vision disappeared, the destroyed forest replaced with two-decade-old devastation. The jackal's deathly magic still lingered, preventing anything from growing.

I staggered a few feet away and sank to my knees, my arms wrapped around my middle as my whole body heaved. I wasn't sobbing. There were no tears in my eyes. The violent shaking was the result of my heart collapsing from renewed grief.

Hearing my parents' voices again after almost twenty years. Seeing their faces. Seeing them again so clearly, so perfectly as though they were right there, alive, in front of me, as though I could reach out my hand and touch them, hold them, be *held* by them—

But they weren't here. They were dead.

It took several minutes to get myself under control. Finally, I pushed to my feet, my limbs unsteady, and turned. Farana had retreated. She stood on the roots of her cedar, watching me anxiously.

Zak stood several long paces away, staring into the trees. Staring at the spot where Bane had dragged his child self out of sight. Just staring, his face expressionless but his eyes—his eyes made the broken shards in my chest writhe.

"Did you know?" I whispered. "Did you remember this before now?"

It seemed to take a long time for my words to reach him. He dragged his gaze off the trees and focused on me.

"I don't remember seeing you," he said, his voice low and raspy. "But I remember the rest. I remember your father. That's why Bane told me when he died. He knew how much I'd wanted to be saved, and hearing that the only person who'd ever tried to help me was dead … it …"

He went silent, his eyes shuttering, and turned his head away.

"When he died," I repeated quietly. My hands curled into tight, painful fists. "You get what happened, right?"

Zak didn't move. He said nothing.

"Dex and Ellanira together kept my parents safe in Hell's Gate. Ellanira alone wasn't enough to protect them." I squeezed my eyes shut. "Bane killed Dex, and before that summer was over, Luthyr killed my parents."

It'd probably been a murder of convenience. Luthyr couldn't be bothered to take on Dex, Ellanira, and two druids who were mostly keeping to themselves. But when my parents had wandered too close to the crossroads while searching for the lost hiker, with only Ellanira for protection, Luthyr had taken the opportunity to fertilize more seedlings with three new corpses.

I had remembered, on some level, that Dex was dead, but it was no surprise I hadn't recalled any details. Why would I remember that terrifying encounter with Bane when, mere weeks later, the most horrific thing to ever happen to me had overtaken all other traumas? How could I remember that battle compared to my parents' sudden deaths?

I opened my eyes to find Zak watching me. Lines creased his mouth—bitterness, misery, maybe distress.

"Do you think it's fate?" I asked him hoarsely. "We first met when we were little kids. Then we found each other again by pure chance when we were teenagers. Then somehow we ran into each other as adults."

His eyes moved across mine as though trying to pry into my head.

"Do you think it's fate?" I repeated.

"No."

"Me neither." My fingernails cut into my palms. "It isn't fate. It's a *curse*. Every time we meet, something horrific happens. Every. Fucking. Time."

Zak's face went blank and cold, all emotion wiped from his expression.

I choked on the bitter grief flooding my chest. "The first time we met, Dex and my parents died. The second time, you betrayed me and I went to prison. And the third time ..." I shook my head, not bothering to list all the shit that had torn my life apart since he'd shown up two weeks ago. "It's nothing but tragedy whenever we get close. It's nothing but pain and suffering."

Zak half turned away, his gaze sliding across the rotting forest where his master and my father had battled.

"If it's nothing but tragedy when we meet," he rumbled so quietly I almost missed his words, "why do we keep meeting?"

The razor shards grinding in my chest were spreading up into my throat, and I swallowed hard. I had no answer, no explanation. Two chance encounters might have been a coincidence, but three? And not mere encounters, but life-changing events that had altered the trajectories of our futures.

Zak stood for a moment longer, then walked away, striding past the dead trees where he'd once hidden, hoping and praying as only a desperate child could that he would be saved.

That my father would save him.

Tears finally came, flooding down my cheeks. "Dad," I whispered as Zak disappeared into the gloom. I wrapped my arms around myself. "You bleeding-heart fool."

He'd seen that hopeless, haggard little boy, and even with his daughter right there, barely hidden and in danger too, he'd tried to save him. Because Killian Orien could do nothing less. Part of me was bitterly furious for the risk he'd taken—and the other part of me knew that, in his place, I would have done exactly the same thing.

He'd risked everything. And he'd lost everything.

And I might do the same tonight trying to save Ríkr.

26

THE WANING HALF-MOON cast a silvery light across the mountain slope, illuminating our way. It was dark enough that I should've needed a flashlight, but Zak had provided me with a sage-flavored potion for enhancing night vision. I'd almost refused it—I hated alchemy—but breaking an ankle in the dark would've ruined everything.

Ahead of me, the former Winter King strode with easy steps, showing no signs of weariness or fear even though his shoulders and arms were draped with Luthyr's luminous vines, the delicate tendrils swaying with his steps. Maybe this was just another battle for the millennia-old fae. He was a warrior, familiar with combat and death.

Zak's footsteps followed behind me, steady and unfaltering. Like Ríkr, he hadn't shown any apprehension during the past two hours of hiking. He'd been exposed to powerful, evil fae since he was a small child; he'd lived with Bane's jackal beast and its toxic shadow magic. Maybe nothing scared him now.

Fear wasn't what I felt either, but I almost would have preferred it. Instead, I kept seeing Dex disappear into the jackal's crunching jaws. I kept seeing my father on his knees in front of Bane, about to die. I kept seeing the forested spot where my parents had been murdered, and I couldn't stop imagining their bodies with their torsos ripped open. Blood-soaked saplings sprouting from their gaping chests. Ellanira's slain corpse lying nearby. Luthyr standing over the massacre, his sunlight eyes merciless and cold.

The harder I tried to change the direction of my thoughts, the deeper I sank into them. Farana's vision had cracked open my defenses, and as I relived her vision over and over, a thought kept driving through me.

My and Zak's encounters always ended in tragedy. Would this night become the tragedy of our third encounter?

Stupid, pointless thoughts, but I couldn't stop them.

In single file, we traipsed along a shallow mountain pass. Short, patchy grass grew among the boulders, and a burbling stream raced downslope, reflecting the moonlight. Pine and spruce trees stood in clusters, but the area was fairly open, the wind sweeping across it with a chill that cut through my sweater. The air had a summery-sweet tang. Luthyr's power dominated here, far stronger than in my parents' meadow.

My enhanced vision made out a widening of the pass two hundred feet ahead. The terrain sloped down into a shallow, forested valley. Along with Luthyr's energy, I felt a soft thrum of ancient power from that location. Somewhere in that valley was the crossroads.

Ríkr halted. I stopped behind him, and Zak stepped up beside me.

"This will be our battleground," Ríkr murmured.

With effort, I forced myself to focus on him.

"Upon Luthyr's arrival," he continued, "we must strike quickly. He cannot retreat into the valley or our fates will be sealed."

I nodded. Ríkr had already warned us that the crossroads' potent energy and ancient fae magic would be impossible for a druid, or even two, to take over with an aura sphere.

"Will he come out to meet us?" Zak asked, flexing his right fingers. His sword's black rune darkened the back of his hand.

"He will have monitored my approach, and now that I have halted here, he will not be able to resist discovering my intent." Ríkr canted his head, his short golden horns catching the moonlight. "See? Already he comes."

Zak stretched his arm into the space between us and closed his hand around mine, just as we'd practiced. I glanced at our hands—and when I looked up again, Luthyr was there.

He stood near the burbling stream, his silk robes rippling in the breeze and a faint golden glow emanating from him in the darkness. His yellow eyes were fixed on Ríkr. He didn't acknowledge Zak and me standing behind the dying Winter King.

The visions I'd conjured of my dead parents, their bodies consumed by Luthyr's trees, flashed through my head again. A sick, raging sort of despair clogged my throat.

"Have you tired of your slow decline, Arawn?" he asked in his smooth, controlled voice. "Do you wish me to extinguish your life?"

According to our plan, Lallakai should be nearby. I didn't know where or how she would ambush him, only that we had to keep our adversary's attention.

Ríkr spread his hands. "I have spent these past hours in deep reflection. After our long contest, it seems tragic to part in distasteful animosity. So, Luthyr, Master of the Forest, Lord of Summer, warrior prince of Rhiannon, the Summer Queen and ruler of the Summer Court, I ask you …" He dipped into a shallow, insolent bow. "… will you accept my *sincerest* apology for wasting a thousand years of your existence?"

Luthyr's features tightened with anger. "Do you think to provoke me into—"

Darkness rushed up out of the ground like black flames, engulfing Luthyr in a cloud of shadow—then sparkling amethyst light burst to life inside it. The flowing fabric of the Carapace of Valdurna unfurled, illuminating Lallakai, her black eagle wings spread wide as she dropped on top of Luthyr, the cloak stretched out between her hands.

She landed on the Summer Lord's back, sweeping the cloak over him. Clamping her arms around his shoulders, she trapped him in the enchanted fabric as sparkling light spiraled into it. Glowing streams of black and gold entwined around both fae as the powerful relic sucked their magic out of them, absorbing it into its shimmering folds.

With a furious roar and flash of amber light, Luthyr threw off Lallakai and the cloak. He staggered, angling toward the Night Eagle.

Cold and frost burst out from Ríkr as he launched himself at his nemesis.

Zak's hand bit down around mine. Lallakai had done her part, Ríkr was charging into battle, and it was our turn to unleash our shared aura sphere, weakening Luthyr and strengthening Ríkr. We had one chance to get it right—one chance for Ríkr to strike with everything he had before Luthyr could recover from our ambush.

"Now, Saber!"

The determined snap of Zak's voice sounded in my ears, and I pushed my spiritual energy outward as we'd practiced. Lallakai retreated into the darkness, dragging the Carapace by one corner, and Ríkr was feet away from Luthyr, an ice spear flashing in his hand.

Zak's druidic energy swept across the earth—and mine sputtered like a flame about to die.

His head whipped toward me, his eyes wide with disbelief—then Ríkr smashed his glistening spear into Luthyr's hastily conjured wooden sword, and ice burst from the point of impact.

Sucking in a wild breath, I tried to calm my mind and focus. *Focus.* But my head was a mess, emotions storming through me, and now panic was spiking in my chest as my pitiful aura sphere fell apart.

Concentration tightened Zak's face, and the sense of his presence intensified—he was trying to compensate for my failed aura sphere. Lallakai's gaze slashed to us, then she threw the Carapace aside and summoned a shadowy black blade. Wielding it with both hands, she leaped at Luthyr's back.

I bit down on my lower lip, tearing the skin as I fought to concentrate.

Luthyr dodged Lallakai's strike, and golden light washed over him, dissolving half her sword. His wooden blade smashed through Ríkr's next ice spear.

Panic whirled in my head like a roaring tornado. I tried to create another aura sphere, but it was even weaker than the first.

Ríkr thrust out his hand and blue magic lit up beneath the Summer Lord. A pillar of ice rushed skyward, but no sooner had it formed than cracks webbed across it.

I fought to clear my head, but all I could think was that this was it. The last tragedy. The third and final act of the curse that had destroyed my and Zak's lives.

The ice pillar shattered, and Luthyr reappeared, glowing faintly with his summer aura, unharmed. Plants erupted from the ground and Lallakai backpedaled, slashing at the ensnaring vines.

My pathetic aura sphere disappeared completely.

Ríkr lunged for the Summer Lord with another ice spear, the ring of frost around him shrinking. Zak's aura was vanishing, overpowered by the sickly sweet perfume of a hot summer day.

"Saber!"

Zak's shout pierced my ear as he wrenched me forward. He was running—fleeing from something. But what? I looked over my shoulder.

The trees were moving.

The clusters of towering pines dotting the grassy mountain path rocked and swayed. Their roots tore out of the ground, writhing like thick snakes, and the trunks lumbered forward. The earth shook. The trees were rampaging toward us, gaining speed, unstoppable one-hundred-and-fifty-foot giants that would crush us beneath their roots.

Zak ran toward the battling fae, dragging me with him.

Just ahead, Ríkr spun in an agile evasion of Luthyr's sword. His azure eyes passed across us, then he swung his hand toward

Luthyr. Another spiral of blue light flashed beneath the Summer Lord, and a wave of ice encased him.

Zak hauled me past the trapped fae in a full-out sprint. My head jerked on my neck as I looked desperately back.

Ríkr stood beside the ice formation. Calm. Accepting.

Escape, dove.

"Ríkr!" I screamed, resisting Zak's relentless pull.

The ice shattered, and Luthyr leaped from the sparkling shards. As Ríkr whipped toward the attacking Summer Lord, pine-tree soldiers closed in around them. Lallakai transformed into an eagle, wings beating hard. The pines bent forward, caging her—and blades of shadow erupted, slicing through their trunks. As branches flew in every direction, she burst free, soaring into the night sky.

I couldn't see Ríkr anymore.

"*Run*, Saber!" Zak snarled.

The pines were still coming. Still gaining speed. Still closing the distance.

Our feet pounded across the trembling earth as it sloped downward. Luthyr's cloying energy mixed with a deep thrum of ancient power. Pale mist drifted around us, and the feeling of ancient power grew.

Ahead, ethereal trees completely different from Luthyr's pine soldiers filled the valley. Their dark, semitransparent trunks were banded with patterns of neon green and vivid pink, their needles glimmering vibrant orange. The fog thickened, tinged with an eerie chartreuse glow as the fae demesne and human world intermingled.

With the attacking pines thundering behind us, we fled into the mists of the crossroads.

27

The pines had stopped at the forest's edge, but the rocky ground, blanketed in fallen pine needles, bubbled and writhed. Shoots, saplings, and vines wriggled up out of the soil, blindly reaching for our ankles. The trees creaked and groaned, their crowns shaking as they came to life, called to attack by Luthyr's power—power that kept getting stronger.

Beneath the canopy, gloom filled the forest, but vivid neon markings decorated the flora, transforming the crossroads into a nightmarishly beautiful palette of pink, yellow, orange, cyan, and purple. The faintly luminescent mist of the fae demesne made the bizarre contrast of intense color and looming darkness eerier.

Zak swerved between trees, still dragging me by my hand. I stumbled after him, wanting to stop, to go back and find Ríkr and—

And what? My chance to help, to do something useful, had come and gone. Our only chance now was to get away while Ríkr distracted Luthyr—but cutting through the crossroads was a gamble. It wasn't merely a spot where fae could move between different locations in a single step. It was also a pocket of intense power and magic where the fae demesne blended with the earthly realm in dangerous ways.

A fallen log blocked our path. Barely slowing, Zak leaped over it, giving me no choice but to follow or crash into it. I jumped.

We landed with a crunch—and thin branches wrapped over our ankles. A patch of low-growing mountain heather, hidden by the log, spun its thin, tough branches around our legs, its bell-shaped flowers shining in the crossroads' ghostly light. Struggling to tear free, I fell onto my hands and knees.

Zak yanked a vial off his belt and dumped it onto the heather. A puff of metallic-scented smoke billowed outward, and the plant wilted. I ripped my feet free and staggered upright.

A thick, leafy bough swung out of the mist and smashed into the side of my head. I landed hard on my side, vaguely hearing Zak shout my name. Tree branches were creaking, groaning, roaring.

I shoved up and raised my hand above my head. Cold flared in my wrist, and blue light sparked on my palm, flashing into a spear-shaped shaft of ice.

Another swinging branch plunged down and hit the spear. It shattered into a starburst of heavy ice, and the bough snapped, crashing to the forest floor. Panting, I spun around. I couldn't see Zak. I couldn't see the fallen log or the patch of heather. It was easy to get lost in the crossroads, he'd once warned me.

Plants sprouted around my feet. Needle-laden boughs reached for me.

I sprang through a shrinking gap between trees and ran. No idea where I was going. No idea what else I could do. The entire forest was after me, merciless and unstoppable, and my only chance was to outrun it.

Outrun Luthyr's power? He owned this valley, this mountain. He controlled Hell's Gate.

Movement flashed among the trees—three large bucks with white antlers, running in bounding leaps. As I fled, woodland fae fled too, as desperate to escape the murderous forest as I was. Tiny pixies zoomed through writhing branches, serpentine sylphs undulated through the air, and a golden fox swerved around the underbrush in search of safety. Luthyr's deadly magic flooded the valley.

Pale mist glowed through the trees. I burst out from between two pines and into a circular clearing. The mist eddied across the ground, hiding everything below my knees.

My foot caught on a hard edge and I pitched forward. My palms scraped across chiseled rock. The fog swirled, revealing flat stones carved with patterns of leaves.

I shoved up and stumbled into the center of the clearing. The trees leaned in, but they didn't uproot to reach me, and as the mist rippled, I caught glimpses of the structure beneath my feet. A perfectly round stone platform. Flora squirmed and thrashed, unable to cross the stone barrier.

Power thrummed through the circle. This had to be the heart of the crossroads, the spot where fae could step across realms, and not even Luthyr's magic could penetrate it.

Chest heaving for air, throat on fire and head throbbing, I sank to my knees and braced my hands on the stone. Tears welled in my eyes, and a violent sob shook me. It hadn't been enough for me to get Ríkr killed. I'd dragged Zak and Lallakai into my mess too. They'd been counting on me to play my part.

And I'd failed.

I'd thought that Zak and I together were a curse. But I'd been wrong. He had nothing to do with it.

I was the curse.

Sobs shook me, choked me. I couldn't breathe, and it didn't matter. I wasn't getting out of here alive. I would die, and so would Ríkr and Zak, all because I'd fucked up. I'd gotten stuck in my own head, consumed by old grief, convinced we would fail before we'd even tried.

A harsh laugh escaped me in a gasp before the next sob racked my body. Who the hell had I been kidding, thinking I could do this? Thinking I could be a druid? Thinking I could accomplish *anything*? I'd fucked up everything important I'd ever attempted.

My unsteady fingers slipped into my pocket, and I pulled out my switchblade. Four inches of steel popped out with a quiet snap. I gazed blearily at it, this tiny little blade I'd relied on to make me feel strong. But I'd always been weak.

I didn't want to be weak anymore.

The maelstrom inside me was spinning, tearing, grinding. Could I ever be strong like my mother, with her stern kindness and steady calm? Could I ever fight like my father, fierce and confident in his compassion? Could I, this cold, violent, mercurial woman who'd rejected her druid power, ever be anything but weak?

My legs burned as I rose. I faced the thrashing, restless, hungry forest. I breathed in, razor edges slicing my lungs as air filled them. Sound built inside me, but not a song. No melody could match the ferocious storm of emotion rising through me like a roaring inferno.

My chest expanded, my head tilting back. Everything inside me wound tight, awaiting release. A still, tense moment pulsed through the forest, where even the trees went silent.

And then I unleashed it all in a throat-tearing scream that challenged the whole fucking world.

My voice exploded through the writhing woods. The mists of the crossroads burst as though hit by a shockwave. The sound swept outward, but it wasn't sound.

It was power.

It was essence.

My essence.

And in it, there was no "obedient Rose," shaped by Ruth's controlling cruelty. There was no "nice Saber," dampened by insecurity and inadequacy. There was no "terrible witch," crippled by the past and hiding her scars. The crossroads flooded with all that I was, good and bad and everything in between.

Quiet settled over the forest. The trees didn't move. The plants didn't thrash. The mist didn't swirl. All was still, all was silent.

All was *mine.*

A moment passed while I absorbed what I had done. Or maybe it was several minutes. All I knew was that I could feel my power humming quietly through the earth, the ancient energies humming with it—but Ríkr had said it was impossible for a druid to control a crossroads.

A spike of golden energy drove through my aura sphere.

A tree at the edge of the circular clearing split with a *crack* like a gunshot. A section of the trunk bowed outward, opening a gap in the center.

Luthyr stepped out of the tree, gold-green light flickering around him. He showed no signs of injury, but he wasn't as composed as before. His neat braid of pine-green hair was mussed, smudges of dirt on his silk-like robes, and his face held a hardness that hadn't been there before.

His intense yellow eyes fixed on me.

Cold burned across my wrist, and with a blue flash, I summoned a three-foot-long shard of ice. I closed my fingers around it, drew my arm back, and hurled it at Luthyr.

He sidestepped the spear. It flew past him, hit the tree he'd appeared from, and burst into icy crystals.

The Summer Lord curled his fingers. A wooden sword sprouted from his palm, polished and deadly, its double-edged blade gleaming. He stepped onto the circular stone platform.

I'd lost my sense of fear on the night I killed Ruth, but I wasn't fearless in a smart, savvy way. I was fearless in a wild, borderline psychotic way—and I used that now as I summoned another ice spear and hurled myself at the ancient, powerful, undefeated fae lord.

His wooden sword met my ice spear, and the latter exploded into a crackling starburst around his weapon. The ancient fae magic of the crossroads sizzled as his power pushed into my aura, slowly but inexorably spreading.

No druid could out-magic a fae lord, but I didn't care about that either.

His blade sliced across my upper arm as I lunged in again, my complete lack of self-defense catching him off guard—and

I smashed a half-formed spear into his arm. It burst into a block of ice, encasing his elbow. The weight pulled his arm down, and faster than I could summon another ice spear, I slashed with my other hand.

My switchblade raked up the side of his face, slicing across his right eye.

He recoiled—and his free hand smashed into my chest. Agony blazed through my ribs as I flew backward. I hit the stone platform, nauseating pain whiting out my vision.

I squinted at the sound of shattering ice. His arm freed, Luthyr raised his hand toward me. Blood ran down his mutilated face, dripping off his chin as his expression twisted in an enraged snarl. Green light sparked across his slender fingers as he conjured magic that would kill me instantly.

Racing footsteps thudded across the platform, and Luthyr turned sharply, pivoting toward the sound.

Out of the mist, Zak launched at the Summer Lord with his black sword swinging.

28

LUTHYR LURCHED BACKWARD. Zak's blade swept past the fae lord's chest, shadows rippling off it. Zak spun with his momentum and brought the weapon around again, the blade meeting Luthyr's wooden sword with a reverberating whoosh.

I gasped for air, each breath like a knife in my ribs. They were either bruised or broken, but I couldn't let that stop me.

Zak drove in hard, sword thrusting and striking with rapid movements. The crystal pendants on his chest glowed, and as he dodged Luthyr's counterattack, he pulled a potion off his belt and smashed it on the ground. Pale smoke swirled out, filling the air with a metallic stench.

Luthyr reeled back, his bloodied face contorting with revulsion. Instead of pushing his advantage, Zak retreated with quick steps and pulled another vial off his belt.

"Saber!"

I barely got my hands up in time to catch the vial he'd thrown. Fizzy gray liquid sloshed inside it—and I recognized the same heavy-duty painkiller Zak had dosed himself with after his fight with Balligor.

As Zak lunged for Luthyr again, I pulled the cork and poured the potion into my mouth. It burned like intense, acidic mint, and I swallowed with difficulty. A cooling sensation rushed through my limbs, deadening the pain in my chest.

Luthyr slashed at Zak, faster and stronger than the druid. His wooden sword raked a shallow line across Zak's abdomen through his shirt.

Pushing myself up, I created an ice spear and launched it at the fae's blind side.

He spun at the last second, smashing the spear with his sword. As ice erupted from the impact, Zak grabbed one of his crystals. An incantation snarled off his lips, and he flung a ball of sizzling blue magic into the fae. It splashed over Luthyr's shoulder, staining his clothes like a liquid, and his sword's point fell to the ground as though his arm were too weak to hold it up.

Spinning his blade in his hand, Zak thrust at the fae lord's chest. I rushed in behind him, forming another ice spear.

Luthyr ducked Zak's blow with inhuman speed. Coming up under Zak's guard, he grabbed the front of Zak's shirt and flung him into me. We slammed down onto the stone platform, and excruciating pain broke through the numbing potion, seizing my lungs.

Gold light flashed—and an invisible force hit me, hurtling me through the air. I tumbled off the platform onto a soft bed of pine needles. Zak landed on my legs, thrown by the same magical attack.

The ground beneath us split. The same thorny vines that had captured us in our first encounter with the Summer Lord twisted around me and Zak with absurd speed, crushing us together as they lifted us off the ground. Thorns ripped into my skin.

Blood dripping off his chin, Luthyr walked to the center of the platform. He raised his arm, palm pointed toward us from twelve feet away.

"Worthless maggots," he snarled softly.

Three wriggling branches sprouted from his palm and spiraled together into a sharp spear point—and it shot toward us like an arrow fired from a bow.

Darkness bloomed over the clearing, and black wings flashed overhead.

Plunging out of the sky, Lallakai slammed down on top of me and Zak, her momentum snapping the vines and shoving us into the ground—then she was thrown backward. She crashed down behind us, wings awkwardly bent.

Luthyr's spear had driven straight through her lower chest.

"Oh?" Luthyr murmured, the twisting length of the weapon stretching across the platform to his palm. "How gallant of you, Lady of Shadow."

He snapped his fingers wide, and the spear ripped out of her torso as it retracted back into his hand. She lurched with a pained gasp, blood gushing down her stomach, then rolled to her feet. Lifting her chin defiantly, she stepped between us and the fae lord.

Beside me, tangled in vines, Zak stared at her with wide, shocked eyes.

Lallakai extended one hand, swirls of shadow dancing around her fingers. In her other hand, she held a folded square of purple fabric—the Carapace of Valdurna.

A quiet, derisive laugh rippled from Luthyr's throat. He raised his hand—and I raised mine.

This time I didn't need to scream my challenge. In silence, I threw the full force of my energy into the earth, commanding it to submit. The mists shivered, and Luthyr's summer aura dimmed.

Zak grasped my outstretched hand. His energy swept out with mine, blending in perfect harmony, intensifying my aura sphere.

And the temperature dropped.

A wintry chill swept through the forest. Frost spread across the ground and crept up tree trunks. Icicles formed on the branches, dripping downward, and as my disbelieving exhalation puffed white in the frigid air, snow rushed down from the sky in thick, dancing flurries.

Snarling, Luthyr raised his hands. His gold-green aura glowed around him, melting the snow and pushing back the frost. "Where are you, Arawn? Show yourself!"

Pale azure light gleamed beneath the shadowy boughs of the ethereal trees. As Luthyr whipped toward it, the glow flashed to white.

Ice crashed through the trees. It flowed as though it were still liquid, shattering and reforming so fast it was like a spinning fractal, dizzying and beautiful. In the shape of a huge white serpent, the ice creature launched across the clearing with its mouth gaping hungrily.

It slammed into Luthyr, jaws snapping shut around him. It soared across the clearing, carrying the Summer Fae in its mouth, and smashed into the trees. The ice serpent exploded into a massive cluster of ice spires.

From the woods where the serpent had attacked, the Winter King appeared.

He walked with unhurried steps, a flurry of snow swirling gently around him. Everything in his vicinity froze solid, ice caking the trees and coating the ground. His eyes glowed, the markings on the left side of his face gleaming.

Luthyr's magic-consuming spell spun around Ríkr's body. The pale blossoms had opened, and the small flowers shone in a mockery of beauty.

Amber light glowed within the massive formation of ice that had entombed Luthyr. Cracks boomed from deep within it, then it broke apart. Trees collapsed as the weight of ice dragged them down. Luthyr appeared in the midst of the breaking ice, his clothes frosted and his shoulders heaving.

Ríkr conjured an ice spear and flung it across the heart of the crossroads. As it flew, he sprinted after it, closing the distance to his enemy.

The Winter King and the Summer Lord came together in a detonation of conflicting power.

Icy blue magic and warm greenish-gold light exploded in sharp bursts. Ríkr drove the Summer Lord into the woods, away from the clearing. Spires of ice exploded outward, toppling trees as they roared, shuddering to life.

Do not let him reach the platform!

Ríkr's command slammed into my head, and I launched up, tearing free of the broken vines. Zak's hand pulled away from mine as I sprinted onto the platform, angling for the spot where the two fae had disappeared.

Cold flared over my wrist, and as light coalesced in my palm, Luthyr barreled out of the trees. He didn't slow—because he didn't see me, half his vision erased by my little switchblade.

I charged full-tilt into his side. We collided, and I went down. He landed on top of me, hands slapping the stone platform beside my head. I tightened my grip on the cool, slick cylinder I held.

The other end of the ice spear was buried in his gut, a jagged cluster of ice protruding from the point of impact.

His wide, sun-yellow eye stared down at me, the other eye a mess of blood, then his face contorted. Power surged through him.

But Zak had reached us—and with one smooth motion, he unfurled the Carapace of Valdurna and flung it over Luthyr's back.

As the shimmering folds fell over the fae lord, Zak grabbed my reaching hand. He swept me out from under the fae—and the cloak—and swung me up onto my feet.

Luthyr convulsed, his magic swirling into the cloak in streams of green and gold. He flung the Carapace off, losing his balance with the motion. As the fabric fluttered onto the smooth, engraved stones, he collapsed onto his back, the half-melted ice spear jutting from his stomach.

Ríkr stepped onto the platform. Ancient, merciless calm radiated from him like the deadly stillness of a deep freeze.

Luthyr gasped and snarled, limbs jerking as he tried to rise. Walking to the struggling Summer Lord, Ríkr grasped the melting spear I'd embedded in Luthyr's gut. Horror widened the Summer Lord's eyes, and Ríkr met his nemesis's fear with a wintry smile. Frigid cold rushed out of him.

Frost spread from the spear and covered Luthyr's entire body. The frost thickened to a snowy crust, then thickened into ice, then thickened even more. The icy prison encased the fae lord until only his shadow was visible inside it.

Ríkr's soft blue magic rippled over the ice—then it shattered into tiny, sparkling specks.

And Luthyr shattered with it.

The glittering ice drifted in the air, then swirled into a spiral around Ríkr. It rushed over him, spiraling tighter, then the minuscule crystals sucked into his body until none remained. The burning cold draped over the forest deepened.

With a soundless shimmer, the translucent, cancerous plant Luthyr had embedded in Ríkr's body dissolved into nothing.

The tension left me all at once, and I sagged against Zak. He wrapped an arm around my waist, supporting me before I collapsed. My aura sphere fizzled away, and as the feeling of my presence in the valley faded, I sensed something else.

Something *wrong*.

In unison, Ríkr, Zak, and I spun toward the Carapace of Valdurna.

Magic rippled off the fabric like a giant inferno. As its indigo light spilled outward, shimmering streams of color were sucking into it. The earth trembled, and the ethereal mist shuddered and thinned.

The Carapace was lying right on the heart of the crossroads.

I stepped toward the fae relic, thinking I could grab it—and cracks shot through the platform, stone crumbling under my feet. The Carapace flared brighter. Magic was rushing into it with even greater speed, and wind whipped through the valley in a howling maelstrom, the mist spinning with it.

I gasped as Zak hauled me backward. Ríkr hastily retreated, a step behind us. At the edge of the clearing, Lallakai was poised to run, one hand pressed to her bleeding chest.

Indigo light burst out of the Carapace, and as the fabric fluttered in the wind, its edges dissolved. The cloak was disintegrating as the ancient, immeasurably powerful magic of the crossroads flowed into it. The radiance turned incandescent.

The earth quaked, the forest trembled—and then it stopped. The wind died, and silence fell.

I squinted my eyes open, blinking away light spots.

Shreds of purple fabric were scattered across the cracked stone. The mists of the fae demesne had vanished, and the neon-colored, semitransparent trees had shifted into a mundane, earthly forest. The quiet, formidable energy of the mountain reverberated through the earth, but I couldn't sense the ancient thrum of the crossroads' magic.

We'd destroyed the Carapace of Valdurna—and the crossroads.

29

Ríkr's gaze turned at my quiet words.

The ice and snow blanketing the valley was swiftly melting as the summer night's warmth swept back in. Ríkr and I stood at the edge of the crumbling stone platform, while a few yards away, Zak examined the wound that had pierced Lallakai's lower chest.

"I completely blew it," I whispered, unable to speak any louder. "We all nearly died—"

"But then you achieved a feat only the most powerful of druids could accomplish." His lips curved up. "As should be expected of a druid that I would offer to take as my consort. I have excellent taste."

I didn't let his teasing derail me. "I'm not extraordinary. I'm a fuck-up."

"If you are unhappy with your capabilities, then improve them. Embrace your power. Train your strength. You have the potential to inspire fear, rather than suffer it yourself." His gaze sharpened. "But I think you have already realized that. I felt the fierce conviction in your aura."

Mute with emotion, I could only nod.

"I am pleased, dove. Weakness never suited you. You belong upon a pedestal of greatness, and I am eager to help you climb to new heights."

"What about you? What will you do now that Luthyr isn't hunting you?"

He canted his head. "I must give the matter considerable thought. My immediate concern is Rhiannon's retribution, but with the crossroads undone, it will take time for her to realize something is amiss and even longer to act."

"You said before that you wanted to start again—a new life." I hesitated. "What sort of life?"

"Something moderately thrilling, at least." He smiled impishly. "Living as a fugitive for so long was quite tedious."

I shook my head. "I have trouble imagining you as a king."

"But I am so stately and noble."

"More like—"

A muffled groan came from behind me and I turned.

Lallakai sat with her back against a tree, her long hair tangled and her face tight with pain. Zak was dribbling a potion into her wound, steam puffing off her flesh. A sulfuric scent scratched my nose.

"Are you sure you can heal from this?" Zak asked in a low tone, tipping a few more drops into her wound. "You need proper treatment."

"I am not as fragile as you think."

"I've never seen you injured this badly before. That strike could've killed you. A few inches higher ..." He capped the vial. "Why did you do it?"

She let out an annoyed puff that didn't sound much like the composed, seductive enchantress I was used to. "Can I not protect my druid?"

"By sacrificing yourself?"

She hesitated, then huffed again. "I didn't want you to die."

Kneeling beside her, he was silent. I could only see the edge of his face, his expression a mystery.

"You've grown so reckless since ... the events this past winter. When you asked for a powerful weapon, I thought ..." Trailing off, she steeled her expression. "Zak, we must return to the way things were between us."

He shook his head. "I can't do that, Lallakai."

She sat forward, ignoring the blood trickling down her stomach. "But if this continues, you will die. It is inevitable. Your enemies are too many and too strong."

"I'll find a way to survive."

"I cannot protect you if you don't let me." She pressed her hand to his face, cupping his cheek. "It worked before. You embraced our partnership. Why is it so terrible now?"

"Because I've changed."

She opened her mouth, then closed it. Her eyelids fluttered over emerald eyes as she struggled to process his meaning.

"Before," he murmured, "the only thing I cared about was power. I wanted to be strong enough to never fear someone like Bane again, so I took everything you offered and didn't care about the cost." He gently pulled her hand down from his cheek. "But I'm not that person anymore."

Her lips thinned in an angry frown. "Then what person are you?"

"I'm still figuring it out, and that's why I need you to respect my autonomy—or end this."

She recoiled, her back hitting the tree. A grunt of pain escaped her, and she squeezed her bleeding wound. "End this? Your commitment to me is for life. You cannot rescind your role as my consort."

Again, he was silent.

"He has grown." Ríkr swept past me toward the druid and Night Eagle. "If he has changed, then you must change as well, Lady of Shadow. Did you not claim to be more adaptable than me?"

Her glare snapped up to him, then swung back to Zak. "Is that what you want? For me to change to suit your desires?"

"Yes," he said bluntly. "And it's not something I want. It's something I need."

She drew in a long breath, then released it. "You have needed this for some time, haven't you?"

"Yes."

Leaning back, she swept locks of long raven hair from her face. "Since it is you who asks, Zakariya, I will try." Her eyes narrowed. "I would not make a concession like this for any other."

A faint smile crossed his lips, and he offered her his hand. "I know."

She took his hand, and he pulled her to her feet. As she leaned on him for support, his gaze shifted. Our eyes met.

Then he looked away.

"Well, Winter King," Lallakai declared huffily. "You cannot deny my commitment to our victory. I have earned my boon."

"Indeed." His eyes gleamed. "And I will share the magic of The Undying as soon as you are hale."

"That will not be long."

A low buzz of anxiety rolled through me, and I wished Ríkr had promised the Lady of Shadow something else in exchange for her help.

Zak pulled her into motion. "We should get moving. It's a long walk to the truck."

A long walk to the truck, then a long drive out of Hell's Gate and back home. Exhausted, heartsore, and aching with pain that was growing steadily stronger as Zak's painkiller potion wore off, I couldn't think any further than that.

Home first, and I would figure out the rest later.

I WOKE UP in my bedroom.

My eyes flew open, and the intense ache in my ribs hit me a second later. I blew air in and out, then carefully sat up with a low groan. In addition to my battered ribs, my head throbbed, my dry eyes stung, and my raw throat burned. Sharp pain pulled at my upper arm.

Warm sunlight streamed around my drapes, and the clock on my bedside table read 1:48 p.m. How long had I slept? The last thing I remembered was sinking into the truck's passenger seat in an exhausted stupor, Ríkr curled up on my lap in cat form.

I slid the blanket off. I was wearing the same tank top and jeans from last night, dirt and blood and all, but someone had removed my sweater. The slice on my arm from Luthyr's sword was wrapped in white gauze, and all my other scrapes and cuts had been cleaned. I lightly prodded my temple. Hidden under my bangs was a bandage where a tree branch had clubbed me.

Moving carefully, I lowered my legs off the bed and pushed to my feet. An excruciating pang ran through my ribs, but I was fairly certain they were just bruised. I'd broken ribs before, and it had hurt much worse than this.

A little unsteady, I wobbled across the room and opened the door. There was no one in the main room, and no sign that anyone had slept on the sofa. No dishes in the kitchen, no extra towel in the bathroom.

An uncomfortable, uneasy weight settled deep in my gut.

Tucking my feet into a pair of my sandals by the door, I descended the stairs and exited the building to find the weather sunny but cool. The pain in my ribs eased as my muscles warmed, and I extended my stride as I passed the stable.

Reaching the edge of the yard, I stopped. There was no black truck parked on the gravel. I stretched my senses out, searching for a telltale presence, but I felt only the soft, calm energy of my home.

Turning, I hastened back up to my apartment and into my bedroom. On my nightstand were a handful of items I hadn't noticed when I'd woken up. My breath caught, and I approached cautiously.

Two vials, one containing purple liquid and the other holding fizzy gray painkiller, sat on a scrap of paper with "Drink these" written on it in a masculine scrawl. My phone lay beside them, and resting on top of the screen was a small river stone with a rune etched on its face.

Swallowing against the dryness in my throat, I picked up the river-stone pendant and rubbed my thumb across the rune, then set it on my nightstand and lifted my phone. Unlocking the screen, I opened my messaging app. No new texts.

Switching to my contacts, I tapped "CD" and lifted the phone to my ear.

The line clicked and a robotic voice informed me that the number I had dialed was temporarily out of service.

Out of service? Where the hell was Zak?

A panicky feeling rose through me. I pressed a hand to my chest and concentrated. *Ríkr?*

It took only a moment for a white hawk to fly through the wall and land on the bed beside me. *My fair dove has awakened,* he declared. *What concerns you?*

"Where did Zak go?" My voice was a raspy croak.

He left after seeing to your comfort.

"Why?"

He did not share his intentions, and I did not question him as I was ill-disposed with fatigue. He blinked, softening his harsh raptor's stare. *Before departing, I overheard him and his lady in heated discussion. Whatever they debated, it was a matter of contentious urgency.*

"Urgency?" I bit my lower lip. "Did he say whether he was coming back?"

He did not.

Zak and Lallakai had argued, then left in a hurry? My hand tightened around my phone. Whatever had made him leave, that bastard could've spared five minutes to tell me where he was going. He'd had time to leave potions and a note. Why hadn't he woken me up instead of disappearing without a word?

He'd said he couldn't leave me alone, and I'd believed him.

I bared my teeth. He wasn't getting off that easy. He'd inserted himself into my life, and I wasn't letting him leave it until I was done sorting through all the shit twisting me into knots, from my future as a druid to the truth of what had happened between us ten years ago.

Saber? Ríkr ventured, observing my mood swing.

"Do you accept me as your consort?" I demanded.

I am delighted to take you as my consort.

"Good. Then let's—"

My phone chimed in my hand. Hope sprang through me, only to sour with resentment when I saw it was a message from Agent Kit Morris.

> Heya Saber. Remember how I asked you not to leave town? Good job on that one. :P

My irritation increased threefold as I read. A second message popped up.

> The arrangements are made. Meet me at this address at six. I'll wait for you out front.

As I peered at the address he'd sent, a third text appeared.

> Don't stand me up, ok? It'll be fun, I promise.

I seriously doubted that, but I couldn't blow him off. His "arrangements" involved my new guild, and I had no choice but to cooperate if I wanted to stay out of prison.

Finding Zak would have to wait—briefly.

Tapping my phone against my palm, I looked at Ríkr. "I'm assuming there's a ritual or ceremony involved in becoming your consort. How long will that take?"

A few hours, no more, he answered promptly.

"Let's get started, then. I want to be ready for this evening."

And what is this evening?

I smiled—my real smile, the one I so rarely allowed to show. The savage, unyielding smile that revealed who I really was. "I'm not in the mood to play any more of the MPD's games. I'll see what Morris has set up for me, but if I don't like it …"

Ríkr flared his wings, his eyes bright. *What better opportunity to test your growing power?*

Still smiling, I picked up the painkiller Zak had left me, uncorked the vial, and downed it like a shot. I had a lot to do before my meeting with Morris, and no time to dawdle.

THE TIME ON MY PHONE read 6:00 p.m. sharp.

Cold rain pattered on the hood of my jacket as I slid my phone back in my pocket and studied the building across the street.

The brick structure, windowless on the main floor, sat on the corner of the intersection, drab and unwelcoming. The neighboring business was boarded up, and graffiti decorated every wall in sight. Garbage blew down the street in the chill rain, and the nearest streetlamps were dark.

Vancouver's big-city stench filled my nose, the discordant energy of concrete and pollution buzzing unpleasantly across my senses. Even ignoring that, this was a rough area of town, known for crime, drugs, and homelessness. I hadn't been in this neighborhood since the days of Ruth's crime-den visits, and I wasn't pleased to be back.

"Nice weather, eh?"

My head snapped up. Standing beside me, Morris grinned, the hood of his hunter-green jacket pulled over his head.

Where the hell had he come from? I hadn't seen or heard his approach.

A white ferret poked his head out from the front of my jacket, his whiskers twitching and his small eyes narrowed.

Reminded that this young agent, for all his joking around, was a dangerous mythic who'd earned Zak's respect, I gazed at him coolly. "You're late."

"I'm a busy man. Busting crooks, saving damsels—"

"So?" I cut in. "What is this place?"

"I'll get to that, but first"—a corner of his mouth quirked up as he scanned me—"I've gotta say, the cute ferret really takes your badass druid look to the next level."

I scowled.

"And yeah, I know that cylindrical rodent is actually a big, bad, scary fae, but he's still ador—"

"Get to the point, Morris."

His smile faded, his mood sobering. "You're short a guild and a rehab supervisor, and you need both ASAP. I couldn't let them put a druid like you in with a bunch of poor little witches or, worse, stuff you into some suffocating, judgy, holier-than-thou guild that'd drive you to murder again within a week."

"And you think *this* place is the best option for me?" I asked with a disparaging glance at the brick building.

He answered with a grin and stepped off the curb, heading for the guild's front entrance. I matched him stride for stride, my hands shoved into my pockets. At the door, he paused with his hand on the wood and looked back.

"This is your last chance, Saber. It's this life or the rogue life—and having tried the latter, I don't recommend it."

My eyebrows arched. He'd been a rogue?

"You can find a home here—or they'll eat you alive and spit out your bones. Your choice."

With that, he shoved the door inward. I caught a glimpse of the emblem on the worn wood before light hit my eyes, half blinding me. Morris's silhouette moved inside.

My vision adjusted, revealing a warmly lit pub with a dozen tables and a long bar stretching across the back. Exposed beams and dark walls gave it a moody feel, the various wood-grain surfaces scuffed and worn. A dozen people were scattered among the chairs, the low rumble of their conversations filling the room. With Morris's entrance, unfamiliar faces turned our way.

Quiet fell, expectant and distinctly ominous.

My last chance, Morris had warned. This guild, whatever it was, might eat me alive—but I wouldn't go down without a fight. The "terrible witch" Saber was no more, and this druid wasn't rolling over for anyone.

But one step at a time.

I strode forward, and as I crossed the threshold into the guild, Morris spoke into the silence, his words taunting, teasing, and cautioning all at once.

"Welcome, Saber Rose Orien, to the Crow and Hammer."

ABOUT THE AUTHOR

ANNETTE MARIE is the best-selling author of The Guild Codex, an expansive collection of interwoven urban fantasy series ranging from thrilling adventure to hilarious hijinks to heartrending romance. Her other works include YA urban fantasy series Steel & Stone, its prequel trilogy Spell Weaver, and romantic fantasy trilogy Red Winter.

Her first love is fantasy, but fast-paced adventures, bold heroines, and tantalizing forbidden romances are her guilty pleasures. She proudly admits she has a thing for dragons and aspires to include them in every series.

Annette lives in the frozen winter wasteland of Alberta, Canada (okay, it's not quite that bad) and shares her life with her husband and their furry minion of darkness—sorry, cat—Caesar. When not writing, she can be found elbow-deep in one art project or another while blissfully ignoring all adult responsibilities.

www.annettemarie.ca

SPECIAL THANKS

My thanks to Erich Merkel for sharing your exceptional expertise in Latin and Ancient Greek.

Any errors are mine.

THE GUILD CODEX
UNVEILED

A vigilante witch with a murder conviction, a switchblade for a best friend, and a dangerous lack of restraint. A notorious druid mired in secrets, shadowed by deadly fae, and haunted by his past.

They might be exactly what the other needs—if they don't destroy each other first.

THE GUILD CODEX
DEMONIZED

Robin Page: outcast sorceress, mythic history buff, unapologetic bookworm, and the last person you'd expect to command the rarest demon in the long history of summoning. Though she holds his leash, this demon can't be controlled.

But can he be tamed?

STEEL & STONE

When everyone wants you dead, good help is hard to find.

The first rule for an apprentice Consul is *don't trust daemons*. But when Piper is framed for the theft of the deadly Sahar Stone, she ends up with two troublesome daemons as her only allies: Lyre, a hotter-than-hell incubus who isn't as harmless as he seems, and Ash, a draconian mercenary with a seriously bad reputation. Trusting them might be her biggest mistake yet.

GET THE COMPLETE SERIES

www.annettemarie.ca/steelandstone

The only thing more dangerous than the denizens of the
Underworld ... is stealing from them.

As a daemon living in exile among humans, Clio has picked up some unique skills. But pilfering magic from the Underworld's deadliest spell weavers? Not so much. Unfortunately, that's exactly what she has to do to earn a ticket home.

GET THE COMPLETE TRILOGY
www.annettemarie.ca/spellweaver

Red Winter

A destiny written by the gods. A fate forged by lies.

If Emi is sure of anything, it's that *kami*—the gods—are good, and *yokai*—the earth spirits—are evil. But when she saves the life of a fox shapeshifter, the truths of her world start to crumble. And the treachery of the gods runs deep.

This stunning trilogy features 30 full-page illustrations.

GET THE COMPLETE TRILOGY
www.annettemarie.ca/redwinter

9 781988 153643